WOMAN MISSING

A Mill Town Mystery

by

LINDA NORDQUIST

HARDBALL

PRESS

Dedication

This book is dedicated to the steelworkers who helped
build this country, only to be rendered obsolete by
widespread plant closures and off-shoring in the
corporate drive for profits.

Published by Hard Ball Press.
Information available at: www.hardballpress.com
ISBN: 978-0-9862400-3-4
Cover art by Patty Henderson
www.boulevardphotografica.yolasite.com.

Exterior and interior book design by D. Bass

Library of Congress Cataloging-in-Publication Data
Nordquist, Linda J
Woman Missing A Mill Town Mystery /Linda Nordquist
 1. Steel mills (PA) 2. Unions - industrial. 3. Cory Johnson.

WOMAN MISSING

A Mill Town Mystery

by

LINDA NORDQUIST

Major Characters

Cory Johnson: Ph.D., searching for her mother
Ginny Johnson: Cory's mother, past steelworker and union activist
Charles Mobley: taxi driver, ex-mill worker
Rashid Mobley: taxi driver, nephew of Charles Mobley
Mrs. Gromski: past baby-sitter of Cory
Beatrice (Blinky) Davis: ex-steelworker, friend of Ginny Johnson
Sheila: steelworker, friend of Ginny Johnson
Dorie: ex-steelworker, friend of Ginny Johnson
Jeff Staniewski: witness to a murder
Danny McCormack: Cory's father, witness to a murder
Pete Davison: past local chief KKK
Tony Blasko: steelworker, KKK, vice president Local 1610 in 2004

Union Officers

Tim Fester: Past President Local 1610
Jerry Chonski: past lawyer for International Steelworkers Union
Johnny Kelso: thug

American Steel Company:

Ron Antoli: past metallurgy foreman, BOP shop superintendent
Franklin Blake: past director Employee Relations,
Chairman of American Steel
Moe Perdue: security

Other characters:

Chief Brayton, April and Mrs. Chestnut, Marian McCormack, Janice Gregorich, Bob Lofton, Al Luwanski, Ralph Owens, Chuck Ellwood, Mike Samuels, Skinny Rich, Curly, Catfish, Horizontal Bob, Champ

June 2004

A prickling sensation crept across the scalp of Dr. Cory Johnson. She felt her client's hand, clammy like the belly of a dead fish, gripping her arm. The moment had finally arrived, the one they both welcomed and dreaded. There were no seats left on the wooden pews. The reporters, scrunched together, leaned forward in anticipation.

"Has the jury reached a verdict?"

The jury forewoman rose from her seat and glanced nervously at the crowded courtroom.

"Yes we have, Your Honor." Her hands trembled as she read from the paper.

Except for an occasional twitch of his upper lip, the defendant sat motionless, staring straight ahead, an insolent smirk on his face.

Behind the two prosecutors sat the frail woman whose life had been shattered the day her mother brought this man into their Pittsburgh home. She had been seven years old when he first fondled her, eight years old when he raped her, and nine years old when she watched, hidden from view, as he beat her mother to death. At that moment pieces of her mind splintered like chunks of wood jumping off an axe, taking with them all conscious memory of the terrifying events.

Years later, when her own daughter reached the age of seven, snippets of those horrific scenes began to appear, paralyzing her with terror. She could feel his presence but could not see his face. She watched, as though from a deep-freeze, disjointed scenes of fists in the air as the sound of bones being crunched roared in her ears. In time she withdrew from everyone she loved and closeted herself away in a dark bedroom.

Finally, in the safety of Dr. Johnson's office, she began her journey back to reality. It took four years to weave a whole cloth from those tattered pieces. With the memories restored, she returned to Pittsburgh to identify the perpetrator of those heinous crimes.

"That's him," she'd testified in court, pointing a quivering finger at the defendant.

"That's my mother's brother...my uncle."

Now, in the stifling heat of the courtroom, she sat with her head bowed, chewing on her lower lip.

Dr. Johnson, her professional reputation hanging in the balance, began to tremble. In that second, she saw a vague image of a woman with wild red hair moving toward her, smiling, arms outstretched. Just as quickly, the image vanished. Johnson shook her head and uncrossed her legs, planting both feet squarely on the floor in an effort to ground herself.

Something wasn't right.

The defense attorney, his dark hair streaked with silver, had conjured up a clever argument. "This is more than a case of mistaken identity," he said in his opening statement. "This is a case of implanting false memories into the head of a susceptible woman during the course of years of alleged 'psychotherapy'. Twenty-five years after the tragic death of her mother, she suddenly remembers who did it—as though she just woke up from a coma. But she hasn't been in a coma. She has been in a psychologist's office twice a week for four years. It is there that fact became fiction."

In a sleight of hand worthy of Houdini, the defense had replaced the defendant as the perpetrator of unconscionable crimes with Dr. Cory Johnson. There had been two weeks of expert testimony. The prosecution's witnesses included experts in the workings of human memory.

"Yes," they all agreed, "dissociative amnesia may occur in response to a traumatic event. And it may be limited to only that event."

"Yes, dissociative amnesia can last for years."

"No, it is not uncommon for a current life event, perhaps a daughter reaching the same age as the victim when the trauma occurred, to precipitate flashbacks and memory with great specificity."

The defense presented experts who debunked the idea that human memory is accurate, especially after the passage of years. "More importantly," one psychologist testified, "there have been ample studies to show that memory is prone to suggestion and can be manipulated."

Two jurors appeared to doze. That was the problem with experts. They muddied the waters with their conflicting opinions.

It came down to the believability of the therapist. Had she led her client along? Made suggestions about sexual abuse?

The jury deliberated for three days while radio and TV talking-heads asked the question: Could false memories of sexual abuse or murder be implanted in someone's head? Were prisons housing men falsely convicted of sexually abusing a child or committing murder? Many inmates had their fingers on the dial prepared to call their lawyers and start their appeals.

Or, could an event be so horrific that it overwhelms the mind and obliterates every vestige of conscious memory? Could those memories explode in vivid color and with accurate detail upon the mental screen of the victim years later?

As the jury forewoman read the verdict, a collective gasp rose through the courtroom.

"We find the defendant, guilty."

2

Cory Johnson closed the door to her hotel room and leaned against it. The entire courtroom experience, from the first volley of pundit criticism aimed at her weeks ago to the verdict, had drained every ounce of energy from her body. She dropped her briefcase on the floor, kicked off her wet shoes and collapsed upon the bed with a groan.

It was dusk. Although the room was stuffy, she couldn't stop shivering. Her temples throbbed. She rolled up in the bedspread and closed her eyes. The nightmare was over, yet she felt like she was unraveling. The rhythmic sound of rain drops against the window lulled her into a fitful sleep.

"Ladies and gentlemen, don't be fooled. This little girl is a cold blooded murderer!" the lawyer shouted. He loomed over the witness box and thrust his forefinger in the face of the child defendant. "You killed her, didn't you? Didn't you, Cory Johnson?"

Confused, the freckle-faced ten year-old screamed and sobbed. "No, I didn't! I didn't do it!"

His fat lips sneered as the purple veins in his temples pulsed. "Where is she then? Did she simply disappear?"

"Y...Yes," the girl stuttered, her body shaking. "Sh...she never came home again."

The jury shook their heads in disbelief.

"It's true!" she cried. "Please, you've got to believe me. It's true!"

The jurors pointed gnarled fingers at her and chanted in unison, "It's your fault! It's your fault!"

The child melted into a puddle of tears and disappeared, taking her guilt and shame with her. Then she heard her mother. "Cory, wake up! You have to help me clean the aquarium. C'mon now." A bright orange goldfish poked at her mouth.

"No, I wanna sleep."

"Cassandra!" her mother commanded, flames shooting from her brilliant red hair. She began to plead as blood flowed down from the top of her head. "Cassandra. Please. Help me. Help me..."

Cory bolted upright in the darkened hotel room, her pupils wide with fear. The pumping of her heart echoed in her head. She hadn't heard the name Cassandra in 20 years. Not since the day she had waved good-bye to her mother from the back of a station wagon as it peeled away from the curb. Why now?

She pushed a lock of hair away from her face and undressed.

The blast of hot water from the shower stung her body. Steam filled the small bathroom, fogging the mirror and the glass shower door. She wanted to stand there for days watching the scum that had become a second skin get sucked down the drain. She felt sullied by the weeks of accusations. The sheer volume of attacks on her professional capabilities had shaken her confidence, adding to her secret chamber of self-doubt. It was doubt that made her a perfectionist and perfectionism that often kept her awake at night.

Cory towel dried her hair and wrapped herself in a white terry cloth robe. Room service delivered a club sandwich, French fries, and a diet coke, which she wolfed down. Her flight was scheduled to leave for Los Angeles at ten the next morning. She needed to sleep, but her mind was on fast-forward.

She sat on the edge of the bed and watched the blurry lights. The rain that had started up again was coming down with more force. In that moment she was no longer a tall, graceful, self-assured professional woman. An old memory shinnied up out of a black hole and found its way to the streets of her childhood in Munhall, PA.

The sound of her mother's voice rang out, calling her from the porch. "Cory, dinner's ready! Come in, now!"

How many times had she hidden under that porch, peeping up through the cracks in the wood, stifling snickers? How many times had her mother turned to go into the house and, just before entering, issue her final warning, "I know you're down there Miss Cory. C'mon. Your dinner's getting cold."

Cory shivered. She had been so focused on the trial that she hadn't thought of how coming back to Pittsburgh might bring up memories of her childhood. She was opening a time capsule, releasing bits and pieces of a life she had long buried in a dark place under a heavy lid.

"You weren't expecting this, were you Cassandra?" she said aloud.

She stared hard at her image on the glass, her mouth open. There it was again, slipping out as easily as sliding on an oil slick. No one called her that name. Only her mother, and only when Cory was in trouble.

"Holy hell! I'm losing it."

Her tense neck muscles throbbed. Returning to bed, she tried to sleep, but was too agitated. Too busy straining to shove the thick cement lid back into place over her memories. She tossed and turned, punched pillows and wrestled with blankets until midnight. Try as she might, the lid remained ajar allowing bits of scenes, fragments of conversations and frightening emotions to slip out.

Amidst the turmoil, a plan emerged.

3

Cory pushed her way to consciousness. Her throat was parched from the recycled hotel air. Going to the window, she opened the drapes and beheld a city cloaked in grey soup. At six in the morning there was no sign the sun would make an appearance any time soon. Somewhere out there was the city she had left as a child. Now she was a stranger in need of a street map. She went to the lobby to buy one.

Dressed in sweat pants and shirt, she sat cross legged on the king size bed surrounded by the Want Ad section of the Pittsburgh Press and a street map of Allegheny County. In a notebook she began a "to do" list: rent apartment near mill, rent car, visit old neighborhood, check police records in Braddock, check library microfiche for old newspaper articles, find someone who knew Mom!!

Within an hour she had made an appointment for later that morning to see a furnished three room cottage in West Mifflin, one of numerous small steel mill towns that had sprung up over the past hundred years.

Studying the map, Cory found 10th Avenue in Munhall where she and her mother had lived for five years in a rented flat. The diner where her mother had worked was in Homestead, another mill town right next door.

That's convenient, she thought. Mama's steel mill was in Braddock, the Rankin Bridge over the Monongahela River connects Braddock to West Mifflin: Braddock...West Mifflin...Munhall...Homestead. Maybe the answers lie there. That is, IF a neighbor remembers anything, and IF the diner still exists and IF it's owned by the same person with the same staff. Talk about a needle in a haystack.

She leaned back against the pillows and dozed. For the first time in several weeks she felt calm. Tired, but calm.

Cory awoke just in time to change her clothes and make a dreaded telephone call. She slipped into black jeans that hugged her long legs and rested elegantly on her hip bones. The roomy white cotton blouse was comfortable and airy. She clamped down her unruly red hair with a large barrette, and then picked up the phone and dialed her 82-year-old aunt.

"Cory, dear, I didn't expect you. I didn't forget. I've got a note in red letters on the kitchen table to remind me that I'm to pick you up at the airport tomorrow morning at eleven. Has something happened?"

Cory balked at telling her the reason for not returning to LA as planned. Ora was the last person on earth that Cory would ever want to hurt.

"Yes, I guess something did happen. I...I started thinking about Mom." She hesitated, inhaled deeply, then plunged ahead. "I have so few memories of her. When I look at those old photographs you have, I see her but I don't *feel* her. Do you know what I mean? I don't feel a part of her. I had her for such a short time and then she was gone."

"Oh, Cory. You're the spittin' image of your momma, Darlin', what with your red hair and freckles. Your eyes may be a different color, but they've got that almond shape and they're as big as hers. Plus you have the same funny way of crinkling your nose when you get angry, like you're smelling sour milk. You've got her spunk. Her intelligence. And you're tall and strong like she was."

For a moment Ora fell still. Cory tried to fill the void. "You have told me these things before but..."

"You've got her big heart, too" Ora interrupted. "She

cared about the wrongs in the world, and she really wanted to make it better. You care a lot for others, too. Think about all the people you help. That's why you're in this profession— you're a caretaker same as your mom."

Aunt Ora stopped long enough to take a deep breath and then continued. "You probably don't remember, but some of Ginnie's steel friends had a little meeting, kind of like a memorial meeting. They wanted to get together and talk about what might have happened, but no one knew anything. I put out one of those funeral type sign-in books. I thought it would be good for you to have it when you grew up. I remember seeing people standing in line to sign it. But when I went to get the book, it was gone. It just disappeared into thin air."

Caught up in her own thoughts, Cory said, "That's why I've decided to stay on here for a bit longer. I want to know everything that happened. It was so long ago. No one else is going to be interested anymore. If I want answers, I'm the only one who is able to get them."

Silence grew between them. Finally, Ora said, "I understand. I guess I always knew that someday you would have to do this. But I'm gonna be worried about you every minute."

"Aunt Ora, I don't mean to worry you, you're my only family."

"Darlin', you wanting to find out what happened to your mother is the most natural thing in the world. I'm just sorry that I didn't have more information to share with you over the years."

"Thanks, Aunt Ora. I knew you would understand."

"You remember to call me. And if you need me, I'll hop on the next plane and be there. Ok?"

"I will. And don't worry. Maybe I'll find some information. More than likely not. It's been such a long time. You take care of yourself. I'll be back in no time."

Cory hung up the phone. A sign-in book of friends of Momma? She felt the rush of adrenalin in her body. *Maybe there's a name of a person or a place, something that can tell me where to begin. As quickly as hope appeared, it vanished. That would be way too easy, and nothing about my mother was ever easy.*

Bewildered, Cory shook her head and spoke aloud to the empty room, "How do I know that? How the hell do I *know* that nothing was easy about Momma?"

4

Jeff Staniewski had not slept soundly. It was one more fitful sleep in an endless line of bad nights that stretched out for twenty years. In the beginning, the nightmares — ghoulish, savage, hideous nightmares — tortured him throughout the night. Long boney fingers charred beyond recognition snatched him by the throat and pushed him down into putrid sludge. He awoke on a sweat soaked mattress and lay, night after night, heart thumping, fists clenched, staring at the ceiling.

By the sight of him it would be hard to fathom that these visions could paralyze him with fright. He was a big man with tattoos of dragons on his beefy arms and barreled chest. But try as he might, drunk or sober, he could not erase the image of a toothless gaping mouth balanced on a raw esophagus that came to him nightly.

He had tried to conquer the beast with booze, tried to drown it in vats of vodka, piss it out in a river of beer, strangle it with his own vomit. Drugs had given him no relief. He had tried them. Lots of them. He didn't want to sit in some rat-infested crack house, back against some crumbling plaster, feeling armies of termites crawling up the wood while he chattered away to dead bodies. At least that's what they looked like, a bunch of dead bodies. No, drugs didn't do it, they just made him feel like shit.

The speed with which he succumbed to alcohol had been dizzying. But each night the nightmare barreled back with a vengeance.

What did that dike doctor in the ER call it? Some fuckin' fancy label. Oh, yeah, said I was hallucinating. Seeing things.

You mean them snakes ain't real, doc? That big boa ain't crawling up your leg looking for some snatch? Shit, doc, you and me got a serious disagreement.

Just gimme the meds, bitch. Gimme the god-damn meds!

He'd landed in detox centers plenty of times, where he would shake all over, his teeth rattling, and roll on the cold linoleum. Yeah, that's it, shake, rattle, and roll.

Finally they got it right. Gave him valium to take the edge off. Then there were *two* monkeys catching a ride on his back. But he didn't care. So long as the image of that body with its arm jerking a second before the stream of red hot steel turned it into a vapor didn't come back.

But it always did. Twisted his nuts and made him howl into the night like a beaten mutt.

Jesus, why didn't he stop the heat from pouring? No. No! He'd been through all that, there wasn't time to stop it. Hah! You lying sack of shit. There was plenty of time. You just stood there. A god damn deer caught in the headlights.

Jeff had been working on the furnace crew that night. Just a kid, really, only twenty-three years old. A big kid. A big hunky. One of those Eastern European, thick-necked, broad-faced, short-legged kids with thin blond hair that would fall out by the time he was forty. Pure-bred Slavic stock. He had one hundred years of Pittsburgh steel history pumping through his veins.

The men in Jeff's family, all the way back to the turn of the twentieth century, had worked in the mills. In 1890 his great-great-grandfather was shot dead by a Pinkerton detective. Sacrificed to the cause of unionism.

Half asleep from his latest sleepless night, Jeff stood in

the kitchen listening to his grandfather, Karl Staniewski II, ramble on. Old Karl retired after forty-four years in the mill. Now, 68 years old, having devoted his life to work and family, he was nearing the end of his journey. Cancer rotted his lungs. His knees and hips were crippled with arthritis. His short-term memory was shot. But with a keen memory for distant times, reliving those events was about all he had left. The kitchen table was his podium.

Old Karl's speech was slow, hesitant, like he was waiting for his tongue to catch up with his thoughts. The old man rubbed his chin and took another swig. Jeff leaned against the kitchen wall poking his teeth with a toothpick. He'd heard these stories his whole life. Knew them by heart. But Jeff also knew that if he tried to bolt from the kitchen his father, Lenny, would bring him up short.

"My Pa was younger than you when he went into the mill," the old man said. "Fifteen was all. They didn't work any eight-hour day with two days off. No sir. They worked seven days a week, twelve hours a day." He paused to take a large swallow of rye. It mingled with the wad of tobacco tucked in his cheek. Brown spittle bubbled up in the corners of his mouth.

"I did it the first year I was in the mill and I can tell yunz it was pure living hell." His head swung from side to side like an old bull. "I never saw anything but the backside of my pa when I was coming up. He was always sleeping in the bed. And when he wasn't in that bed some other mill hunkie was. Ma took in borders to help pay for food. That bed never got cold."

He scratched the stubble on his chin. "Lots of the men died too. Lots of accidents in the mill. That's how my Daddy died." A tear wobbled down his flabby cheek. "Crushed between them train cars in the dead of winter. So much steam from them hot ingots, the engineer never saw him."

17

He swallowed the last of the whiskey. "Steelworkers built this country. We did it with our blood. Back then we didn't have no government agencies to check on things."

"They ain't checking on things now, Grandpa," Jeff said. "OSHA tells the bosses time, date and place they're gonna inspect, company gets everything cleaned up, puts on a pretty face for the visitors. Hell, they need to show up without telling anybody. Show up at three in the morning. But then they might have to do something besides rubber stamping company reports."

Jeff never considered a different life. He played football in high school, one of those hulking defenders on the front line. And he had one girlfriend, Ruth, who was steady, loyal and uncomplicated. They married two weeks after graduation. Seven months later Ruth gave birth to a daughter and, ten months later, a son.

In 1978, his life preprogrammed, he marched through the security gates of the mill on his first day of work, proudly following in the footsteps of family tradition. He became a man that day, a steelworker, a union man. And he made good money. It was the best job he could imagine.

Then one night fate dragged him into life's seamier side. As he worked in a dark corner stacking bags of chemicals, two men ran past him towards the metal platform that stuck out over a waiting ladle. One led the way. The other pushed a wheel barrel with a shiny asbestos coat in it. He saw them hoist the barrel up and send the coat flying over the edge.

No! Oh my God, no!

A body flopped out and dropped like a sack of cement to the bottom of the ladle. Jeff stood rigid, shocked out of his wits. His mouth gaped open. His gut retched like a sump pump. As the men turned to run, Jeff recognized one of them. His blood turned cold. It happened so fast that he never saw the other man. The minutes ticked by as he stood hidden in the shadows. Did he will himself to move? Did he even try? If they saw him, they might come back. Invisibility was the key to survival..

When he finally did move, he made a curious decision. It was one of those puzzling decisions that alter the course of a life. In that moment, he stood at the crossroads between hero and coward. There was precious little time. Yet, instead of racing to the furnace office to tell the foreman to shut it down, he stood in the dark corner second-guessing himself. Maybe he had made a mistake. Maybe he hadn't seen what he'd seen. Maybe it was some kind of joke.

At the last second, just as the furnace began tipping downwards to release one hundred tons of molten steel into the ladle, when it was too late for the entrance of a hero, he raced onto the platform.

He saw it. The body had landed on its back. The legs were twisted and rested up against the wall of the ladle. He leaned forward and saw what should have been a face, but was a bloodied mass of shredded skin and bone. There was a black hole where the mouth used to be. Just as the steel began to pour, he saw an arm move towards the head, towards the crushed jaw bone.

"Jesus," he whimpered. "Jesus." But even then he didn't move. He stood there, riveted to the spot and watched as the fiery liquid flowed into the cavernous ladle. That was part of his job, to double check that everything was all right.

Only this time hot piss ran down his legs. He felt like he had been splayed open, his guts exposed. And hanging out for the world to see was his singular lack of courage. He had witnessed a murder without ever lifting a finger. There was no escaping the magnitude of his discovery: he was a coward.

The only saving grace bestowed upon him that night was the lack of witnesses to his cowardice. He was the only one who knew.

Now, twenty years later, long after Ruth and the kids left; after losing job after job because he couldn't meet the reasonable expectation of showing up; after drinking his way through Pennsylvania, New Jersey and Delaware; after failed suicide attempts and, lest he forget, after an endless number of detox and rehab tours of duty, Jeff Staniewski, was clean, sober, and sleepless. It was the end of his sixth week. No medications and no mind altering chemicals. This was the old-fashioned "cold turkey."

A few nights before his momentous decision to sober up, he reeled down an alley near the parking lot of the mill. It was midnight. The shift was changing. Men walked to their cars, jesting with each other. Once again Jeff could be found hiding in the shadows. He leaned against a light pole and tried to focus on the faces of the men as they passed under the security lights at the main gate.

Suddenly Jeff saw him. He recognized him immediately. The man hadn't changed much. Short, wiry, powerful with sinewy muscles that sprung to life as fast as a rat trap snapped shut. His bald dome shone under the street lamp. He strutted like Marine brass towards the gate talking to some guy. Suddenly the son-of-a-bitch practically doubled over laughing, high-fivin' the security guard. A yellow sports car idled on the outside of the gate with a pretty little blond in the driver's seat.

"Hi, Dad. Do you want to drive?"

"No, honey, it's ok, you do it." As he dropped into the passenger seat, they sped off.

Jeff slid down the wooden pole and sat in the alley. At first he was confused, his brain awash in cheap wine. It was damn difficult to sling together a coherent thought. But then he got it. This guy was living a grand old life, while he, Jeff Staniewski, had spent twenty fuckin' years trying to obliterate the image of a mangled body and the big yellow streak that ran down the middle of his back. Meanwhile, that sick bastard never missed a night's sleep.

Spasms of cramps twisted his belly. He pitched forward and puked, heaving up out of the depths of his weary soul years of hatred. It was the kind of hatred that aims at the self, leaving no options except slow agonizing destruction. Deep convulsive contractions consumed him, while strings of saliva swung from his lips. His ribs hurt as he sobbed and heaved. These were not the tears of self-pity, his pity tank was empty. These were the tears of rage.

He needed to sober up. He needed to fix things. He needed to dispense some justice. For once in his sorry life he felt a stirring of courage in his heart.

5

Cory stood in the middle of a vacant lot in Homestead clutching her map. The early afternoon sun blazed down on her head and shoulders. With droplets of perspiration dotting her hairline, she could feel the freckles multiplying on her face. She raised her hand to block out the glare and studied the area where the diner had once been.

Her day had started out successfully. She had rented the furnished cottage in W. Mifflin for a month. The cottage suited her needs perfectly, with a large sunny kitchen and living room, a small bedroom and bath in the rear. There was a weather-beaten deck that skirted it. The cottage sat on an acre of land, surrounded by tall oak trees. The only drawback was that it was up a steep hill and far from public transportation.

She had hiked down the hill to Eighth Avenue, turned left and walked towards Munhall in search of the old flat where she used to live. Twelfth Avenue in Munhall was four blocks up another precipitous hill. The two-story brick houses with wide wooden porches sat peacefully along the tree-lined streets. It was noon on a Tuesday and the neighborhood was deserted.

Cory was breathing hard as she turned onto Twelfth.

Thank God this part is flat, she thought. Another block up and I would be spread-eagle kissing the sidewalk.

Her pace slowed as she approached the house where she and her mother had lived. Her heart had been pounding from the hike up. At the sight of the house, it began to race as if she expected a ghost to fly out the door. Shards of memory were starting to fall into place.

The yellow-brick house appeared the same except for the front door, which was painted brown instead of red. Lace curtains covered the row of windows along the porch and a metal swing hung from rusty hooks in the ceiling.

Cory was surprised. Little had changed over the years. Indeed, time had stood still.

She was feeling edgy. Tension grabbed hold of her neck. A headache began to throb in her right temple. "Oh no you don't," she muttered to a budding migraine. "I don't have time for you today." She forced herself to climb the porch steps.

Cory knocked on the front door. No one answered. She tried the houses on both sides. Empty. A postal worker, her blond ponytail swinging back and forth, approached the house next door.

"If you want to find anybody, the best time is around six o'clock. This whole block is a cemetery during the day." She climbed the stairs and stuffed some circulars in a mailbox, then walked in Cory's direction.

"Maybe you can help me," Cory said. "Is there anyone living on this block that has lived here for twenty years or more? I'm trying to find someone who may have known a family back then."

The woman stopped, pulled some envelopes out of her pack, and grinned. "Hah! I got it! Someone got left an anonymous inheritance and you're the agent trying to find 'em?"

"Something like that," Cory said, smiling back.

"Twenty years ago? I really can't say. This has been my route going on eleven years and the neighborhood's changed some since I started." She glanced left and then right. "There is a man lives in the red brick house down there. He just put his mother in a nursing home. They've been here a good long time. He might be able to help. That is, if he wants to, he runs hot and cold. Never know which he's gonna be. But he's lived here a long time."

"That red brick five houses down?"

"Yeah, that's the one. But he ain't there now. Probably at the nursing home with his mom. Putting her in the home was hard on him. You know the type, momma's boy and then some. She's all he has."

The postal worker started on her way, cutting across the lawn to the next house. "Oh, yeah, way down at the end of the block there's an old woman, but I doubt she can help you. She's almost blind and her memory's not so good. If you don't find anyone to claim that money, my name's Cheryl. You can find me here most days. Sure wouldn't mind an early retirement."

"Thanks a lot!" Cory yelled after her. "I'll remember that!"

She decided to take her advice and return that afternoon, feeling confident that some little tidbit of valuable information could be found in one of those houses. Now, after a greasy hamburger with fries, she had come up against her first dead-end. Weeds sprouted through the cracked cement that had been the foundation of a building. Rusted cans, cigarette butts and rumpled candy wrappers lay strewn on the ground. A path was worn from the alley-way to the sidewalk where people had carved a shortcut to Eighth Avenue. On either side of the lot were abandoned buildings with plywood covered windows that once opened onto a vibrant city street.

Cory scanned the skeletal remains, deep in thought.

A slow moving taxi pulled up to the curb.

"You lost, Ma'am?" a bass voice echoed from inside the car.

Cory jumped.

"No, I don't think so," she said, turning to face the man who possessed a vocal pitch so deep it resonated in her inner ear. Through the windshield of an old Chevy Impala she saw a massive body crammed behind the steering wheel. The driver's seat listed backwards at a forty-five degree angle.

Cory walked to the sidewalk and bent down to speak through the passenger side window. She peered at a gentle face under a prodigious forehead. He gazed at her with curiosity and kindness. A narrow band of pure white hair circled around the blue-black skin of his scalp.

"What I'm searching for seems to have disappeared," she said.

"If you don't mind my askin', what might that be?"

"An old diner. My mother worked there in the seventies. I'm trying to find someone who might have known her. She disappeared twenty years ago."

"I'm sorry to hear that," he said. "There used to be a diner here but it closed many a year ago. Not long after the mill shut down. Practically the whole town closed up then. The couple that owned it, well, they passed on some time ago and the city tore it down 'cause there weren't no chilrin' to make a claim. That was back when Homestead had money to tear things down."

He nodded towards the abandoned buildings. "They don't have any money now, even after them developers moved in and built that big shopping mall over yonder." He gestured with his thumb in the direction west of the Homestead High Level Bridge.

In the distance she could see tall red-bricked smoke stacks—all that was left of the famous Homestead Works.

Cory felt deflated.

Taking a long shot, she asked the taxi driver, "You

wouldn't happen to know anyone who used to work there, would you?"

"No, Miss, I sure don't. To be honest this was a white folk's restaurant, if you know what I mean. I never was inside." He turned off the engine and, improbable as it seemed, leaned further back in the seat.

"Are you investigatin' something in particular, Miss? Maybe I can help. I've lived in this area my whole life and the Good Lord has blessed me with a long one. I'm seventy-six years old, but my girlfriend, Tildie, she's sixty-three, she says I don't look it."

He puffed up his mattress sized chest in a proud fashion and displayed the warmest grin Cory had ever seen. "We been knowin' each other for a good many years. Sing in the choir at Ebenezer Baptist Church over in Rankin. Brenda, that was my wife, she passed on fifteen years ago. Cancer. The Lord took her real fast, so she didn't suffer much. Brenda sang in the choir, too. A person could hear her a *mile* away."

When he stopped talking, the sound of his voiced lingered in the air. He seemed a bit puzzled, as though he'd lost his way.

Cory waited a moment. Then, with a soft voice, she intruded upon his recollection. "Maybe you can help me," she said. "I'm not going to be here long, no more than a month. I need a driver for five or six days a week. Someone who is dependable and knows his way around."

"Well now, Miss. I don't do no long distance drivin' no more."

"Oh, that's ok. I'll be concentrating between Braddock and here. Do you know Braddock?"

"Yes, Miss. I know all these lil' towns. But I don't work every day now. I don't work on Sundays because of Church and Wednesdays for Bible Study. I rest on Fridays. So, you see, I'm only workin' four days a week. And I don't drive at night. Can't see good enough."

"Yes, I understand. I just —"

Suddenly, he interrupted her. "Well, now. I don't know if this will suit you fine or not, but my grand-nephew drives my taxi on my off days. He's a good boy. Name's Rashid. He's my brother's grandson.

"His Daddy died in a gang shootin'. He wasn't in no gang, he was in the wrong place at the wrong time. The boy was with him when it happened, but he was pretty young. I doubt he remembers much. I'm the only family Rashid's got, what with my brother passin' on and his mama dead, too. Her heart gave out."

"I'm so sorry to hear that," said Cory.

"He lives with me. I guess you could say we kind of take care of each other. He talks kind of funny, you know how these young folks do, but his heart's big and he's honest. He's a good driver, too. If you don't mind havin' two drivers, well, then, I think we can be at your service."

Relieved at having solved this problem, she readily agreed. "Sounds fine. There won't be much driving. Probably a lot of waiting while I talk to people. And if I need any long distance trips, maybe to downtown Pittsburgh, I'll save them for Rashid. How much will that be?"

He cleared his throat and sat up straighter. "Let's see, not much drivin' but plenty of waitin', for me that's plenty of nappin'. For Rashid that's plenty of time on his cell phone. He'll probably spend way more than he earns. How about fifty dollars a day?"

Cory did some quick calculations. She had enough money to see her through three weeks. Smiling, she stuck her arm through the window to shake his hand. "It's a deal! My name is Cory. Cory Johnson." She watched as her freckled hand vanished from sight, lost in a grip the size of a catcher's mitt.

The big man laughed heartily as he pumped their hands up and down. "Well, Miss Johnson, I'm mighty glad to make your acquaintance. My name's Charles Mobley. Is there somewhere I can drive you now?"

Cory felt fatigue spread through her body after her long day. She decided to skip the old neighborhood and set up her little cottage instead. "Yes, Mr. Mobley, there is. I want to buy some groceries. And, if it's ok with Rashid, I would like to start tomorrow morning around nine."

"Yes, Ma'am. There's a big new supermarket where the Homestead Mill used to be."

"So long as they have the makings of a salad and some feta cheese, I'll be happy," Cory said.

Mr. Mobley gabbed away as Cory climbed into the back seat. She found that the tonal quality of his voice was not only a joy to hear, but reassuring.

Later that night, after eating one of her traditional large salads, Cory crawled into bed, exhausted. She rang Ora to reassure her that she was safe and had solved two major problems in one day. Then she turned out the light and was instantly asleep.

Late that night a thunderstorm rolled across southwestern Pennsylvania. Jagged flares of lightning streaked across the sky. Thunder roared like an angry bull elephant. Sheets of rain rode a furious wind that whipped in all directions, sending water cascading down the hilly city streets, overwhelming sewage systems and flooding sidewalks at the bottom. Electrical generators were blown out. Power was lost.

The massive oaks surrounding Cory's little cottage swayed, bowed, and shed weaker limbs. The brittle sounds of snapping branches were muffled by the force of the storm.

Undisturbed, Cory slept like the dead.

6

At nine the next morning, as Cory picked up branches and debris from the storm, Mr. Mobley's red Chevy Impala squealed around the corner and screeched to a stop at her walkway. A young man unfolded his daddy long-leg extremities and exited the car.

"Yo, you Miss Co?" He ambled up the yard in her direction. "Sir Charles said you be expecting me at nine."

"Ah, you must be Rashid," Cory said.

"You got that right, Miss Co," he said, tipping his black and gold Pittsburgh Pirates baseball cap, which was on sideways and frayed around the edges. "Rashid Mobley! Ready, willing, and able. Just point me in the direction, put a bead on the line, and you be there in no time. No frills, just chills."

Cory studied the young man, who appeared to gear up his propensity for constant motion the closer he came. He bounced an imaginary basketball with one hand, then pivoted, sashayed left, then right and tossed it up towards a non-existent hoop.

ADHD run amuck, she thought. She would be hyper too if she had watched her father being gunned down in the street.

"Rashid, my name is Cory Johnson," she stretched out her arm to shake his hand, hoping he would pick up on her full name.

"Yes, ma'am, Ms. Co. Master Charles said I was to drive you today, it being Wednesday." His oval-shaped eyes flitted everywhere, even on her chin, but never directly at her.

"Ok. I'll just get my jacket and we'll go over to the Braddock Police station." She trotted off to the cottage, harnessed her wild red hair with a large black clip, and grabbed her jean jacket off the bed. She guessed she would be 'Miss Co' for a while. Could be worse, she chuckled.

Cory climbed into the front seat of the car. Rashid's body was folded up like a portable poker table. As he turned the key in the ignition, the sound of a rapper burst forth from the rigged sound system.

"Rashid!" she yelled. "Please, can you turn it down?"

"Oops. Sorry, ma'am." He snapped off the radio and pushed down on the accelerator. The big Chevy peeled away from the curb. A red streak blazed down the hill, sloshed through puddles, crossed the Rankin Bridge, turned onto Braddock Avenue and headed for the local police station.

Rashid slowed the car as he drove through the dead town. The avenue was reminiscent of a funeral. There were no signs of life, only ghosts in a graveyard of boarded up shops.

"Before we talk to the police, let's drive by the mill, ok? I'd like to see it up close."

"Cool," he said.

∽∽∽

Rashid withdrew into himself during the warp-speed drive to Braddock. He was at a loss for words, which was a rarity for him. This woman was an oddity sitting there beside him. Older woman. Older white woman. Older white woman with a secret. At least that's what his uncle had said the night before at supper after announcing the steady taxi job.

"She's sad, Rashid. Sad or lost. Said her momma went missin' some twenty years ago." Mobley put down his fork and wiped his lips with a paper napkin. "Funny thing to go searchin' for someone who knew her momma back then. What's that gonna do?"

Rashid, the heel of his right leg jumping up and down, was making his way through a second mound of mashed potatoes. "Maybe she's owed some dead presidents. Maybe she be wantin' that."

"Owed what?"

Rashid rolled his eyes. "C-notes, cabbage, cash, money," he said, with exaggerated patience, as though Master Charles had recently checked out of the mental department. "Maybe someone owed her momma some money and she wantin' to collect."

Mr. Mobley, accustomed to Rashid's quirks and jingoism, nevertheless demanded that a certain level of English be spoken between them. He shot his nephew a warning glance over the empty platters of food on the kitchen table.

"No, she don't seem to be hurting for money. It's a different kinda hurt. She's searching for an answer to something. An important something. Seems she keepin' it to herself. Some kinda secret."

Rashid hadn't given it another thought. That is, until she was sitting next to him in the car. What was he s'posed to talk about? Was he even s'posed to talk? She sure outta place in Braddock. We gonna be mugged, man, mugged. Peeps be eyein', tryin' to figure out what's what. She gonna be stirrin' up a lot of interest. No way to keep her outta sight. She boss, though, plenty good lookin' in a funny kinda way. He was okay with her. Just do the driving, don't have to do nuttin' else.

As they cruised slowly down Braddock Avenue he found it more and more difficult to handle the silence of a ride without the radio. Silence was always dangerous. It was easier for those memories to sneak out of the boxes in his brain, boxes he tried to keep locked but were never failsafe.

It didn't take much to remember the sound of his father's head splintering as the bullet ripped through his skull, or feel the warm blood squirting down upon him, splashing across his seven year-old face.

Those memories had a way of creeping up on him, especially in the night when sound and motion stopped. Now in this quiet car driving down these deserted streets, he was dangling by a thin thread and about to fall if he didn't do something quick.

"Master Charles used to work here," he blurted out. "He retired 'bout fifteen years or so."

"Where?" Cory asked, gazing out at the grim streets.

"There." He pointed a finger down the avenue at a seven-story fabricated blue building. It had a large metal tube that ran along the spine of the roof. Steam poured out of smoke stacks at either end of the building. A large dirty white sign was painted on the wall that faced Braddock Avenue. It said: "American Steel — Andrew Carnegie Works."

Rashid parked the car. They peered through the fence at the sprawling steelmaking complex. It was surprisingly quiet. One man, dressed in a silver asbestos coat and a yellow hard hat, leaned against a doorway. He took deep drags off a cigarette as he gazed up at the hills around Braddock.

Rashid nodded towards where the man stood. "That's the BOP shop where they make the steel. And over there are the blast furnaces where they make the iron." The furnaces were upright like missile silos silhouetted against the sky.

Rashid pointed further left. "Uncle Charles worked

down in the slab mill. It ain't there no more."

Cory barely heard Rashid, her attention was riveted on the massive blue structure in front of her. She remembered now. The BOP! That was where her mother had worked. Cory felt drawn to the place, as if an eerie force was trying to yank her through the fence.

"I have to get in there. Somehow. I *have* to see it."

"I don't think they let peeps — I mean people. They don't let people inside who don't work there."

But she was only half listening. Her thoughts were of the families who often go to the sight of a disaster to say good-bye. Some need to see it, to imagine each detail of the last minutes of their loved ones. This was no different. She needed to understand it. All of it. Besides, there might be some answers in there.

Her knuckles were white from gripping fence wire. "I'll find a way," she whispered.

They returned to the car and sped off to the police station. Rashid pulled up to a no parking zone in front of the station.

"Do you think this is wise?" Cory asked, glancing up at the traffic sign and down at the yellow line along the curb.

"It's cool," he said. "Master Charles is tight with the main Bro. So I be waitin'. Chillin' like a villain." He reached for the radio knob and was instantly immersed in rap.

"Chillin'? Villain?" If she was to understand him, she would have to start asking for definitions or hire a translator.

The station was awash in light that glared down upon the highly polished linoleum floor. As Cory's pupils contracted, a dull pain began near her right temple.

"Can I help you?" Adelene, a middle-aged black woman with short hair and a penchant for low-cut blouses, was busy banging out reports on an old typewriter.

"Yes. That is, I hope so. I am hoping to get some information about the disappearance of a woman twenty years ago."

Adelene coughed. "Twenty years ago? This woman disappeared in Braddock? Who was she to you?"

"It's kind of complicated. She was my mother. Her name was Ginny Johnson. She was working at the mill down the street. She went to work and never came back. I'm trying to find out what happened to her. I'm hoping the police might have investigated her disappearance and have a report on file."

"Twenty years ago? And you're just now trying to find out what happened?"

"I was only ten when this happened," Cory said, resenting the implication. "I was taken to California to live with my Aunt. This is the first opportunity I've had to come back here. It happened in July, 1984. Do you keep records back that far?"

"It depends on if there was anything to make a record of. Have a seat, I'll speak to Chief Brayton."

Within minutes a voice boomed from a back office, "C'mon down the hall, young lady! Let's see what we can do for you."

As Cory walked into his office, she saw a man with reddish brown hair and cocoa colored skin. When he stood up to shake her hand, she was taken aback by how short he was; short and thick as a stump. Towering over him, Cory wondered how he had slipped under department height requirements.

"I see we got something in common." He laughed and he pointed to the freckles on his face. "I don't know why people don't appreciate having freckles, do you? They sure help a lot in identifying folks in a line-up. My whole family's got 'em. Your's, too, I suspect. Goes with the red hair."

He motioned for Cory to sit and settled back into his desk chair.

"Adelene told me a little bit about what you want, but how about you start from the beginning."

Cory recapped what she had told Adelene. "Do you keep records back that far?"

Chief Brayton sat back, dwarfed in the big black leather chair. He seemed to be slowly and deliberately turning the pages of his memory. Finally he gave a brief nod in the affirmative.

"I remember something about a woman gone missing from the mill many years ago." He paused and frowned. "But, we weren't called in on that because there was no sign of foul play. Plus, no one in the family made a missing person report. I was a beat cop at the time and not a part of the administration, but I don't think anyone here had anything to do with it."

He gazed at the cement block wall across from his desk. "Yeah, that's right. We heard rumors, but nothing official came through here."

Cory gasped in disbelief. "Chief Brayton, how is it possible that a worker is on the job for part of a shift, disappears into thin air, and the mill or some part of management, some part of American Steel, doesn't make a report to the local authorities? Is this normal procedure?"

"They run a pretty closed operation over there," he said, shifting his weight in the chair. "They have their own private police on the grounds. Guards at every gate."

Cory opened her mouth to question him but was cut off. "They don't like outsiders poking around on their private property. Now, if it was a homicide or assault of some kind, they would have to contact us. But if a worker just disappears and there are no witnesses or evidence of foul play, why they might just think that worker walked off and left the mill." He scratched his forehead. "If I'm not mistaken, I think that's what they said about your mother."

Cory inhaled sharply. She was stunned. This was the first time she had heard an explanation, and it was the one she dreaded hearing the most. Her voice seemed to catch on a hook. "They said she...she just walked off?"

"I believe so."

Could this be true? Maybe she did just leave. Maybe she had grown tired of the single mother life. Cory leaned forward in the chair. "Do they have much of that? Homicides? Assaults?"

"No. Might have had some rough-housing during a strike, but it's been a long time since there's been any labor unrest at AC. They've had a couple of suicides, but there was witnesses to that."

"Suicides?"

"Yes, ma'am. About five years apart. Both did it the same way. Jumped right into a hot ladle. Damn thing full of molten steel. They was serious, that's for sure. Ain't no changing your mind once you step off the edge into one of those things. Other men on the job saw them, but it happened so fast, they couldn't stop 'em. Those men must have wanted to die real bad."

Cory shuddered.

"Did the mill report the suicides?"

"Yes, Ma'am. But they had witnesses. In your mother's case, there were no witnesses that came forward and no one filed any missing person report."

Cory stood up to leave. "I was only ten then. I remember staying with a school friend for a couple of days until my aunt flew in from California to get me. She would have been the only family to make a missing person report. She was probably too upset and worried about me to do something like that. We left for California right away. This is the first time I've been back here. I was hoping to find an official report. Something on paper."

Her finger traced a figure eight on a thin layer of dust on his desk, lost in a hazy memory of the school friend's bedroom. Until that moment she had forgotten that piece, and now it absorbed her. Where did they live? What was her name? Cory frowned with frustration.

Chief Brayton stood and extended his small hand, "I'm sorry I can't help you. If you need anything in the future, you just let me know."

"Thank you, Chief Brayton, I appreciate your offer." She shook his hand and turned towards the door.

"There is one place you can check. Ask at the union hall down on Eleventh Street. Somebody down there might remember something."

"Thank you, I'll do that. Maybe something will turn up." She left, feeling dispirited by another dead-end.

When Chief Brayton heard her footsteps fading down the hall, he shut his office door and picked up the telephone.

A gruff voice answered, "Local 1630. Luwanski speaking. Can I help you?"

"Al, its Red. You ain't never gonna guess who was just in my office."

"I don't have time for this, Red, I got a meeting downtown. Just tell me."

As far as Chief Brayton was concerned, Luwanski always had a meeting to run off to. It seemed more like he had an aversion to law enforcement. "I'll give you a hint. Twenty some years ago, female, Ginny something or other..."

There was silence on the other end of the line.

"You there, Al ?"

"Yeah. Don't know what you're talking about."

"Remember when that girl went missing in the BOP? No one knew what happened to her?"

"Yeah. So what? That was a long time ago."

Chief Brayton had the impression that Luwanski was hedging. There were long memories in the mill. A missing red-headed woman would have become part of mill lore.

"Well, her daughter was just in here. She's wantin' to find out what happened to her momma."

"*What?* You're joking, right?"

"Nope. She was asking about a police report but we were never involved. I told her she might get some information from the local union. She'll be coming your way."

"Yeah, ok, I'll keep an eye out," Luwanski said. Hanging up the phone, he felt panic seize his chest.

He walked quickly across the meeting hall and peeked through the Venetian blinds. No one was out there. He hurried to the front door, locked it, and snapped off the ceiling lights. Then he ran back to his small wood paneled office, slammed the door, and grabbed the phone.

"C'mon. C'mon. Answer the damn phone."

Finally, a man's voice said, "Harley Security."

"It's Al down at the hall. We got a problem."

7

The big semi barreled eastbound on the Ohio Turnpike. The driver looked over at the dozing hitch-hiker.

"Hey, Bud. The next exit is Youngstown. That's where I get off. There's a service area near there. It'd probably be easier to catch another ride there than at the exit."

The rays of the afternoon sun pierced the passenger side window. Under his thick, black hair his scalp perspired and itched. There were deep creases around his eyes, the kind that come from a lifetime of squinting in dark places.

"Hey, Bud. You gotta wake up now and tell me where you want to get off."

"Service area's ok," he mumbled.

Within minutes he swung down out of the cab. "Thanks," he muttered over his shoulder as he walked towards the restaurant. He bought a hamburger, French fries, and a root beer and sat outside under a tree.

The parking lot was crowded. Parents and their kids spilled out of vans with TV screens hanging from the ceilings. A man bent over the hood of his car reading a map. A pair of young lovers laughed, their arms wrapped around each other as they tried to walk in sync. Truck drivers wearing t-shirts that fit snug around their bulging bellies leaned against their rigs smoking cigarettes, seeming at ease in their freedom, comfortable and confident.

Danny McCormack watched the scene warily, then he snickered. So this is normal. Thirty years in a nut house. He shook his head. How the hell was he supposed to know what's normal?

His mood turned nasty when he remembered his imprisonment in that loony bin and the train wreck that had become his life. His big-knuckled fingers ached with arthritis, the result of swinging a wet mop up and down the dimly lit tunnels that connected buildings at Ypsilanti State Hospital. He'd figured it out the day before he left: six fuckin' hours a day, five fuckin' days a week, fifty-two fuckin' weeks a year, eighteen fuckin' years. That's 30,000 hours of my fuckin' life down in them tunnels. One hour of daylight inside a ten foot tall chain-link fence topped with barbed wire and electricity.

For a minute his Irish green eyes, bright as a neon sign, followed the flight of a yellow jacket. When it came within reach, he snatched it and crushed it in his palm.

All them years. For what? For trippin' with that girl. That's it, man, nothin' else. Just got high. Trippin', having a good time. They said he killed her. But they got it wrong, man, all wrong. Danny McCormack is no killer. It was him that did it. He said he was gonna fuck her up. What for, man? We're just having a little fun. He said she was a cop. Are you nuts? She's been trippin' with us for three days, cops don't do that, man. Said he'd had enough of her, of the whole scene, and he was going back to the 'Burgh.

The cops didn't believe Danny, although they had a problem with the evidence.

He shouted from the defense table. "Where exactly, Your Honor, is the fuckin' weapon?" He glared out over the crowded courtroom, the veins in his neck pulsating. "Anyone here have it?"

Spit shot out of his mouth as he screamed at a stranger.

"You, Sissy, you with the big tits, you got it? How 'bout you, you prick!" He glared at the prosecuting attorney. "You got it? Naw, ain't nobody here got it 'cuz it's in Pittsburgh!"

The judge stood up, red-faced with fury, and banged his gavel down on his desk. "Get him out of my courtroom! Get him out of here now!"

Two deputy sheriffs grabbed Danny's arms.

"Get your hands off me, you cock-suckers!" he roared as he wrestled against the manacles wrapped around his wrists and strapped to his waist.

From the jail, he made one phone call.

"You gotta believe me, Ginny, I didn't do this. You know me, Gin. You know I couldn't do anything like this. Jesus, God, Gin, I'm no animal. We did a lot of drugs. There's a lot I don't remember."

He paused, his eyes darting up and down the hall. A guard stood nearby. McCormack listened to the tearful voice on the other end of the phone.

"Yeah. Yeah." His voice rose. "God damn it, I know you got problems! I know money's tight. What the fuck, you think I'm on some kind of holiday here?"

He forced himself to stop yelling, but the tension made his teeth grind.

"Ok, Ok. How's the kid? She ok? Yeah, well, I'm gonna beat this. I'll be back. I'll get a job. You, me and the kid, ok? Listen, I know who did it, some mother-fucker from the.... Hey, I got time left. Hey god-damn it, don't you disconnect this phone. HEY!"

He stood staring at the receiver and then he smashed it into the phone box over and over, sending metal and plastic flying along the tarnished linoleum floor until the guards shut him down.

Not guilty by reason of insanity. Too nuts for the prison system where at least there was an end date. The doors slammed shut behind him, the locks engaged, and he became an indefinite guest of the State of Michigan.

A State Trooper cruised through the parking lot. The

officer looked left and right, and then straight at him. Danny took a long, slow drink out of the super-sized root-beer that covered half his face. His watched the car, watched it park, watched the trooper lock the doors and stroll into the restaurant.

It was time to move on. He stood up and took a last glimpse of an enormous orange-red sun that was beginning its descent below the flat Mid-west horizon. Then he ambled off to the line of semis parked at the back of the lot.

"Any chance I can catch a ride to Pittsburgh?"

"You bet. I'm making a delivery in McKeesport. Should be there in about two hours. Glad for the company."

Two hours. Not long now. A chill shot down his spine.

8

The Local 1630 union hall had been closed when Cory and Rashid back-tracked

to the mill. She decided to make the best of her time and visit the main branch of the Carnegie Library near the University of Pittsburgh. Traffic was congested and parking nearby, impossible. Rashid pulled the big Impala into another no parking zone and turned off the ignition. Cory, resigned to her law-breaking driver, hopped out of the car.

"I'll just be a few minutes," she said.

Rashid nodded as he punched numbers into his cell phone.

A librarian set her up at a monitor with microfiche film of the Pittsburgh Press and the Pittsburgh Post-Gazette editions dated July, 1984. Since there was no police report, Cory doubted there would be a newspaper article, but she wanted to cover every idea on her limited list of possibilities.

Headlines trumpeted panic in tunnel of Mecca: The lead story speculated on Walter Mondale, Democratic Party presidential candidate selecting a woman as his running mate. Pittsburgh Pirates were on a winning streak. The body of a security guard employed at Andrew Carnegie Works was found on the shoreline of the Monongahela River, an apparent suicide. More severe thunderstorms were expected.

After an hour of searching in vain for an article or announcement about a missing steelworker, the flicker of hope vanished.

A dull pain was threatening to burgeon into a full scale migraine as Cory returned to the car. "Let's take a break," she told Rashid. "I'll go home for lunch. Can you pick me up at six tonight? We'll take a spin over to Munhall."

"Sho' Ms Co," he said, peeling away from the curb, the cell phone in his ear. "It's been real, man, hit me up when you get the digits," he said into the phone.

"Hit me up when you get the digits?"

"Yeah," he snickered. "Hit me up means call me later and digits is someone's phone number. You gonna need some kind of notebook so you can study at night."

"You've got that right," she laughed.

In the cottage, Cory pulled the blinds and stretched out on the bed. With the noon day sun beating down on the roof, the cottage was heating up, but she was shivering. She pulled the blanket up to her chin and waited for her migraine medication to kick in.

As she dozed, the dirty blue BOP shop came alive. She was a little girl in coveralls running alongside the metal wall, banging on closed doors. Round and round she went, yelling, "Momma! Momma! I can't get in! Don't worry, I'm coming! I'm coming!"

She awoke drenched in sweat.

∿∿∿

Rashid sat across from his uncle at the kitchen table. Having downed two roast beef subs, a bowl of baked beans, and coleslaw, he fixed his sights on the raspberry Jell-O.

"How'd it go this morning?" asked Charles Mobley.

"Cool," he said.

Uncle Charles waited, tapping his wide forefinger on the table. He shifted his bulk and gave an exasperated look at his much loved nephew.

"Cool? That's it? Y'know, if you used as many words to talk as you do mouthfuls of food to eat, maybe we could have a real conversation. Now I been waiting real patient for you to finish the last tidbit like you haven't seen food for a month. And don't even think of touching that Jell-O, unless you planning on drinking it. It's not set yet."

Rashid looked up at the ceiling. Then he launched into a retelling of the morning's events, from the mill to the Braddock Police Station to the Union Hall to the main Library.

"I think whatever she be poking around for has to do with AC. She got real strange actin' when we was there. I thought she was gonna start bawlin', but all she said was she had to get in there. I told her they don't let peeps in there, but she said she would find a way."

Charles frowned. "AC? What in the worl' could she have to do with the mill?" The creases in his forehead deepened as he studied a jar of mustard on the table, as if answers could be found inside.

"I don't know," Rashid said. "She was serious about getting in there. If anyone can find a way, she can."

"Twenty years ago thereabouts her momma went missing...from the mill?" Mr. Mobley scratched his head. "Well, I'll be. I'll betcha that's it. Got to be."

"What's that?"

"There was stories going 'round the mill about a redhaired girl who went missin' in the BOP. There was lots of rumors about what happened to her. Some said she died in an accident or been killed or walked off the job. The mill was always full of rumors, especially about the women who worked there. I knew who they were referrin' to because she used to speak up a lot at union meetings." He chuckled. "She used to tie the local union president in knots with her fast words."

"You think that was her momma?" Rashid asked, suddenly showing more interest.

"It fits together now that I think about it. My memory isn't so good for names, but that red hair and those freckles say a lot."

Mr. Mobley took a long swig from his glass of ice tea.

"Maybe I can help her. I know some of them women used to work in the mill back then. Most of 'em lost their jobs when the mill downsized. Didn't have enough seniority to hang on. I'm pretty sure one lives in the projects in Rankin. I'll stop over there early tomorrow morning before I pick up Ms. Cory, see what I can find out. Don't you say nothin' though. I don't want to get her hopes up."

~ ~ ~

That evening, while Rashid waited in the car, Cory canvassed the residents on Twelfth Avenue in Munhall. She didn't have much luck. Reaching the last house at the end of the block, she said a silent prayer, hoping for a break.

She studied the brown brick dwelling, with its rusted gutters and splintered shutters hanging askew. The wooden porch and steps were warped, in sore need of replacement. Surely it must be abandoned, she thought. Yet, there was a familiarity about it that puzzled Cory.

Cautiously she climbed the stairs, testing each plank with her foot before putting her full weight on it. She was about to knock when the door creaked open. A frail woman dressed in a faded blue-checked house dress, her spine curved by osteoporosis, peered up at Cory through glasses as thick as plate glass. Her sparse white hair was pulled back in a disheveled bun.

"I thought I heard these old boards groaning. Can I help you?" she asked, stretching her wrinkled neck upwards.

Cory's knees weakened at the sight of her. "Mrs. *Gromski?*" A lump swelled in her throat. "It's me, Cory. Cory Johnson. Do you remember me?"

The old woman leaned closer to the tattered screen door and squinted up at her. "Cory? Cassandra? Is that really you?"

"Yes, Ma'am, it's me." A sudden vivid memory struck Cory. She was a little girl leaning against the kitchen counter as Mrs. Gromski kneaded dough for rolls. She could smell the cinnamon on her baby-sitter's apron.

"Cory. My word." A tear moistened her cheek. "What a nice surprise. Come in and sit down. What are you doing here? Let me turn on the light so I can see you. My word but you have grown. I always knew you were going to be tall because you were such a leggy girl and your momma was tall. How old are you now? Do you want something to drink? Coffee? Tea? Where have you been young lady? What have you been doing?"

"I've been living in California with my Aunt. I turned thirty-one this year. I'm a psychologist. But, how are you? How is your health?"

"Thirty-one! My word but where does time go? I'm getting along just fine. I'll be eighty-eight this September. Social Service hasn't been able to warehouse me yet. I want to die in my own bed." The resolve in her voice reminded Cory that Mrs. Gromski had always been a force to be reckoned with.

The living room was crowded with old oversized furniture. A rocker sat directly in front of the TV with an end-table off to the side. The newspaper was opened to the sports section with a large magnifying glass on top. Mrs. Gromski loved the Pittsburgh Pirates.

Cory followed the old woman towards the kitchen in the rear of the house.

Mrs. Gromski slowly maneuvered her way from coffee pot to cups to sugar canister. When she sat down, she peered through her glasses at the tall young woman with her unmanageable tresses.

"How lovely you are," she said, sipping her hot coffee. "You're not that gangly girl with scabs on her knees, whipping around the corner on her bicycle. You're all grown up and quite striking. You look exactly like your mother."

"I do?"

"Definitely." She stirred her coffee. "Tell me, what are you doing here? Have you moved back from California?"

"I came back to try to find out what happened to my mother. I know it's been a long time, but this is the first opportunity I've had to...to.... You see, I don't know what happened to her." Cory took a sip of coffee to get control of her quivering lip. "I have so few memories of her. In fact, I don't remember much about my childhood."

Mrs. Gromski was not surprised at Cory's return. She had expected that someday the girl would return to search for her mother. It was the reason why she stored that box in the back of a dresser drawer.

"It was a long time ago, but that's one of the good things about decrepit old brains," Mrs. Gromski said. "I can't remember if I brushed my teeth this morning, but I remember your mother. Ginny would be hard to forget. She was special."

She paused to add a tad more sugar to her cup. "There were only two things she cared about: you and the state of the world. And you were the only one she had any control over. You were her home base while everywhere else was raining fly balls. The problem with Ginny was she believed she was the only outfielder. She was always blowing in and blowing out, always on the move, dragging a burlap sack of clanging problems behind her. She just raced from one to another, waving her solutions in the air. She had a heart of gold, that one, and she wanted wrongs to be set right."

Cory soaked these words up like a dry sponge afloat in a sudsy tub. Up to now the memory of her mother always felt like a momentary brisk wind. It swept over her, gathered force and then disappeared around a corner, leaving her dazed and alone. What had been missing were the stories that made her mother a real person.

"If you have the time, Mrs. Gromski, I would like to hear anything you can tell me about her. The only family I have is my aunt in California. She was really a distant relative and doesn't know much about Mom's life."

"Well, now, Ginny never said much about personal things. She was one to go on and on about issues but she would clam up about her private life."

Mrs. Gromski stirred her coffee as bits and pieces of a conversation with Ginny took form in her mind.

"There were a couple of times when she spoke of her family. I could see it was painful for her, so I never asked any questions. I let her talk when she needed to and I just listened..."

～～～

"There's another lay-off coming," Ginny said as she folded the clothes that she'd taken off the line. "It couldn't happen at a worse time. I've been trying to save money for a newer car but I'll have to forget that idea. If that old junk breaks down again, I'm gonna claim the mechanic on my tax return."

"Any idea how long the lay-off will be?"

"No, just rumors. I've been thinking of trying to get hired in a coal mine. There's lots of mines south of here. Maybe I could get a job there."

Mrs. Gromski frowned. "That's dangerous work, Ginny, and they get laid-off, too. Plus, they have those long strikes. You know what they say about coal miners. The first year of a 3-year contract they make up what they lost for the strike the year before. The second year they earn money. The third year they save up for the next year's strike."

Ginny stopped folding clothes and stared at her empty hands.

"I know," she said, her tone subdued. "My daddy died in a mine explosion when I was just a baby. I never knew him, but my grandmother would talk about the accident from time to time. She believed that the mining company was playing fast and loose with the safety rules. The local union was about to call a walk-out when the explosion happened. It killed three miners. Daddy was one of them."

"I am sorry, Ginny. It must have been difficult for you and your mother."

"I didn't really know him, so that part wasn't so bad." Her voice became hoarse as she bent over and began to brusquely fold towels.

"It was a lot worse on my mother. She was lonely and depressed for a long time. At least that's how I remember her. Then one day she was gone. Packed her bags and took off with some guy. I was eight years old."

Ginny went to the kitchen sink for a glass of water. She remembered watching her mother shove her clothes into an old suitcase.

'I'll be back for you as soon as I can,' she said, but she wouldn't look at me. She was in such a hurry to get into that shiny red convertible that she never took a moment to explain how and when we were going to be together again. 'You tell Alma I'll send her money as soon as I get a job and you mind her. She's your grandmother, she'll take good care of you.'

"The man she was leaving with could see me standing at the screen door, but he wasn't too interested in me. He stayed leaning against the car, blowing circles of cigarette smoke into the air. That's how I felt, like one of those exhaled puffs, set adrift to nowhere. Mom grabbed her suitcase, gave me a quick hug, and ran out the front door. That was the last I saw of her."

Ginny set the stacked laundry on the kitchen table and sat down with her glass of water. This was more talking about her past than she had ever done before. It was both liberating and exhausting.

"I was raised by my daddy's momma, my grandma Alma. There was just the two of us living near Johnstown. My granddaddy had worked on the railroad. He was one of those radical Wobblies. I never knew him either, but grandma filled my head with stories about him so I felt close to him. He died in the Johnstown flood in the thirties."

"Nineteen thirty-six to be exact," Mrs. Gromski said.

"Yes, that's right. Funny thing was, Grandma Alma didn't say much about my daddy. Maybe it was just too painful to talk about her only child being blown up seven hundred feet underground. She had a photograph hof him she kept on the fireplace mantle. Sometimes, if I woke up earlier than her, I would find the photograph on the table next to her rocking chair.

"And she never mentioned my momma. She came home that day and found me hugging a doll on the back porch, crying my eyes out. When I told her what happened, she hugged me long and hard and then said let's get supper ready, and that was it. It was like a teacher erasing yesterday's lesson off the blackboard. I guess she figured we would start with a clean slate. Maybe it was for the best.

"I waited for my mother for a long time, but she never

showed up. Never sent any money. Never even sent a birthday card."

Ginny shrugged off the memories. "I guess you could say I inherited two things from my family. A strong belief in unionism and my momma's red hair."

~~~

Cory grew quiet. The only sound was the ticking of the kitchen clock. She realized that, while many people who suffered painful losses in a lifetime continued to make new connections, but she had wrapped herself in a sheath of armor, a superb defense against the possibility of any emotional risk. It was an uncomfortable insight.

Cory stirred her coffee with a spoon. After a few moments, she asked, "Did Mom have a boyfriend?"

Mrs. Gromski clapped her hands and laughed.

"Your mother was a very pretty woman. So yes, there were always men interested in her. One fellow in particular, his name was...oh, dear, I can't recall. But she wouldn't make any commitments. She would go to the movies or out for a pizza, but, as far as I know, that was about it. She said she didn't want to complicate her life."

Cory took a deep breath. She wasn't sure she wanted to go in this other direction, but since she was plumbing the black abyss, she decided she might as well hold nothing back. "Do you know anything about my father?"

"Not much, I'm afraid. Ginny was young when she got pregnant. She told me she had fallen in love with the emerald eyes of an Irish lad. I think his name was David, no, that's not it...Danny. Yes, Danny. They weren't together long before she got pregnant. I think they moved in with his parents somewhere in Pittsburgh. Then he went on a hunting trip to Michigan and got into some kind of trouble.

I don't know what he did, she never said, but it must have been pretty bad because he was put away for a long, long time."

"In prison?"

"It must have been. She only mentioned it one time. Never said another word about him."

A gentle breeze, fresh with the smell of lilacs, floated through the open kitchen window. "Do you have any idea what happened to my mother?"

No, Cory, I'm afraid I don't. But I would bet what's left of my life that she did not just walk away. That was company propaganda."

Cory gasped. "You knew that's what they said?"

"Yes, I heard that nonsense. AC management sent a man over to your house with a box of her belongings from her locker. I was there packing up your clothes. He told me she left about four in the morning. Said there was some guy in a white pick-up truck waiting for her.

"He didn't think she wanted that job anymore. Well, it's true enough that if she didn't want that job, she was feisty enough to walk off. But she would never have left you, *you* were the reason for her life. There was no way she was walking away from you, especially after her mother walked out on her."

Cory's face began to crumble.

"Are you ok? Goodness, maybe I shouldn't have gone on like that."

"No, I'm alright," Cory said, stiffening her lip. "It's just... well...part of me has believed she did walk away. That being a single mom was too hard and she got tired of struggling. And when I couldn't remember much about her, it was easy for that idea to take hold."

"Here's a tissue, dear. There's more that I need to tell you. I'll be right back."

Cory composed herself while Mrs. Gromski went rummaging around in one of her dresser drawers. She returned carrying a small box.

"I have always believed that something bad happened to Ginny that night. You see, we would always chat after she got off work, especially when she worked the midnight turn. She would get home a little after eight in the morning. I had already seen you off to school and I would have some fresh orange juice waiting for her. She would come dragging through the front door, especially during the summer when the heat was so bad and her working around that hot steel all the time. There were many mornings we would sit out on the front porch and she would talk about the mill, the union, you, her old car.

"But then it changed. She started coming home with a worried air about her. She didn't say much. It wasn't like her, not a bit. I could tell something was bothering her. About a week before she disappeared, she sat down at the kitchen table. I remember like it was yesterday..."

~~~

"Hi Nora, how was Cory last night? I left her a chocolate cupcake for her lunch box. Did she get it? Man, it's humid."

Ginny reached down, untied her shoes and pulled her socks off. Her hands shook when she reached for the juice. She sat there for a while, staring out the window, deep in thought.

"Something wrong, Ginny dear?"

She didn't answer right away. I thought maybe she hadn't heard me. "Ginny?"

"No, it's ok. Everything's ok. I'm just tired."

"Cory's coming by my house for juice and a cookie when school is out, so you don't have to set an alarm. I'm going to go now. You get a good sleep. You'll feel better after."

When I got to the front door, she came running after me.

"Nora, wait. Would you do me a favor?" She reached behind her neck and unclasped the gold chain that she always wore. It had a gold heart that hung on it.

"If something ever happens to me, give this to Cory. I want her to have it when she's a little older."

"Ginny, what is going on? Why are you thinking this way?" But she didn't answer. She shoved the necklace into my hand. She looked sad, but she wouldn't say anymore.

<div align="center">~~~</div>

Mrs. Gromski pushed the little box across the table. Cory opened it and removed the necklace. She opened the heart and gulped when she saw the two tiny photographs. On one side a small girl posing with an ear-to-ear smile, a large gap where her front teeth used to be. On the other side was her beautiful mother, her expression soft and inviting.

Cory studied her mother's face as though evaluating a precious gem.

"Thank you, Missus Gromski. Thank you very much." She closed the clasp of the chain behind her neck and tucked it beneath her shirt.

"I wish I could tell you more. A lot of people knew Ginny. Some of her mill friends organized a little meeting after she disappeared. They sure didn't think that she had walked away from her job. But there wasn't a clue anywhere that something else had happened. Your aunt came and whisked you off to California. She said to give away the furniture and things as I saw fit. I had Goodwill come and get the furniture. I hung onto her clothes for almost a year, then I took them to the Goodwill, too."

She stirred her coffee absentmindedly. "One minute you both were here and my house was filled with laughter, and the next you both were gone—and everything was empty."

The two women sat together quietly. The laughter and shouting of children playing kick-ball in the alley wafted through the open window. Somewhere someone was pushing a lawn-mower. A telephone rang. A screen door slammed shut.

"Mrs. Gromski, I cannot thank you enough. Would it be ok if I came back to visit? You and my aunt are the only family I have. I am so glad to have found you again."

"Oh, Cory. My word. Absolutely! Would Sunday be good? I'm afraid I can't bake anymore. Seems I sometimes forget the oven is on. This aging business can be such a bother. My world keeps getting smaller and smaller."

Knowing she had chocolate chip cookies in mind, Cory said, "Don't you worry. I found a bakery in that new Homestead shopping mall. I'll pick up some cookies and be here Sunday around one o'clock."

Cory hugged her good-bye and gingerly navigated the porch steps.

9

Jeff Staniewski had used his sobering up time to good advantage. Once the tremors in his hands slowed down and his nerves were not so frayed, he was able to get work as a day laborer. At five each morning he crawled out of bed to be first in the boarding house toilet and tub. He turned the hot water on full blast and stood directly under the rusting shower head. Sometimes the steamy water scorched his skin, turning his hairy chest and back red, but he didn't flinch. It was a strange sensation to actually feel something. He'd spent two decades trying to stop what couldn't be stopped: feeling. Now he relished his burning red skin, it sharpened the rage that gurgled in his stomach and strengthened his resolve.

Jeff was a good worker. Why not? Breaking his back for a few dollars a day was in his genes. He sweated over heavy jackhammers, shoveled rocks, spread hot tar, wielded a sledge hammer high above his head and sent it crashing into old wall, and took any other job that required shear brawn. He said little, sat alone at the lunch break, and caused no trouble. In the meantime his muscles hardened along with his bilious hate.

One day he got lucky. The labor boss told him an outfit doing independent contract work for Andrew Carnegie Works was hiring.

"It ain't a bad job. AC's the only mill left around here. You'll be making half as much as them union guys, but it's more than you're making now, and it's steady daylight.

You think you can handle that?"

"Yeah, thanks," Jeff said, trying to control his excitement. This was the break he had been waiting for—a legitimate way to get into the mill. "I'll go see the boss of this outfit first thing in the morning."

"The closing of these mills and the downsizing of AC has been real hard on the people here," the labor boss continued. "A lot of them never found another job, or they had to work two or three jobs to make the mortgage. So if you get hired on, it'll be your lucky day."

Three days later Jeff walked through the Eleventh Street gate of Andrew Carnegie Works. He pulled his hard hat down low and waved his ID badge at the guard from ten feet away, not taking any chances that someone might recognize him.

He couldn't believe his luck. His assignment was in the BOP shooting fireproofing chemicals with an industrial hose over the bricks that lined the ladles. He worked at the far end of a long wide aisle where the lighting was dim and he would go unnoticed. Best of all, he worked alone.

The mill didn't use ladles much since the continuous caster had been installed. So most of the time he sat hunched over in a darkened corner, taking long, deep drags off a cigarette, watching and waiting.

Then one day, near the end of the turn, he saw him. He wasn't a foreman anymore. He'd moved up the ladder; lots of promotions over twenty years.

I'll be damned, he thought. A real success story. He's management now, comes and goes as he pleases. Struts around with his white hard hat. Keeps his fingernails clean and trim and never does a lick of real work.

That ain't changed, he never did work. Back then we could almost smell his fear when he had to get close to the heat. That's why he stayed in his shanty office—except when he wanted to write somebody up for a safety violation.

But when there was trouble on the steel-pouring platform, man, he was long gone.

When the first steel pourer couldn't shut off the ladle, that hot stuff splashed all over the platform. Those guys were nuts to keep workin' the heat. Had to run for cover every time the crane moved up a mold. Then they'd run back and keep workin'. Bend backward, shove them long iron bars up above their heads and slide them 300 pound caps downhill till they stopped on top of the molds. Tryin' to kill the heat in the molds. And the whole time the smoke would be coming up from the bottom of their boots. Everything on the platform caught on fire. Smoke so thick they could hardly see. Yet they kept working, trying to save American Steel a quarter million dollars.

But not him. No way. The bastard was nowhere in sight when the alarm went out over the PA system, "Pit foreman! Pit foreman! Number four platform! Running stopper!" Yeah, he was afraid of the hot stuff. But he sure was a mean son-of-a-bitch. Hated blacks. Hated women. And hated the union. Hated anything that got in his way. He did some mean shit on the street, too.

Jeff stood in the shadows of a ladle and watched as he leaned on the railing high up on the furnace floor. Jeff Staniewski's task had just become a hell of a lot easier—just get past the guard two hours earlier than his normal shift time.

"*Then* what?" he mumbled aloud.

Sparks burned his yellowed fingers as he crushed the cigarette butt against the iron ladle. The time had come to make the plan. A sinister smirk parted his chapped lips, exposing the brown tobacco stains on his teeth.

Oh, yeah. The time had come.

10

The sky was overcast and the high humidity augured a morning thunderstorm. Arriving at the cottage promptly at nine o'clock, Mr. Mobley found Cory sitting in the kitchen sipping a lukewarm cup of coffee.

"Good morning, Miss Johnson," he said, his massive bulk resembling the trunk of the oak tree in the yard. "How are you this grey day?"

"Good morning, Mister Mobley. Please call me Cory. I was trying to figure out what to do next. Would you like some coffee?"

Charles Mobley had been up early knocking on doors in the housing projects in the small town of Rankin. Some of the women who opened their doors were young black mothers on public assistance, living in cramped conditions in run-down government housing with short-term government benefits. They had no connection to the mill and no knowledge of the opportunities it once promised women.

Mobley was about to give up when a bone-thin young woman with a naked toddler balanced on her hip asked warily, "What you want with her?"

"She might have known somebody back then, another woman who worked there. She disappeared and her daughter is trying to find out what happened to her."

"You lookin' to get somebody in trouble?"

"No, Miss. I'm trying to help the daughter get some answers. I used to work in the mill back then and I remember there were quite a few women there for a time. Maybe, if I can find one or two, they might be able to help."

Shifting the child to the other hip, she studied his face, trying to assess his motives. "You be wantin' my grandmother," she said, emitting a bored sigh. "She ain't here. You come back here around eleven, you'll catch her."

If he could have, he would have expressed his glee by skipping down the cracked sidewalk back to his car. His first detective assignment and it was as easy as baking an apple pie. But how was he to break this news to Ms. Johnson without seeming to be interfering in her life?

"Mister Mobley?" Cory said, interrupting his silent replay of the morning. "Coffee?"

"Yes, ma'am. Uh, you can call me Charles if you like. Coffee would be just fine."

They sat at the kitchen table with fresh coffee steaming from their cups.

"I hope you don't mind if I continue to call you Mister Mobley. My aunt would be on a plane tomorrow to wreak havoc over my head if she caught me referring anyone over sixty by their first name."

They laughed at the prospect, then she continued, "I spoke with Rashid yesterday. He told me you used to work in the slab mill at Andrew Carnegie Works."

"Yes, I did. Retired in eighty-six after forty years." He watched the zigzagged flight of a Monarch butterfly out the window. "My brothers and I migrated up from Alabama during the war huntin' for work. Found it in the mill. Over the years I'd been through good times and bad with American Steel. But, in the early eighties, they was goin' through some bad times. They closed mills all over the country.

"There was talk that they were going to modernize the BOP with some new-fangled equipment. Rumor had it that lots of men was gonna lose their jobs. I didn't need to be workin' anymore, so I took my retirement." He patted his enormous girth. "That's when I started putting on an extra me," he chuckled.

"Believe it or not, Mister Mobley, it suits you." Cory laughed. She flicked a piece of lint off her black jeans. "My mother worked in the BOP. She vanished one night without a trace." She brought him up to date on her conversations with the Chief of Police in Braddock, her failed attempt to see the local union president, the research at the main library, and the relevant parts of the talk with Mrs. Gromski. She left out her decision to find a way into the mill.

"I'm convinced that something horrible happened to her. Yet, other than learning she was frightened several days before she left for work that night, I haven't found out much else."

Thunder rumbled overhead as dark clouds moved in. The rain burst from the sky in torrents. Mr. Mobley wondered what had angered the Good Lord so early in the morning. He decided the time was right to report on his investigative activities.

"After I spoke to Rashid yesterday, I thought maybe that was your momma that them rumors were about back then. I remember her."

Cory's head shot up.

Mr. Mobley raised his hand to stop the questions he knew were coming.

"I didn't know her. I never talked to her. But I remember her from the union meetings. She could rile up them union officers, that's for sure. She always had some issue or cause she wanted the union to take up. They wasn't used to thinkin' and doin' like she wanted them to. They could do the little things, file grievances and the like, but her ideas were too big for them."

He chuckled as he thought of the headaches she gave

those guys. "She was a fighter, your momma, and real smart."

"Rumors?" she asked. "What were they?"

"That there had been an accident or she had walked off the job...or...or she...," he stumbled over his words, not knowing exactly how to say it.

"Or she'd been killed," Cory whispered.

"Yes, Miss Cory, there was that. The thing was there was never a body, so the story that stuck was what the Company said. She walked off the job, quit in the middle of the night. I believed that back then, but I don't believe it no more."

"Why?"

"I can't see her walkin' away from you. Why, that'd be telling half yourself to stay put while the other half takes a hike. It ain't possible."

"I believe you're right, Mister Mobley," a broad grin expanding on Cory's face. "Thank you for saying that. I just wish I knew what to do next."

"Well, I hope you don't mind, but I took it upon myself to try and find a woman that might have worked with your momma. I found her granddaughter and she told me to come back at eleven this morning. Maybe she can help you."

Cory jumped up and vigorously shook his hand. "You have saved the day!" she said. She grabbed her umbrella and opened the door. "Shall we make a visit?"

～～～

The old Impala swerved and swayed as it sloshed through the waves of rainwater running downhill. It was a weekday at mid-morning so traffic was sparse. The car sailed over the Rankin Bridge, sending a rooster-tail spray spewing up from the back tires.

They pulled up to the curb in front of a project apartment. A short, light-skinned woman in her fifties stood in the doorway, peering out behind large oval-shaped glasses that gave her the appearance of an owl, and waved them inside.

As Cory entered, the woman led her guest into the middle of the cramped living room. With arms folded over her chest, she examined Cory from head to foot.

"There's no doubt about it, you're Ginny's daughter. C'mon and have a seat." She pointed to the sofa that was piled high with freshly done laundry. "Tashika, come down here and get these clothes so people can use this furniture for what it was intended. This ain't no laundromat."

She kept staring at Cory and shaking her head. "I have to pinch myself so I know I'm not dreamin'."

Mr. Mobley stuck out his hand. "I'm Charles Mobley and this here is Cory Johnson. She's here...."

"I know why she's here. It's about Ginny. Sit down, Mister Mobley, we got a lot to talk about."

"Thank you for the invitation, but I'll be running along. I'd just be in the way, so I'll head home and do some cookin' for lunch." He fished around in his cracked leather wallet, pulled out a wrinkled business card and handed it to Cory. "I'll be by the phone, Miss Cory, you ring when you're ready to be picked up."

"My name is Beatrice Davis," said her host, "but everyone calls me Blinky. You can, too." She ran her fingers through her short black hair that was peppered with strands of grey. Despite the silliness of her name, Cory could tell she was tough as an industrial diamond. Blinky wore men's khaki pants and had her sleeves rolled up to her elbows, lumberjack-style. This was a person who took no prisoners.

"There are a couple other women who are coming over this morning. They knew your mother from the mill. You'll be interested in what they have to say."

"Oh, yes, please, I want to hear everything."

"I'm sure you do. You need all the pieces, don't you? We don't have all of them, some are still missing, but maybe we can help."

"Did you work in the BOP?" Cory asked.

"Yep. And Sheila still works there. She's got a good job on a crane. Dorie worked in the blast furnace. They had a few months more seniority than Ginny and me." She heard laughter outside. "Here they come now."

The door flew open and two women ran in out of the rain. When they saw Cory, their mouths flew open. Once again she was examined from top to bottom.

"Good Lord, honey, you are a carbon copy of your mother!" Sheila exclaimed as she pulled the wet rain slicker off her lean, sculpted body. Her long hair fell in dozens of thin braids ending in a line of brightly colored beads.

"She sure does," Dorie said in a slow Southern accent, her voice raspy like gravel. She was a large woman with a long face pockmarked with acne scars. Her thin blond hair clung to her wet scalp.

"I remember you when you was just a little thang," Dorie said. "You was all Ginny ever talked about."

"You mean, when she wasn't tryin' to change the world?" Sheila laughed, her white teeth like whipped cream against her chocolate skin.

"Sit down, we have business to attend to," Blinky said. She looked at the rocking chair and the recliner and yelled upstairs, "Tashika, what'd you do, girl, move the laundry three feet? This ain't no bedroom. Come down here and take these clothes upstairs where they belong so people can sit down!"

The sound of running feet could be heard pounding down the stairs.

Though the front door was open for ventilation, the room was stuffy from body heat. Seated next to Sheila on the sofa, with Dorie and Blinky seated across from them, Cory told them her story, apologizing for taking so long to return and ending with, "I am not only trying to piece together what happened and why it happened. What is just as important to me is to fill in the gaps in my memories of her." In a soft beseeching voice, she added, "I want to know my mother."

"You don't need to apologize, honey," Sheila said, patting her on the arm. "I always knew you'd be back some day. The important thing is you're here now." She turned to the other women, "Where should we begin?"

"I was telling her how we got hired at the same time," Blinky said. "Remember that ninety-day probation period? We weren't in the union and the company could fire us for any reason. We sure sweated that out. There was one foreman, Kirkpatrick, he was on Ginny like flies on shit. One night we were pushing brooms on the furnace floor...."

〜〜〜

Ginny scowled as she watched the tiny flakes of silvery graphite spout out of the roaring furnaces and like a blizzard cover everything. Flakes got sucked into noses, stuck in throats, even in underpants. She sneezed.

"Can this get any more boring? We just swept that corner and now it's covered in graphite. All we do is sweep floors for eight hours. This has got to be the cleanest damn steel mill in the country."

She caught sight of Kirkpatrick, strutting towards her like a rutting buck.

"You're doing a good job, honey," he said, standing so close that the edge of his hard hat touched hers. A vulgar grin smeared his face. "How 'bout we get together after work? I know a place where we can have some fun. How 'bout it? I give great back rubs, and I bet you give good rubs, too, don't'cha?" He reached out to touch her arm.

Ginny took a step back. She was so pissed off her face turned purple. But she had to harness it or lose her job.

"Can't do it."

"C'mon, Baby. Just you and me."

Ginny began pushing the broom in another direction. He moved in front of her.

"Some other night then," he said with a cocky smirk. "I can wait but not too long. You know what I mean?"

"Ginny told me she was real worried about that mangy dog Kirkpatric. The closer it got to our ninety days being over, the pushier he got. She kept her distance, took jobs in mold conditioning way on the other side of the mill.

"This is the day!" Ginny said, as she and Blinky rode the elevator up to the break room to grab a sandwich. "Our probation is up. You know what that means?"

She marched into Kirkpatrick's office with Blinky right behind her for moral support. He was sitting at his desk when she stuck her index finger in his face and hissed like an agitated snake.

"You get this straight, Kirkpatrick. I'm only gonna say it once. You ever pull that shit on another new female hire and you'll be stacking shelves at the Giant Eagle for minimum wage. You got that?"

"Get your finger out of my face, bitch."

She bent closer to his face. "Now, now, Kirk. You don't want to go any further or we'll be having some meetings at the union hall. Just know that if they ever hire another woman, I'll be watching. There's nothing I want more than to get you busted for sexual harassment. So you keep that disgusting mouth of yours shut. Got it?"

"Get outta here," he snarled. "Get the fuck outta here!"

But he stayed in his chair. The women could tell he was worried.

～～～

"Ginny didn't take nothin' off nobody," Dorie said. "Depending on who it was, she could either shoot 'em down fast with her sharp tongue or kick 'em in the butt."

Sheila jumped in. "Back then, a woman working in the mill had to have a tough second skin or she'd get eaten alive. You couldn't let them guys get over, couldn't let 'em see that they had rattled you. If they found a weak spot, they'd go at it same's a dentist drill. That's how they were with each other, Always searchin' for a soft spot, something to tease each other about. When they found one, oh Lord, they would ride it for a *long* time."

"It could be a raw place, that's for sure," Dorie agreed. "I mean, most of the men were respectful around the women. But we couldn't let our guard down no way. A woman had to draw a line in the sand if she wanted any respect. Your momma was always drawin' lines in that sand and coming up with some clever ways to do it."

A mischievous grin broke out on Blinky's face. "The place that we liked to hang out the most was the pit shanty. The pit was the most dangerous place in the BOP, because that's where the steel got poured into molds. Here, let me show you."

She leaned forward and lined up two small salt and pepper shakers that were sitting on the coffee table. Then she grabbed a sugar bowl and held it over the shakers. "Just pretend that this bowl is a ladle full of steel at 3,000 degrees and it's held up by two iron hooks that are attached to a crane. And these little shakers are molds sittin' on top of flat railroad buggies."

Blinky put the edge of a knife up against the sugar bowl. "This is the iron bar that hooks into what they called a stopper. It was a long bar inside a ladle with a plug at the bottom of it that sat in a hole at the bottom." She pointed to the bottom edge of the sugar bowl. "When you push down on this bar, it pulls the plug out of the hole and the steel pours out into the mold. Get it?"

Cory nodded.

"They'd been pouring steel that way for over a hundred years. Lots of dangerous stuff could and did happen there. For some crazy reason Ginny loved doing stuff that the men didn't believe a woman could do.

"On the nights when we were ridin' those brooms, we used to sneak down to the pit shanty, because that's where the action was. Usually there'd be about ten or twelve guys hanging out in the shanty, playing cards, jiving, sometimes they'd even have a TV in there. I think they were glad to see us. We kind of broke up the monotony.

"The problem was that the wall of the shanty was covered with posters of naked women. Not just your average naked woman. No way. No one was interested in pretty smiling faces. They were interested in body parts. I mean, right above the coffee pot there was a big poster of a woman spread eagle with her vagina up close and personal. Ginny would get into it with them dudes. She'd tell them, 'C'mon you guys, give us a break. We don't want to see this stuff. This is a work place, not some back street massage parlor.'

'What's wrong with this? It's art.'

'This is *art*?' Ginny said.

'Sure. I seen pictures of the Vatican and it's full of naked bodies.'

'You think this is a de Vinci? A Michelangelo?'

'It's art. Beautiful women capture my interest.'

'Well, if that's the case, why don't you have it framed. Put it on your living room wall. Let the whole family enjoy this art?'

'Hah, she's got you there, Haystack. Better give up while you can.'

"Then one night we went into the labor foremen's office to get our time cards, and it just so happened the bottom drawer of his file cabinet was wide open. There was a stack of Playgirl magazines in it. Playgirl! That raised our eyebrows. We grabbed some and ran to the john where we tore out the centerfolds. You know, the ones with the naked men in different poses.

"The next night when the Pit shanty was empty we tore down the girlie posters and taped up the men in their place. Then we sat down and started playing gin rummy like nothing had happened."

"When the guys finished working their heats, they came into the shanty. The funny thing was no one said anything. There wasn't a peep. We were kind of deflated because we expected a big bang of some kind. I think it stunned them and they didn't know what to say. The next night all the center-pages had been taken down. And it stayed that way for months."

ᘒᘒᘒ

Finally, the women, having exhausted their supply of stories, grew quiet. The rain stopped, but the dark clouds hung motionless. The air in the room was thick with humidity.

"Your mother was a special person," Blinky said. "And because of that, she made some special enemies."

73

"What do you mean?" asked Cory.

"Ginny had some pretty strong beliefs," Dorie said. "She didn't just spout 'em off like she carried the list in her back pocket. Uh-uh. She lived by those beliefs. She made enemies of people who didn't appreciate what she stood for."

Cory wanted to know more. "What did she believe in that would make someone want to hurt her?"

Sheila brushed away droplets of perspiration from her brow. She leaned forward and tried to explain. "Ginny made enemies in the union *and* in the company, amongst racists and men who hated women working in the mill. She was always in their face with her behavior and her ideas. That's why I never believed for one second that she walked away from her job. She wasn't about to turn her back on her beliefs. There were a lot of guys who wanted her gone. Some bad enough to mess her up."

Blinky and Dorie nodded in agreement. The lull in the storm was short-lived. Lightening cracked and thunder rumbled.

It was time to tell the other stories, stories they'd witnessed or heard about from some of the men or Ginny herself.

11

"**Y**ou're on the pit schedule this week, Ginny. Just think of that big money you're making," Horizontal Bob teased as they walked into the cavernous BOP shop. His nickname was "Horizontal" because he spent his time between heats stretched out on the shanty's wooden benches sound asleep.

"Yeah, Bob," said Ginny. "Lots of guys on vacation, so I got a steady job for a while."

When she was lucky enough to catch a job in the pit, she worked as a fourth steel pourer, bottom of the rung. It was hot and heavy work, lifting 16,000 pounds in an eight-hour shift. Two men would divide that equally, 8,000 pounds apiece. They weren't going to take on any additional back-breaking work, so she had to do her share. This was not a place for chivalry.

Besides, Ginny didn't want any. She worked hard on the platforms, never let up, and never accepted favors, worried it might come back and bite her later.

On her off days, she huffed and puffed in the gym doing curls, bench presses and squats. For the most part, she was a success, at least among the men on her turn. But, she never worked on the other turns. Many of those guys refused to believe that a woman could do the work. Some said they would go home rather than work with her.

It was, after all, a place where masculinity was defined by physical strength. If a woman could do it, what did that make them? For some, her challenge cut too deep.

"You're a third steel pourer this week."

"I'm loving it, Bob," she grinned. "It won't last long, but I'm loving it."

"Just be careful. Tony Blasko, the guy you're working with transferred in from the blast furnace. Thinks he knows it all. He just spent two weeks training with Shortcut, so he might give you some problems."

"You don't call working with Shortcut training, do you? But thanks for the warning, Bob. These guys transferring in here sure are pissed about going to the bottom of the pile, even if it's temporary. Hell, in two more months, I'll be riding that broom again, so I'll just enjoy it while I can."

"Thatta girl," Bob said. "Just watch your back up on the platform."

The siren blew, announcing that her heat was tapping and would soon be moving down the platform. "Aw shit," she said. "It's a rim heat." She climbed the metal stairs to the platform and saw that nothing had been set up except for two stacks of heavy iron plates that needed to be spread out the length of the platform.

"Great!" she muttered. "Just great."

She ran down the stairs and flew into the shanty. Her fourth steel pourer, pouring a cup of coffee and munching on a sweet roll, ignored her.

"Forget the coffee," she said. "The last crew left us hanging on this platform. There's a lot to do."

"Yeah," Blasko said, and continued to stir his coffee.

"Listen, unless you want to follow the midnight crew out the gate this morning, you better get up on the platform now."

"Who are yunz to—"

John, the first steel pourer, shut him up with the wave of a hand. "Better get going, this heat's almost ready."

"Great way to start the day," Ginny grumbled as she

climbed back up onto the platform.

Rim heats were the toughest and hottest of all. Leaning over wide open molds and beating black slag out with a wooden board was like bending over a lava flow with an oar. Once the slag was out, iron plates were picked up with long iron tongs and placed over the top of the bubbling mass, three in a row. Then hoses were laid over the plates running cold water on top. It was called "killing the heat."

Steam spewed up making it difficult to see a yard ahead. As long as the water stayed on top of the plates, there was no problem. But if it seeped below, the steel would explode like a geyser, shooting 50 feet up, spraying 3,000 degree globs in every direction. The plates hissed like a boiler about to blow seconds before they shot through the air, an iron missile that could sever a head.

The third and fourth steel pourers worked side by side, beating, lifting, dragging hoses, mindful of the gurgling liquid that responded to mysterious chemical forces not three feet from their faces. Their safety glasses fogged over, adding to the peril of working in the blind. They communicated with grunts, pointed fingers or hollered warnings. Their thermal long underwear, sodden with sweat, clung to their backs and legs while their feet squished inside their steel-toed boots.

Dehydration plus the weight of the asbestos coats, the long oversized asbestos gloves, and the fireproof spats that went to their calves took a toll on their energy. Long after the first and second steel pourers had left the platform, they continued to labor until the last mold was done.

It was imperative that they watched each other's backs.

"It's too late for the forklift to move these plates," Ginny said. "We'll have to carry them down. On the way back up, make sure the hoses are in position while I check the boards and tongs."

Ginny grunted as she picked up four of the plates and walked away. Tony Blasko swore under his breath and gave her the finger behind her back before he bent down to pick up some plates.

"She'll be wipin' my ass in another couple of months," he growled. "Anything can happen up here on these platforms. Anything."

They worked through the heat in silence. Near the end she saw a mold that Tony had missed.

She pointed down the platform. "Put a hose on that mold."

Long thick veins along his temples swelled up with rage. "Go fuck yourself!" he shouted. "I don't take orders from bitches. There ain't nothin' wrong with it. Yunz don't like it? Then yunz do it. I'm outta here." He stormed down the stairs and marched towards the shanty.

Ginny walked down the platform and put a hose on the missed mold, angry, yet surprisingly calm. Something would have to be done, but what? She was opposed to complaining to the pit foreman. And the union? Forget it. She'd have to solve it herself.

When Ginny entered the shanty, it was standing room only. She leaned against the wall. Tony wasted no time. "I don't know why yunz been putting up with her crap. She don't belong down here and yunz know it. Yunz been carryin' her ass."

He lit a cigarette. Smoke blew out of his mouth and nose like a snorting dragon.

"She can't do the work. She ain't shit up there. Something bad happens up there, then what? She gonna come to the rescue? Shit. These bitches are going to kill us."

"Whoa, whoa, you don't need to be using that language," one of the men grumbled.

Ginny shifted her weight, her face heating up. She felt

conspicuously out of place.

"Next you're gonna tell me she can lift those three hundred pound caps. No way. Yunz been lifting the cap for her 'cause she can't do it. Well, I ain't breakin' my back for some bitch that ain't got enough sense to stay where she belongs."

Ginny opened her mouth to speak but was silenced by a loud booming voice that erupted from the oldest man in the BOP.

"SHUT UP!" Krank bellowed. His voice reverberated off the flimsy wall. They called him Krank because he rarely smiled or spoke. He was an old-timer who had started in the mill as a kid during World War II. When he spoke, his big pinkish head with its nose shaped like a grenade oscillated slowly.

"Just shut up! Yunz don't know nothin'. Who do you think was working in the pit in the war? Working in them blast furnaces? It was *women*, that's who. Little Mexican women, not women big as this one. There was a camp up yonder where them Mexican women lived. So yunz just shut up, 'cause yunz sure don't know what yunz'r talking about."

"Hey, you go Krank, tell it like it is," said one of the men. Then others jumped in with, "Leave the girl alone, she knows what she's doing." "Yeah, we don't want to hear this crap."

Ginny almost burst out crying. Good God! This is the last place to start bawling. She kept her head down and nudged a gum wrapper with her boot. Behind her she heard the voice of her first steel pourer.

"I've heard enough out of you, Blasko. You been belly-aching about working with Red since I seen you in the bathhouse this morning. Fact is she's one of the best steel pourers we got down here. Ain't nobody works harder than her and nobody works safer than her. So my advice to you is to settle down and pay attention to what she says because she's gonna teach you right."

He turned and faced a shocked Tony Blasko. The door of the male-only club had just opened for women.

"Do we understand each other or do I need to go upstairs with this?"

Ginny never heard the answer because she bolted out of the door and walked briskly to the canteen. A grin slowly spread across her face. She had won the support of the men on her turn.

She had also made a bitter enemy of Tony Blasko.

Later in the week, the new pit foreman, Ron Antoli, jerked open the door and marched into the shanty. A hush fell over the room as heads turned in his direction. Ginny, who was sitting on a bench munching on an apple, watched him warily.

Suddenly her body tensed. He had come for her.

"OK, Johnson, let's get to work," he snarled.

"I am working," she said. "My heat's up next."

"There's a problem with the furnace, so your heat's delayed. I've got a special project for you. C'mon." He motioned for her to follow him out the rear door. She could feel the men watching her as she walked out.

Antoli stood with his legs spread apart, hands on his hips, staring at the platform behind her. Eye contact with women, especially tall women, was not something he had mastered.

"I want you to clean up around here. Cans, gum wrappers. And see those cigarette butts lying all over the place? Pick 'em up. This isn't a pig sty."

"What, just me? There's eleven guys sitting in there."

Antoli's upper lip curled into a sneer.

"You want to work in the pit? Then you keep your

workplace clean. If you don't want to do it, you can go home. And stay out of the pit shanty until you finish."

He turned on his heel and all but goose-stepped down the main aisle towards his office.

Ginny stood riveted to the spot, her face burning with indignation. She wanted to let loose with a blood curdling scream, but she sucked it up. Tight lipped, she bent over and began picking up trash. She took comfort in the thought that the world was round and that he'd meet up with himself someday.

Curly stuck his head out of the door. "Hey, Red, what's up?"

Through clenched teach, Ginny explained what had happened. "Can he do this, Curly? Is this in the contract?"

"He's got it in for you, Red. Yeah, he can do it. Keeping the job site clean is definitely in the contract. Just be careful."

Funny thing. None of them are running out to lend a hand. She figured housekeeping was beyond the limit of their support.

Ginny began keeping a record of run-ins with Antoli. She mentioned it to no one. Word spread fast in the mill and snitches could be found anywhere. She was preparing for the day when he would go too far. Within a month three other minor incidents were added to the list. Finally, emboldened by his successes, Antoli crossed the line.

She and Skinny Rich were sweating over a rim heat. Ginny heard the ominous hissing sound of a mold about to explode. Her head spun to the left. She was blinded by a flash of orange light streaking towards her face.

"*Run!*" she yelled to Rich as she whirled to her right and took off down the platform.

Red-hot steel shot up seventy-five feet in the air. Then it rained down like fireworks. Pellets were in front of her, behind her, on top of her. She could hear them hitting her hard hat and see them splashing against her face shield. The steam spread out thick like an ocean fog and made it damn near impossible to see where she was going. She tripped over hoses that lay entangled along the platform like a swarm of snakes.

A few steps ahead Skinny Rich was tearing ass. She saw him tumble against a wheelbarrow and almost fall.

There was a god-awful stench of burning chemicals... or was it flesh? She regained her balance and ran faster, jumping over boxes like an Olympic hurdler. Finally, she was out from under the shower of steel. Rich was bent over heaving at the end of the platform. Men bolted out of the pit shanty and raced towards the platform, yelling "Are you OK? You get burned?"

"I don't know," she choked, her chest rising and falling in short jerks. "I can't tell. Something smells like it."

"What happened?"

"The third mold exploded...just blew up. I heard it hissing...before I could move there was a flash of light...in my face...I took off running."

Her partner was ashen. "You were damn lucky that steel shot straight up. It could'a blown back at you."

Ginny shuddered.

The men checked Ginny and Rich over. Aside from their head scarves being full of burn holes, they were both ok. But sacks of chemicals were on fire up and down the platform. She and Skinny Rich didn't have time to commiserate. The rest of the heat was waiting for them. He put his arm over her shoulder as they walked back to the hot molds.

"I've never had that 'this is it' feeling before," she said.

"Me neither," he said. "When I ran into the wheelbarrow, I was like, man, you like making this extra money but you never wanted to die for it."

Black slag had crusted over the top of the molds. Her back muscles were on the verge of cramping as she leaned forward with the wooden paddle and beat away at it. The strain and sweat took its toll and, by the end, Ginny felt like a wrung out rag. She took off her safety glasses and wiped the sweat from her face.

At that moment Antoli bounded up the stairs and shouted at Ginny, "Get your stuff, you're going home!"

She glared at him. "Get out of my face, Antoli. When I want to hear from you, I'll yank your chain."

"Get your gear and get out!" he screeched, his hands balled into fists as he took a step toward her. "You're going home. Violation of safety rules. No safety glasses. You're a lucky girl. You got a three-day vacation. No pay." He took the stairs down two-at-a-time and turned towards his office to write up the violation.

"That fucker," Skinny Rich said. "He must've been waiting for you this whole heat, hiding in the dark like some rat. Damn, he sure don't like you, Red."

"It's ok, Rich. I think I got him this time."

It was three-thirty in the morning when she left the mill. Six hours later she was in the union hall telling Ronnie Jones, the BOP grievance man, what had happened. Not trusting the union to see the bigger picture, she laid out her plan. Jones was relieved. "You sure you want it this way?"

"Yeah, Ronnie. If I go down, it will be because of my doing. I don't want to second guess the outcome. It's ok with you?"

"Sure, Ginny. I'll help you any way I can."

"Great. I really appreciate it." She checked some notes she had scribbled earlier. "The first thing is to set up a meeting with Chuck Elwood. I know it's a little out of the ordinary to meet with the BOP superintendent, but this whole situation is out of the ordinary. Can you set this up?"

"I can try. It depends on him."

"Just tell him it's in his best interest. Tell him I'm trying to do him a favor before this gets out of hand. That ought to get him out from behind his desk."

One week later, an obviously annoyed Chuck Elwood sat across from Ronnie Jones and Ginny Johnson in a cramped administrative office. Ronnie was jittery. Ginny, her thick red hair hanging in a long pony tail, sat with a legal pad balanced on her lap. She was anxious but she would have dived off the Fort Duquesne Bridge before she would have let it show.

Elwood was the BOP superintendent, a busy man with heavy responsibilities. Meeting with disgruntled workers was not a part of his job description and he was unhappy with the intrusion into his daily routine. He checked the time on the wall clock and then directed a frown at Ronnie.

"What's this about?"

Ginny answered in a calm and confident tone. "There is a serious problem with one of your employees."

"Then take it through normal channels," Elwood snapped. "File a grievance. You have a union contract, follow it. I don't have time for special meetings."

"I want ten minutes of your time so that you understand what's at stake here," Ginny said.

When Elwood tried to interrupt, Ginny's voice rose. "The fact is you have an employee, Ron Antoli, who is on the verge of creating what could be a national scandal for American Steel. I don't believe that you or the corporate headquarters in Pittsburgh, would want to see this happen. It's in your best interest to listen to what I have to say."

Ronnie Jones busied himself with staring a hole through the floor. Elwood, tight lipped, nodded for her to continue.

"I've worked in the pit for three years under seven different foremen and never had a problem. Your Mister Antoli doesn't have what it takes to be a pit foreman." She listed a long series of incidents involving Antoli, with dates, times and the foreman's own words.

"The job requires cooperation and support. We don't need some petty foreman skulking about in the middle of the night trying to find someone—not just anyone, only me, the only female—who takes off her safety glasses to wipe sweat from her forehead. It's obvious he doesn't like women working here. But it's the law. If you need to keep him on, then I suggest you put him somewhere where he can't harass women."

Elwood stopped taking notes and glared at Ginny. "Anything else?"

"Yes, there is something else," Ginny said, squaring her shoulders and planting both feet firmly on the floor.

"I am prepared to take this information to the National Organization for Women and to the Equal Employment Opportunity Commission if American Steel decides not to protect my rights to work here. We can organize a picket line and invite the press. I think they would find the story of sexual harassment interesting. That's a lot of negative publicity for your corporation. I don't think the big men downtown would want that to happen. Do you?"

Elwood set his pen down, leaned back in his chair and scowled. Ginny could feel a drop of sweat roll down the middle of her back. She felt like she was sitting in a pressurized cell waiting for an explosion. Finally, Elwood sat forward and asked, "What exactly do you want, Miss Johnson?"

"I want to work free of being harassed by Ron Antoli. Whatever you have to do to get him permanently off my back and that of any other female employee is what I want."

"I see." Elwood stood up, as if to assert his authority, and announced that the meeting was over. "You understand, I hope, that we have the right to place our employees as we see fit?"

Ronnie Jones bolted from his chair and reached for the door knob. Ginny stood up and looked directly at Elwood.

"Of course I understand that," she said evenly. "I also understand that there are rules here and your employee is breaking a big one. I'm just trying to save American Steel from public embarrassment. Thank you for your time, Mister Elwood." Ginny walked out behind Jones.

Elwood's fists balled up.

She's bluffing! Call a press conference? They aren't going to come out here because one female has a problem getting along with her boss. Who's going to listen to a bunch of women? Besides, it would set a dangerous precedent if I let her dictate which foreman she's going to work under.

Thing is she may not be bluffing, he thought, heaving a sigh. She's building a case, that's clear. From what I hear she's quite a fighter. She raises hell in the union meetings. Got elected to be head of a women's committee in the union. It could smack of us trying to drive her out because she's a vocal critic. Downtown wouldn't be too happy about that.

Then, too, the men might see her as some kind of hero, some kind of example for standing up to the company. Maybe that's the risk I have to take. Besides, there are other ways to neutralize any influence she might develop.

When the pit schedule was posted a week later, Ron Antoli's name was not on it. He had been reassigned to an isolated desert post. Metallurgy.

Steaming with blistering rage, Antoli glared at the four walls of his new office. He had one thing in mind: to wreak revenge upon the bitch that put him there. It was just a matter of waiting for the right moment.

❧❧❧

Though the rain had stopped, bloated dark clouds hung over the city. Dorie stood up, stretched and turned on a lamp.

"Just thinkin' about Antoli gives me the creeps," Blinky said, her face scrunched up like she had caught a whiff of garbage baking in the summer sun. "The brothers used to tell me stories about his evil ways when he was younger, how he'd lose his senses and go off in his mind to some sick place. He used more than his fists to tear someone apart."

Sheri sat forward on the sofa, twirling a braid around a finger.

"When he first came to the BOP, he didn't even try to hide how he felt about us women workin' in the mill. And, let me tell you, he hated us blacks. Thing was he wanted to go upstairs, be a part of management, so he had to be careful. He had to play inside the rule book."

Sheri took a sip of her cold coffee. "Antoli really lost it with Ginny. She got under his skin same's a blood-sucking tick. She was too much for him."

Blinky burst out laughing. "Yeah she was! She sent him to Siberia. She sure did. And if ever someone deserved it, he did!"

"Problem was," Sheri added, "Ginny made a nasty enemy. Back then she ruined his career. Now he's a big boss in the BOP. The only thing that changed was that Ginny disappeared."

12

"**H**ey Ginny, check this out?" Conway shoved the morning newspaper across the table at her.

She poured a cup of coffee from her thermos and picked up the paper. Her eyebrows rose as she read. "I'll be damned. They're going after our health benefits in the next contract negotiations. They want us to pay twenty-five percent of the first three thousand in medical expenses. Then, they say, maybe we'll pay closer attention to what the doctor is ordering. If we think the doctor is ordering unnecessary stuff, we can just tell him no and this is supposed to keep costs down."

She slammed the newspaper down on the table. "Do I have this right? In order to save American Steel some cash, we're supposed to pay all this money and then tell the doctor what to do?"

"They're serious," Conway said. "I can't afford that, not with Mary Ellen's diabetes. It's hard enough already."

Ginny shook her head. "If something should happen to my daughter and I needed a thousand dollars for medical care, there's no way I could come up with that much money. I'd have to get a loan at the bank."

She went straight to the union hall after work to see the president of the Local . She put the newspaper article on his desk. "Did you read this?"

He nodded.

"How are you going to respond to it?"

Tim Fester grimaced. "It's not up to us, it's up to the

International. President McBain knows how best to handle this."

"This article has lots of quotes from McBain. Says he agrees that doctors are the problem. Says he agrees American Steel's costs are too high. Hell, Tim, they just bought an oil company for six billion dollars. Does that sound like they're hurting?"

Fester sighed. The slack cheeks of his puffy red face were lined with wispy purple veins that tracked his years of alcohol consumption. He had an addled expression, like an aging boxer who had taken too many punches.

Fester was due to retire in another year, having presided over the local union for twenty years. They had been good years for steelworkers and the union, when the union didn't need militant tactics to win good contracts. Now he had a nest of radicals in his local making demands. It had started with that damn federal Consent Decree that forced them to hire these women.

"Ginny, I'm telling you that this isn't our affair. What do you want me to do, organize a strike? A protest? Have everyone go off half-cocked parading around downtown? What will the International think?"

"Maybe they'll think you were doing your job, Fester. You know what? I think the company and the International both need to know that we aren't going to take cuts in our health care. The company is posturing for the next contract negotiations. They're testing the waters. If they get a public message from the rank and file, then they'll understand they're in for a fight. Crap, Tim, how about a simple letter to the editor?"

"No. Plain and simple. This is out of our hands." He bent his head over some paperwork. Ginny was dismissed.

A week later a letter to the editor appeared in the Pittsburgh Post-Gazette.

The corporate heads of American Steel displayed the logic of the rich when they suggested that the way to reduce their rising costs for medical care is to make steelworkers pay 25% of the first $3,000 in medical expenses. This, they said will force us to scrutinize the costs and be less inclined to let the doctor prescribe unnecessary care.

They should re-read our contract. We have NO sick days. A three-day bout with the flu can cost us $300. A long illness costs us one week's pay before we qualify for sickness and accident benefits.

American Steel's scheme won't reduce health-care costs. It will reduce the health of steelworkers who can't afford to pay. This is about increasing profits by cutting our benefits. We steelworkers will be ready come contract negotiation time to fight for our health care benefits.

Signed: Ginny Johnson
Andrew Carnegie Works
ISU Local 1630

༄༅༄

The shrill ringing of the phone greeted Tim Fester as he trudged up the stairs to the union hall. "Yeah, yeah, I'm coming," he grumbled, fiddling with the key to his office.

"Tim, what the hell is going on over there?" It was the agitated voice of Lou Bork, the Director of ISU District Thirty, barking into the phone. "Can't you keep your people in line? Christ, Tim, we don't want any problems right now, we got a sensitive situation going on here what with American Steel shutting down all these mills."

Fester felt the tell-tale signs of a panic attack seizing his chest. He searched through his desk drawers for the small flask he kept hidden for such occasions.

"I didn't have anything to do with that letter," he said.

"She came in here wanting the Local to respond to that article. I told her it was not our business. She did that on her own." He paused to gulp a mouthful of vodka. "She's head-strong."

"Listen to me," Bork growled. "American Steel closed down forty-five steel-making plants last year. They're probably going to shut down the Homestead Works in the next couple of years. You want to be next?"

"No, of course not, but—"

"Then for Christ sake put a muzzle on the radicals. We can't be waving red flags in front of the company's face. We got to show them we can cooperate. Understand?" He hung up, not waiting for an answer.

Fester's hands trembled as he mopped the sweat from his brow with a handkerchief. His heart was beating erratically. Retirement in a year looked less feasible. Death from a heart attack was more likely. He took another swig of vodka.

13

Ginny had just finished the last of five midnight shifts. She stood under a rare hot spray from one of three shower heads in a bathhouse that serviced forty women, content to stand there feeling the warmth, not wanting to face the icy blizzard that was blowing across Western Pennsylvania.

Blinky slid through the slush that had accumulated at the doorway, her hair wet with snow.

"Damn, it's cold!" she hollered to no one in particular. She began to change into her BOP clothes, getting ready for the day turn, when she noticed Ginny.

"Yo, Red, how ya doin'? Where you been? I ain't seen you for the longest time."

Ginny smiled at her friend. Theirs was the kind of friendship that is forged when two people fight battles side-by-side; and being a woman in the mill was like being on the front lines.

On the face of it they were completely opposite: one a short, stocky black woman with close cropped hair, mother of three children, and a laissez faire attitude toward life; the other a tall, lanky white woman with wild red hair and one daughter, who carried the weight of the world's problems on her shoulders. They had been through a lot together since the day they were hired.

"What's up, Blink?"

"They're killin' me. I been a switchman on the railroad all week and I'm about done in. It's freezing out there. There's ice all over the tracks. The hot molds make so much steam,

I can't see the train. I can't see nothin'. One of these days I'm gonna slip right under those railroad cars and nobody will see me. They'll find my body come Spring."

"Come on, Blink, stop talking that nonsense. You're too ornery to give up this big money you're making."

They trudged towards the BOP together, bent forward against a bitter wind, and blew through the doors of the canteen. Blinky shoved coins into the coffee machine.

"Listen," she said as she waited for the grey colored coffee to pour into the paper cup, "Ed told me that AC is definitely going to put in a continuous caster in the BOP. It's a new kind of equipment where the steel pours directly into slabs. But I don't know too much about it. Do you?"

"No. I'll go to the main library tomorrow and see what I can find out." As Ginny opened the door, a blast of frigid air blew in. "Stay on your feet, ok?" she yelled as she disappeared into the blowing snow.

The snow removal crews worked through the night but the roads were still treacherous. The next day it took Ginny over an hour to make the drive to the Carnegie Library in Pittsburgh. Her defroster, a sometime thing, worked well in the summer and hibernated in the winter. Cory, wrapped in an afghan, snuggled next to her mother. Their frosty breaths shrouded the windshield in fog forcing Ginny to wipe the crystals from the glass with her wool scarf.

The immense library, with its marble floors, two-story high ceilings and dark hallways, was practically empty when Ginny and Cory arrived in the afternoon. They sat together at a heavy oak table, huddled inside bulky winter coats. Cory was content to make her way through a stack of Dr. Seuss books while Ginny leafed through steel industry trade magazines searching for information about continuous casters. She made copies of some of the articles, especially the ones that had drawings and pictures of how the caster worked.

It was true. The steel would pour right from the furnace along narrow canals and end up as slabs to be taken somewhere, probably over to Frick Works, for rolling. Those bastards! It will wipe out half the departments at AC. They'll be making a lot more steel with half the workers. More profit with half the cost.

She sat back and stared out the long windows at the gloomy grey sky. "So this is what's called technological advancement," she whispered to the empty room.

"What's wrong, Momma?" Cory asked.

Ginny reached over, wrapped her arms around her daughter and squeezed. The sweet smell of shampoo that lingered on Cory's hair from the morning shower drifted into her nostrils. "Hmmm, you smell so good," Ginny said, as she buried her nose deeper into her daughter's hair.

"Momma. You're not answering me," Cory replied, shaking her head and mimicking the scolding tone her mother used when Cory had pushed her last button.

Ginny squeezed her tighter. "Nothing, honey, everything's fine," she lied. She picked up a copy of the Iron and Steel magazine and mindlessly flipped through the pages.

Suddenly she stopped and turned back to a page with a large red headline that read, "Steel Industry in Danger: How to Save It." Ominous words and numbers popped out at her as she read.

From the government, the steel executives demanded tariff protection, quotas on imported steel, capital investment tax breaks, tax reform, and a weakening of environmental regulations. They'd probably get all that without any problem, she thought. It was what they wanted from the International union that caused her breath to catch. She sat with her fist pressed against her lips, fighting the urge to scream.

One thing was clear. American Steel, the giant in the industry, was going out of the steelmaking business–on purpose! It would continue to sell off steel production assets, divest itself of its coal fields and mineral mines, and downsize. They were branching out into other enterprises, like the more profitable oil business.

Ginny's chest felt constricted and there was a throbbing pain in her temples. She was both frightened and angry.

There it was in black and white. The magazine was six months old. The plan had been out there all that time and no one, not one person in the International, said jack shit about it. They read this magazine. THEY KNOW WHAT'S COMING! Now there were three: the steel industry bigwigs, the International union leadership and Ginny Johnson. She felt like she had uncovered a national security secret. Obviously the union leaders didn't want this to get out. If it became known to steelworkers across the country, the union would look like the tail on the company dog. So what was she to do? Say nothing?

Glancing around furtively, as if her behavior was being scrutinized, she quickly made a copy of the article, bundled up her daughter, and walked out into the frigid day.

∼∽∼∽

It was standing-room-only as 400 members jammed into the union hall to hear a staff member from the International address the rank and file. Up on the stage sat the officers of Local 1630 and a paunchy, middle-aged man wearing a blue poplin jacket with the words "International Steelworkers Union" printed in white above the area of his heart. One hand, soft and well-manicured, clutched a roll of papers, while the index finger of the other twirled an unruly cowlick on top of his head.

Ginny leaned against a back wall. The article from Steel/ Iron Industry Magazine was jammed inside her jacket. She wasn't sure what she was going to do, having shared the information about the continuous caster with the pit crew and some of the laborers, as well as leaving copies of the caster articles describing the increased production and decreased workforce around different shanties and in the bathhouse. The women from other departments had distributed them to their co-workers. Ginny was confident that the caster would come up in this meeting; it was the other article that worried her.

Local union president Tim Fester made a brief introduction. "Mr. Chonski, from the legal department, is here to talk about our contract."

"I'll bet he's never even seen the inside of a steel mill," Curly whispered.

"Curly, you know better than that," Ginny countered. "They get one tour before they settle into their offices in that big skyscraper downtown so they can sound like they know what they're talking about."

Jerry Chonski flattened his notes on the lectern, his round pink face lit by a spotlight. "Thank you for allowing me to address this meeting tonight. I'll get right to the point and be as brief as possible," he said, his voice surprisingly strong.

"As many of you probably know, there are some serious problems in the steel industry and we cannot avoid being affected by them. US companies are taking blows from underpriced steel imports. European and Japanese steel production plants are more modern, using technology that we don't have here on any large scale. Unfair trade practices allow these foreign companies to import their steel into our country and sell it for less than what it takes

Americans to make it. That's why the steel industry needs higher tariffs and import quotas. Let's face it, folks, if the industry can't compete, we won't have jobs. We're asking you to write to your Congressmen and demand that they protect our jobs. I've put a stack of postcards over there on the table. The message is already printed on them. You just have to sign your name at the bottom."

He was poised to continue when Blinky jumped up.

"What about the plans for a continuous caster? Are they planning on putting that in AC? That's gonna cut our jobs in half!"

A man blurted out, "Who are we supposed to send post-cards to about *that*?" Laughter broke out among some in the audience. Others sat stone-faced.

"I don't know about their plans for a caster," Chonski responded, swiping at his cowlick. "I'm here about the upcoming contract. It—"

"We need to know what's going to happen at AC!" Sheila yelled, cutting him off. "Are we gonna have jobs or not? We got families to take care of and they can't eat hot air."

"You'll have to take that up with your local leadership or with the District," Chonski said, his upper lip twitching. "I want to address the next contract. We have some tough negotiations coming up soon. It's not a pretty choice. The company closed down over forty plants last year because of these economic problems. We sure don't want that to continue. We want to protect our jobs, keep them going, so we may have to give a little in order to help keep the industry afloat."

"*Give what?*" a voice bellowed from the middle of the room.

"*Yeah, what?*" someone else cried out.

"They want us to pay a chunk for our health benefits!" Conway shouted. A wave of grumbling rolled through the crowd.

Chonski raised his hands and motioned for silence. "I don't know. We have to wait and see what they come up with."

It was more than Ginny could stomach. She stepped forward and shouted from the back of the hall, "I can tell you what they want because it's right here in their Iron and Steel Magazine! I'll bet you know what they want, Chonski, you can read and so can the International leadership. I'll bet McBain and his buddies have been burning the midnight oil trying to figure out a way to break the news to us!"

The members turned in their seats so they could hear. Ginny waved the article in the air as she spoke. "They want a three year wage freeze, no cost of living for a year and then a fifty cent cap for two more years. You can kiss the thirteen week vacation for senior seniority good-bye."

The noise in the hall began to rise like storm swells in the sea.

"WAIT!" she yelled, "that's not all. The worst is yet to come."

The crowd quieted. Tim Fester was being urged to adjourn the meeting by his fellow officers. Chonski had turned an ashen color and seemed sculpted to the spot with his hand on top of his head.

Ginny took a deep breath and plunged ahead.

"Their plan is to shut down more mills and to cut out 90,000 steelworker jobs. They call it *downsizing*. Then they are going to restructure their corporation, branch out to other manufacturing. They call that *diversifying*. And while we are being downsized, our International union is sending out the Chonskis to tell us to send postcards asking the government to help a corporation that just spent six billion dollars buying an *oil* company.

"They have the nerve to say they don't know what's

happening. DON'T BELIEVE IT!" she roared, jabbing her index finger in the direction of the stage. "They know exactly what's happening. What they don't know is what to do about it!"

For a split second, there was shocked silence. Then, as the significance of what she said burst into the collective consciousness, men shouted out their accusations and complaints. Boos and catcalls reverberated off the wall. Their fear and frustration mounted as they thought the unthinkable: massive layoffs and a decimated future.

Fester, his face redder than usual, tried to descend the steps to reach his office, but he was besieged with agitated union members. Chonski turned abruptly and made a quick, unnoticed exit from a rarely used door off to the side of the stage.

In lockstep behind him was a large, villainous-looking goon wearing a Local 1630 poplin jacket. His twisted nose seemed to take up half of his face. Beneath his jacket was the bulge of a gun sticking under his belt. Before the goon closed the door, he turned and watched Ginny as she stood in the middle of a group of men handing out copies of the now infamous article. Some patted her on the back, gesturing their approval. The thug studied her face for a moment, and then disappeared through the door.

Blinky rattled around in the kitchen making iced tea. Although the doors and windows were open, there was no relief from the hot, sticky air.

"There's something I don't understand," Cory said, the back of her blouse wet with sweat. "Why would the union officers be so against the members?"

"Oh, I don't think they saw it that way," Dorie said. "I

think they believed they represented the best interests of steelworkers. That they knew how to save jobs."

"Like hell," blurted Blinky. "Listen, I'm not against the union. The problem was they had cushy jobs, good pay, no shift work, and they got that by playing second fiddle to the company. Shoot, when it rained on American Steel, the ISU put up its umbrellas. Maybe if they made the same money we did, they would have thought differently. But they made way more than us, so they were afraid of us. Afraid of a rebellion in the ranks. Afraid they'd lose their soft life. That's why they needed to shut us up."

Cory felt the blood drain from her face. "Do you think they..."

"Let's put it this way," Blinky said, pointing to a true crime paperback on the coffee table. "They had motive, means and opportunity."

Dorie stirred sugar into her tea. Her mulish face, flush from the heat, was drawn and tired.

"Ginny was goin' up against some mighty big guns. Men who couldn't afford to risk strikes, protests, or public criticism. She was more than just a pesky ol' gnat to them. Back then she represented potential, and that scared the hell out of them."

14

It was a crisp, clear spring day in downtown Pittsburgh. Several long black limousines cruised to a stop at the soaring American Steel Tower on Grant Street. Chauffeurs dressed in black uniforms hastened to open the rear passenger doors. Silver haired men in tailor-made suits gathered on the sidewalk like members of the royal family preparing for a visit with the king.

They shook each other's hands and inquired after each other's families and golf handicaps as they proceeded towards the massive glass doors of the lobby. There they boarded a private elevator and were whisked to the sixty-third floor; one floor from the top, where the office of the president provided a luxurious sanctuary from the hustle and bustle below.

The men were attending a Board meeting to hear progress reports concerning a recent request made of the International Steelworkers Union.

Coffee, fresh juice and an assortment of breakfast foods were placed atop a long service table at one end of the large conference room. Silver pitchers of ice water sat on white linen placemats in the center of the oval mahogany table.

A new round of handshakes ensued as Chairman Conrad Richards entered with Franklin Blake, Director of Employee Relations, by his side. Finally, the men took their seats.

Franklin Blake was a glib and arrogant fellow in his early forties, with an animated style that was a bit over the edge for the cookie-cutter corporate persona. But it stood him in good stead with union leaders. As chief negotiator for American Steel, he was at his best when sniffing out vulnerability in his opponent and driving a pick-axe through it. A high stakes player, Blake was unaccustomed to losing. More, he detested it.

The tone of his voice as he addressed the Board was as smooth as a fine French cognac.

"As you know, for the past several months we have been in secret meetings with President McBain and the executive committee of the ISU. In March, we presented them with reports that laid out the unprecedented problems our industry faces. We gave them facts and figures that showed our need for greater cooperation in the form of concessions from the union. And even though we are only one year into a three-year contract, we asked them to re-open negotiations.

"At first McBain balked at the suggestion. He was worried about the reactions of the local presidents, who are more sensitive to the pressure of the rank and file members. He was also concerned that if he were to move precipitously, without the agreement of the local presidents, we might risk wildcat strikes and an insurrection against his leadership."

Voices of concern rippled through the room as though a stone had been tossed into their placid waters.

"McBain suggested that we work together in getting the local presidents on board. He invited me to send a letter to all of them outlining the issues. I sent out an eight-page report and then went a step further. I offered to address their members directly with a slide show that would help explain the facts. Most of the locals have responded positively. So," he chortled, "one week from this Saturday we begin the American Steel road show."

The Board members chuckled and nodded approval to each other.

"I am going to start at Andrew Carnegie Works. We've invested a lot of money into that mill, what with the two basic-oxygen furnaces. It's the mill where we are gearing up to invest $250 million in a continuous caster. We have a lot at stake there. I think it is important to assess their reaction early on so we can adjust our campaign as we go along.

"This is a five billion give-back plan. It's a big pill for the International to swallow. We have to be prepared to take less."

"How low can we go and still be viable?" asked one of the VPs.

"We can go as low as two and a half billion," said the First National Bank representative. "But our ability to buy other entities and give satisfactory returns to our stock holders depends on getting as much as possible from the union."

"Yes," Blake agreed. "We have already begun our publicity campaign by raising the issues of over-paid steelworkers in the news media. They are the highest paid industrial workers in the world. We need wage concessions in order to be competitive. If we keep repeating that, we should be able to win over popular opinion."

"It was clever to offer to do the slide show," one of the Board members offered.

"Thank you. I simply could not imagine the mess the local presidents would make trying to explain eight pages of facts and figures. Besides, the working man responds better to pictures, especially if they are in color. Holds their attention longer."

Snickers filled the room.

"How confident are you that the International is going

to cooperate? We have an awful lot riding on them."

"Plain and simple? They're scared witless," Blake said. "As you know, a big part of our restructuring plans are the closing down of most of our steel-making plants. If we do this in stages, it will lessen our public exposure.

"To diversify, to move into oil and energy, which is where we will get the greatest return on investment, we are going to need capital. Steel production is no longer our main concern. The ISU is not blind to our future plans, but they want to hang on to whatever they can. Besides, they can diversify, too. McBain has the support of his district presidents. Believe me, they'll cooperate, of that I have no doubt."

"Is the union asking for anything in return for these concessions?"

"They are demanding we reinvest some of the money we will save into upgrading the mills that are left. Once we get past the locals, it's clear sailing."

A silence pregnant with satisfaction fell upon the room. The idea of plucking bloated profits from the newly acquired oil company and other diverse entities caused their collective hearts to beat a little faster.

A Board member raised his hand. "Conrad, where do we stand with the government? Are they on board with the import quotas?"

In his early sixties, Chairman Conrad Richards had the appearance of a no-nonsense five-star general. He responded brusquely.

"The Secretary of Commerce is in meetings with representatives from the European Union as we speak. He has phoned several times to keep me informed of their progress. We will most assuredly achieve our goal of quotas on imported steel from Europe. And, the Director of the EPA is doing her utmost to downgrade the environmental regulations that place an undue burden on our industry. The government is cooperating at the highest levels."

Applause rang out. The prize was close at hand.

Chairman Richards checked his watch. He had a one o'clock tee time at the Sewickley Country Club. He shook Franklin Blake's hand. "Excellent job, Franklin. I expect to hear good reports about your meetings with the local unions. Perhaps it would be wise to send a couple of our security personnel with you. Sometimes things can become unruly."

"I will do that, sir. I am not expecting any serious problems, but I will take you up on your idea, thank you."

Blake watched as Conrad Richards went to each individual Board member and shook their hands, sharing a joke, making small-talk. Some day that would be him, the CEO of one of the biggest corporations in the world.

As he watched Richards enter his private elevator to ascend to the top, Blake thought, *I want what he's got.*

～～～

At eleven o'clock in the morning the ringing phone shattered Ginny's sleep. She had been in bed for two hours. She fumbled with the receiver. "Yeah?"

"Ginny, it's Blinky. You got to get up, girl, and come to the union hall now. Fester's invited American Steel to send someone out here to talk to us. There are a lot of guys giving Fester hell right now. C'mon. Get up, you can sleep later."

Ginny hopped around the floor, pulling on her jeans.

"Ok. If that piece of junk of mine will start, I'll be there in fifteen minutes. Tell 'em not to start the revolution without me!" she hollered as she slammed down the phone. She fastened her bra and pulled a t-shirt over her head.

She was exhausted, her two hours of sleep only making her feel worse. A dull ache in the back of her head competed for attention with the pain she felt in her knees. She winced from the strain on her back muscles as she bent down to tie her shoes.

Twenty minutes later her car screeched to a halt in front of the union hall, sputtered and died. Ginny dashed up the stairs, stopped outside the door to compose herself, and then strode into the hall.

Tim Fester, looking weary and helpless, was standing in the middle of the hall surrounded by a group of angry rank and filers who were shouting questions and derisive comments at him.

Blinky sidled up next to Ginny and said under her breath, "These guys think Fester's up to something. They think he knows more than he's telling."

"About what?" Ginny whispered.

"About why this guy from Employee Relations is coming to the union meeting next week. Listen."

"They been shuttin' down mills all over the country. Is that why he's coming here? They tell yunz they're gonna shut down AC?"

"I keep telling you no one has said anything about closing down this mill. He's coming here to explain some of the problems the company is having."

"Since when does American Steel give a rat's ass if we know about their problems? There ain't never been a company rep in this union hall before. Something's behind this and you know what it is."

Fester shifted his weight from one foot to another as though he had to piss.

"The guy is just coming to give a little speech. Why don't you wait and see what he has to say?"

"Because they got something up their sleeve and we

need to know what's coming. We need to be prepared. That's why."

Ginny had inched her way through the group until she was face to face with Fester. His red face blanched.

"Don't worry, Fester, I'm not going to bite you," she said, disgust in her voice. "Have I got this right? He's coming a week from Saturday?"

Fester nodded his head.

Although the men tried to hide it, Ginny could sense the panic they were feeling.

"I bet this has to do with the contract," she continued. "He's coming here to soften us up, make us feel sorry for their problems. We've got a little over a week."

Blinky said, "Fester, the Women's Committee wants to have a meeting here tomorrow at four-thirty, so don't leave early, we need the doors open."

Ginny turned to the group. "If any of you guys want to join us, just show up. We're going to prepare for this bozo's visit."

15

Eleven days after Ginny confronted union local president Tim fester, she stood with four other women outside the union hall handing out leaflets and tissues on a warm May morning.

"Here's a fact sheet and some questions you might want to ask. Here are some tissues to use when you start crying over American Steel's problems."

Hundreds of steelworkers who had come to learn their fate jammed into the union hall. The temperature began to rise as bodies pressed against bodies. A mushroom cloud of tension hovered over the room. Some sat with beefy arms folded over thick torsos. They sensed that big changes were coming. Some were willing to cooperate, hoping to save their jobs. Others stood around in small groups, jabbing fingers in the air, making angry points, casting glares in the direction of the stage where the blank slide screen stood, poised like a guillotine. A few laughed and joked. All were worried. The impotence that accompanied the inability to control their lives lapped at their feet.

In his office, Fester could feel his gut quaking. He leaned against the closed door and drained what was left in his flask. He opened his office door and scurried up the steps of the stage, where he busied himself moving metal chairs into position, while Franklin Blake, unconcerned that the odds were decidedly not in his favor, made adjustments to the slide projector, which was set up in the middle aisle.

Ginny stood at the back, squeezed between Curly and

Haystack. Her skin was galvanized with the electricity of anticipation.

When an anemic-looking Fester called the meeting to order, a hush fell over the room.

"Brothers and Sisters, we have been asked by the corporate headquarters and by our International to invite Mr. Franklin Blake, Director of Employee Relations for American Steel, to speak to us today. He has some important information for us, so please give him your full attention. Mr. Blake?"

As Blake approached the podium he removed his navy blue sports jacket, handed it to Fester as though the man was his valet, and rolled up the sleeves of his oxford shirt. He exuded an air of confidence as he swept the audience with his steely grey eyes. His infectious smile soon had some in the audience smiling back at him. Others studied him cautiously, their instincts warning that he was a rare breed of carnivore.

"Thank you for coming out today. I know you are busy people, so I am going to jump right in. We at American Steel want to give you important information so that you will understand the challenging position we find ourselves in. And when I say we, I am not just talking about management, I am talking about all of you because *you* are the backbone of this company."

With a nod of his head to someone along the wall, the lights dimmed. "I brought along some slides, which I hope will present the material in a clear manner."

What followed was a dazzling display of brightly colored bar graphs, line graphs and pie charts designed to convince the workers that the industry was in desperate need of their cooperation. It was as plain as the noses on their faces, was it not? The invasion of imported steel from Europe and Japan, selling at fifteen percent less than American-made steel, was a big part of the problem.

"Our government is negotiating with these countries to put limits on the amount that can be brought across our borders. These are countries that reaped the benefits of our generosity after World War II and built technologically advanced steel producing plants."

Flipping through the slides with his remote control, Franklin Blake rolled on like a puffing steam-engine. American steel production, which had for decades enjoyed top thoroughbred status, was no longer in the lead on the world track. They had fallen to the rear of the pack, garnering only nine percent of world steel production. Sales were down, capital expenditures were static, operating income was fifty percent lower than a year ago, and stock performance was lackluster.

"American Steel has had to pull in its belt. You know perfectly well that no individual or business can continue to spend more than it earns. We've had to sell some assets to keep afloat. We've had to close down the plants that were losing money.

"Some of you might suggest that we should cut our prices and compete like Kaufmann's department store does when its competition has a sale. But we can't do that because our operating costs are at an all-time high."

A bright blue pie graph positioned against a fiery red background popped up on the screen. It dissected the financial lives of the steelworkers and showed what a drain their labor had become on the company. A pink slice of the pie representing wages and salaries at the AC totaled $3.6 million yearly. The chartreuse slice depicted employee benefits at $1.2 million. A skinny orange slice portrayed the growing number of pensioners who were tapping into the pension fund. When these costs were compared with income, a bar graph quickly came up on the screen with a towering red column for costs and a shrunken black column for income. Well, anyone could see it was an impossible situation, couldn't they?

The lights were turned on. Blake, sweat staining his shirt around the armpits and rolling down his back, mopped his face with his monogrammed handkerchief. Hands shot up from the audience as a few voices shouted out questions, but he remained composed.

"Please. I will answer your questions in a moment. I want to impress upon you that we are in this together. Believe me, I wouldn't be here if it weren't an emergency. If we don't act now, act together as a team, we will face even tougher times in the future."

He clicked the remote, bringing up a line graph that depicted a thick red line tumbling downward toward impact with a flat bottom.

"We all have to make sacrifices in order to keep our ship afloat. Thank you."

The angry tone of a man's voice carried throughout the hall. "What kind of sacrifices are yunz talkin' about?"

Blake had prepared for this moment; the game was on and he embraced it.

"That will depend on you," he said. "When American Steel and your International leadership sit down together, they will develop a workable plan. But because we are in an emergency situation, we have asked that the latest contract be re-opened and re-negotiated."

A wave of grumbling rolled through the room. Blake raised his voice. "Hold on a minute! That contract was negotiated before the full impact of our difficulties was known. Knowing what we know now, all of us have to reconsider our options."

Another voice rang out, "Our options are pretty limited. We get paid for our work and we receive health and pension benefits. It doesn't take a genius to see what will be up for grabs if this contract is re-opened. Do you think we're that stupid?"

"Yeah," someone else yelled, "give us some specifics."

Blake clasped his hands like a penitent. "I apologize if I've given you the impression that I want to mislead you. The truth is that I do not know what specifics will be discussed in the months ahead. But nothing will be discussed unless the contract is re-opened. That's why I'm here today—to explain why that needs to happen"

Blinky stood and turned to face the union members. "It's hard to believe he doesn't know what the company's plans are. Maybe if I go down the list of things they want that showed up in the Iron and Steel magazine almost a year ago, it will help him remember." She shouted out the items on the list. The members listened in silence.

Blake, caught off guard, cut her off. "Those are what the industry believes it needs in order to remain in business. As negotiations take place there will be a natural give and take of ideas. Compromises will be made."

He nodded at another man with a question.

"American Steel has made a lot of money over the years. Why haven't they invested it in the mills? They only have two mills with basic oxygen furnaces, yet Europe and Japan built a lot of new plants using BOPs. Where's the money gone to?"

"In their pockets, that's where!" Curly hollered from the back of the room.

"And in your pockets," quipped Blake, trying to refocus their attention off the company. "You are the highest paid steelworkers in the entire world. The Japanese, the Germans, they don't earn the wages nor have the benefits that you do."

He was revving up like a politician on a stump. "And,

yes, the company has made profits. I'm not going to apologize for profits, that's what keeps American business marching forward. That's our economic system. You want communism? Then you're in the wrong country."

No one wanted communism. And yet they were made to feel that a decent standard of living was un-American. Though some were outraged, many felt resigned to their fate. Besides, what difference did their opinions make? They neither discussed nor voted on their contracts. Everything was taken care of by the International, the district, and the local presidents. The belief in their powerlessness had deep roots.

"It's really very simple," Blake powered on with the patronizing tone of a teacher tired of explaining that the world is round. "You have a choice between making some temporary concessions and keeping your jobs or hanging onto a contract that will put everyone out of work."

Blake saw the red-head waving her hand in the back of the room. He'd been warned that she was a prime agitator and he should ignore her. At the time, Blake had agreed, but now he was having such a good time. Not wanting to stop the game, he pointed at Ginny.

All heads turned as she walked toward the center of the room. Slim, tall, her long curly hair falling freely around her shoulders, she had a commanding presence.

"The fact is we are going to lose our jobs anyway. That's what is not being said here today. Right now American Steel has 150,000 steelworkers on its payroll. In the next few years they plan to send 95,000 of us to the unemployment lines permanently. They are going to downsize us."

Slowly she scanned the crowd. "You, Regina, you can forget about buying that little house you want for you and your kids. And you, Frankie, you can forget about sending your boy to college. Conrad, you can forget about the health insurance that takes care of your sick wife. I can forget about buying a newer car.

"Mortgages are going to go into arrears for tens of thousands. There will be long lines around the offices of bankruptcy lawyers. We won't be carrying cash into the supermarket, no sir, we'll be paying with food stamps. That's the future they are planning for us."

As her voice rang out, a low rumble of frightened and angry voices could be heard in the background.

She turned to face Franklin Blake. "The truth is American Steel is moving out of the steelmaking business. They have milked it dry and can't cut a big enough profit. Why can't you just fess up to the truth, Blake?"

She turned back to the audience. "They just bought an oil company for six billion dollars. When they go shopping, it's not the same as you and me. We don't take the food from our children's mouths so that we can go buy a TV, but they do. They take the food from OUR children's mouths so they can go buy other industries."

The rumble was threatening to become a roar that drowned out Blake's voice as he struggled to find some way to stop her devastating remarks.

16

With the union members growing more and more angry, Ginny raised her voice over the din. "It costs them a lot of money to buy industries. You know how it is when you play Monopoly and you land on Broadway or Park Place. If you want to buy hotels, you end up selling off other properties to get the cash. That's what these concessions are all about. They need our money so they can diversify."

She reached into a pocket of her jeans, pulled out a wrinkled ten dollar bill and dangled it in the air. "Here, Blake, here's my contribution to the growth of your blood-sucking giant."

The crowd roared with laughter and shouts of derision at Blake.

Blake was livid. He had been so close to winning and now she had snatched what should have been his glorious moment out from under him.

"Just a minute, young lady," he growled into the mike. "You are just—"

"You shut up!" Curly shouted from the back. "You're in our house now. We listened to you, now you listen to us. Go on, Ginny. Tell it like it is, girl!"

The color of Blake's face turned as red as the sinking line displayed on the graph still on the screen. As he gave a slight nod to the big thug who had accompanied him, the man sidled along the wall towards the back of the room.

Ginny paused, waiting for the clamor to die down, then she continued, her voice resonating off the wall.

"As long as we do not have the right to vote on our contracts, as long as we do not have the right to strike, as long as we have a union leadership who forgot a long time ago who the hell they represent, and as long as we have politicians who have never walked a picket line, then we may seem to be helpless."

She pointed at Blake and said, "But we are NOT helpless. You came here wanting us to rubber stamp our death sentence. That isn't gonna happen. We will take back our power and shut the industry down. Maybe it needs to be nationalized. I don't have all the answers, but I know one thing: we will fight! We will go to all the locals. We will organize like the mineworkers. We are not going to lie down and let you steam roll over us. We will fight every step of the way!"

Pandemonium broke loose as the men and women of Local 1630 rose as one from their seats. They shouted at Franklin Blake, at Tim Fester, and at each other.

Some were angry and pumped their fists in the air, shouting, "Strike! Strike! Strike!" Others, confused and frightened, pushed their way through the crowd and surged towards the door.

In the confusion the slide projector toppled over, sending the slides spilling onto the floor. Franklin Blake's road show of meticulously prepared color-coordinated facts and figures crumbled under the feet of the very people it was designed to hoodwink.

Blake and Fester climbed down from the stage and shoved their way through the jostling crowd. They dodged pointed fingers, raised fists and a few well-aimed globs of spit until they reached Fester's office. It took the two of them to shove the door shut and lock it.

Bright purple blotches popped out on Fester's face as he bent over, sucking in air. Blake moved to the window and peeked through the Venetian blinds trying to judge the distance to his Mercedes sedan. Seething with rage, he rubbed his clenched jaw, trying to undo the tension that had clamped his mouth shut.

Bodies pressed in on Ginny as her union brothers and sisters offered support. Her shirt was soaked with sweat and wet ringlets of her red hair clung to her neck. She was being carried along by the crowd, moving towards the exit.

"Remember," she repeated several times, "there is an organizing meeting Wednesday at five o'clock. We're gonna build the biggest demonstration of steelworkers ever."

Ginny felt someone pinching her arm. She glanced up at a man's face that looked devoid of cheek-bones and as flat as a tombstone. He had no lashes. Worse, his eyes expressed only emptiness, a place where human intimacy had never taken up residence.

Ginny instinctively recoiled.

He motioned with his fingers for her to bend toward him so that she could hear something he wanted to tell her.

"How is your daughter?" he hissed.

"What?"

"Your daughter. Cory. How is she?"

Ginny raised her head to see if she knew this man, but he pinched her arm tighter, drawing her closer. "I'd forget about organizing if I were you."

Fear gripped Ginny's heart. She yanked free of his grasp with such force that she fell sideways against Blinky.

"Hey girl, slow down, we're almost out of here," Blinky said, missing the alarm on her friend's face.

Ginny turned her head, wanting to point out the man who had threatened her daughter, but he had disappeared into the surging crowd.

"This man, he asked me about my daughter," she said.

"Man? What man?" said Blinky.

"I never saw him before, and I hope I never see him again."

"Well be careful, girl, you've stirred up a hornet's nest. We don't want nobody getting' stung."

~~~

"It's true," Dorie said, as a clap of thunder rattled the windows. "Your momma flustered the company. It wasn't only her, there were lots of us out there speechifying at other locals, passin' out leaflets at supermarkets, doing lots of stuff. For them few weeks, we were workin' hard to get the word out about the protest demonstration. We wanted steelworkers and their families to know what the company had in mind for us."

"But Ginny had a peculiar way of attractin' a lot of attention," said Blinky.

"She was beautiful," Sheri said. "And quick on her feet. The media loved to interview her. Problem was she got a lot of publicity. She became the company scapegoat because she stood out more than any of the rest of us."

Blinky rose from the rocking chair to open another window. The humidity in the room was stifling.

"Plus, she wasn't afraid of them," Blinky added. "She would take them on, sassy and all. I'd tell her, girl, these guys are defending an empire. Don't you think they'll do any evil deed to get to their goal? But she wouldn't listen. She was fearless at a time when the company wanted us to be afraid. They wanted to make an example of her."

Cory struggled to digest this new information about her mother. Vague impressions of phone conversations she had overheard, steelworkers coming to the house to pick up leaflets, animated discussions around the kitchen table late into the night took form. Her memory began to unfold like the first petals on the bud of a rose.

"Hold up," Dorie said. "It wasn't just the company, there was a *lot* more going on besides. A lot more."

17

At twelve-twenty in the morning Ginny had just finished up a rough night in the pit. Because she had been late to work that afternoon, she was forced to park in a dark corner behind the metallurgy lab.

Her car listed to one side. A tire was flat as a board.

"Shit! Just once I'd like to catch a break." She looked up at the black sky. "Is this some kind of *test*? You got some special *plan* for me? Something real nice at the end of this life?"

Silence was her answer.

"No, I didn't think so," she grumbled as she opened the trunk and pulled out the jack and spare tire. Fifteen minutes later she laid the flat tire in the trunk. She was about to close the trunk when she suddenly heard the sound of a familiar voice behind her.

"Gotta problem, Miz Johnson?" Ron Antoli jeered. He was standing on the other side of the fence leaning against the back door of the metallurgy lab.

"Crawl back in your hole, Antoli."

"You better inspect that tire. It doesn't look like a nail hole to me."

"You know something about this?"

"Not me," he said with an expression of mock innocence. "But maybe someone else has a special plan for you. How did you put it, something real nice at the end of this life? Could be that's sooner than you think." He burst out in a shrill cackle.

Ginny jumped into her car and sped off. She pulled up under a street lamp in front of her house, grabbed the flashlight from under the front seat and raced to the trunk, where she ran the light over the tire.

Then she saw it, a three-inch gash ran parallel to the ridges of the tire. Antoli was right. How did he know? Had he done it or had he watched someone else do it?

Suddenly she heard a scratching sound behind her. A tingling sensation circled the back of her neck. Slowly she took hold of the carjack and strained to hear anything beyond the sound of chirping crickets.

Then, in one sweeping movement, she spun around, raising the jack above her head, ready to bring it crashing down on someone's skull. Instead, she saw an empty street with a circle of light from the lamp above.

It was deathly still. Even the crickets had fallen silent.

My imagination is in overdrive, she thought. But not taking any chances, she slammed the trunk closed, grabbed her keys and raced to her front door. Once inside, she bolted the door and leaned against it, panting.

Mrs. Gromski was asleep on the sofa, her soft snoring filling the room.

Ginny checked on Cory and straightened the blankets that were twisted around her daughter's spindly legs. Then she went to the kitchen and popped open a cold bottle of beer. Thirty minutes later she crawled into bed.

∞∞∞

Ginny didn't know how long the phone had been ringing. At first it was a part of her dream. Her mother was calling, calling from a far off place, wanting to tell her something she needed to know right away. She tried to grasp the receiver, but the phone inched further away. The ringing became louder as the phone became smaller until finally she reached consciousness.

She grabbed for the phone. *"Hello? Who is it?"* she shouted.

"Whoa, Baby, it's Mike. You still in bed? If that's the case, I'll be right over." He chuckled. Hearing no banter in return, he asked, "You ok?"

"Mike?" she said, shaking her head, trying to jump-start her brain.

"Yeah, Baby, what's wrong?"

"I was having a bad dream. Where are you?"

"Getting a new muffler put on the car. You up for a matinee? There's a new Star Trek flick that starts at one o'clock in Monroeville. I know how cheap you are, so I'll buy the popcorn," he laughed. "I can pick you up at twelve-thirty."

The clock on her bedside table said ten-twenty.

"Yeah, ok, I'll be out front. But I'm not *cheap*, I'm broke."

She buried her head in the pillow and felt every aching muscle in her lean body. She groaned. This was the beginning of her short week-end: exactly 48-hours off, from midnight to midnight, in the middle of the week. Today Mrs. Gromski would pick-up Cory after the Brownie meeting at school, so Ginny was free until five that afternoon.

Mike Samuels was a tall, athletic, handsome man with a square-jaw, full lips and amber colored eyes flecked with green. He had played football as a running back throughout college and aspired to a professional football career. The reality that he lacked that extra bit of talent that carried athletes into the pros forced him to change plans. He graduated with a degree in physical education and a teaching certificate.

Mike fathered twin boys, married the mother and shortly after, at the age of twenty-six, divorced. Since that time he had been devilish with the women in his life, enjoying a variety from the buffet that was ever present. The resolute avoidance of any long term commitments was a necessary part of the feast.

Now, twelve years later, he was smitten by a lanky red-head with the spirit of a lioness. He found himself barreling along that emotional roller-coaster, up and down steep slopes, around cramped curves; feeling, at one and the same time, immobilized with trepidation yet as flighty as the moth that flirts with a flame.

He would have given anything to backtrack to his roguish ways where he was in control of the situation and, more importantly, of himself. Instead, his body tensed as he rounded the corner and spotted Ginny sitting on the front porch. She waved and gave him the gift of her dazzling smile.

It's not so much her beauty, he thought. It's her enthusiasm, her optimism that the world could be made a just place. Yes, today is the day he would have that talk with her. It has to be today.

~~~

They settled into seats in the middle of the movie theatre balancing large drinks and buckets of popcorn. There were a few people sitting towards the rear, but otherwise the theatre was empty.

"It's hard to catch up with you these days," Mike whispered. "What gives?"

Ginny stifled a yawn. She was so tired she felt dazed. "It's this union stuff. Nothing too important, just fighting to keep our jobs," she replied, a slight testiness to her voice.

"Hey, it's me, remember? I'm not the class enemy," Mike said.

Ginny realized that she had stabbed at someone who didn't deserve it. "I'm sorry, Mike. It's just that since the big union meeting when that American Steel guy came to speak, I've been doing nothing but working and going to meetings. I hardly see Cory anymore. The demonstration is three-weeks away. Did I tell you we got a permit to march from the International Headquarters to American Steel?"

She didn't wait for an answer.

"And now there are rank and file committees at local s in Ohio and Illinois that want us to speak at their meetings. That means long distance driving. To top it off, someone slashed my tire last night in the lot at work."

"*What*?" Mike leaned towards her, his face darkening with concern. "How did that happen? I thought they had guards there!"

She explained the circumstances and what Antoli had said to her. "I guess it was bound to happen. I know I'm pissing some people off. They're worried that if the local is seen as a trouble-maker, then the company will shut it down."

"Ginny, you've got to be careful. Let some of the other guys do this. You don't have to be a one woman show."

"I'm not and they are. It's just that I spoke up in that meeting, so now I get to wear the label."

She did not mention the weasel that had ambushed her with threats about Cory at the meeting. The movie began and they fell into silence. Sitting close together, they were unaware that hate-filled eyes were drilling holes into the backs of their heads.

After the movie, they sat in his car in the parking lot of the cinema.

"There's something I want to talk to you about," Mike

said.

"What's that?" she asked, suddenly wary.

"It's about us." He ran his index finger along the nape of her neck. "You know I care about you a lot. I was thinking maybe we could ratchet this up a notch."

"Aren't you the romantic," she quipped. "What exactly does ratchet this up a notch mean?"

"C'mon, Ginny, you know what I mean. Get a place together, live together. Then we wouldn't have any more next times. We'd be together all the time."

His voice trailed off.

Ginny sat quietly. She liked Mike. He was an honest, intelligent man and a good father to his sons. She knew she was lucky to have him in her life. She traced the veins along the back of his hand with her finger. His skin is such a beautiful color, she thought, brown like aged copper. She did not want to hurt him nor did she want to lose him, but he was asking for something she was incapable of giving, at least for now.

In a soft voice she asked, "Can't we be just as we are?"

Mike shifted his position, staring out the driver's side window.

"For how long, Ginny? It's been a year already." He turned back to face her. "I know I have a playboy past. I'd like to tell you I was searching for Ms. Perfect, but the truth is I was scared to death to get involved with anyone. I think you've been scared, too. But, hell, Ginny, don't you think it's time we ditched the people who hurt us so bad so many years ago? I mean, we carry them around like every junkie with a monkey on his back, only ours isn't drugs, it's being afraid that we'll get hurt again. Plus..."

"Mike, stop. Please." She swallowed a sob. "I just can't right now. There's just too much going on right now."

"Excuses," he said. "Nothing but excuses."

"No, it's true. Besides I have to think of Cory."

"Don't you think I know that? I have to think of my boys, too. But if we talk to them and show them that nothing is being taken away from them, that actually good things are being added, they'll come around. Besides, what's the alternative? Wait until they're grown up with kids of their own? That's not fair to us or them. It's not giving them a realistic picture of life."

"You've plotted this out, haven't you?"

"I want you, Ginny, right here beside me."

She knew he was right. Knew she loved him. She knew they were good together. Yet she felt this inexplicable apprehension that went deeper than the usual jitters of making a commitment.

"I need some time to think."

As he began to speak, she put her fingers over his mouth. "You've been figuring all this out for yourself. Now I need to do the same. So I'm asking you for a little more time."

"How much time?"

"Two months, ok? Two months."

He put his arm around her shoulder and drew her to him. She buried her face in his chest. "I want you for a lifetime," he said. "I can wait two months."

The couple sat in silence for a long time, unaware of the eyes focused on them from a man in a car parked 100 yards behind them. A man who loved the darkness.

18

A family birthday party was in full swing when Tony Blasko burst through the gate of Pete Davison's backyard late that afternoon. Hot dogs and hamburgers were sizzling on the grill; large bowls of potato salad, baked beans, and salad were laid out on long folding tables covered with checkered plastic table cloths. Kids were tumbling on the grass while the adults sat and gabbed at picnic tables.

Pete was tending a makeshift bar offering whiskey, vodka, or scotch. A keg of beer sat in a vat of ice nearby. He watched as Tony made his way through the raucous family grouping. Although Pete didn't like Tony, he tolerated the steelworker, since the man could be useful on certain occasions. Occasions that required a heightened element of persuasion.

Both men were the same age and both had enlisted in the Army during the Vietnam War. Pete had made sergeant and re-upped for an extra tour. He thrived on the tension, the killing, and the whores. Tony, on the other hand, had spent time state-side in an Army hospital screaming at incoming helicopters.

That, plus a shared ideology of hate, was the sum total of their similarities.

They differed markedly in physical appearance and temperament. Tony was a medium-sized man, boorish and crude, who cinched his pants below his swollen belly in a self-delusional move to deny his sizable girth. He didn't speak, he bellowed.

Pete Davison, on the other hand, was adept at concealing his emotions. Normally, he was disengaged and distant. But when he stood on a stage, he was transformed into a fiery preacher, spitting out words of warning against wicked thoughts and sins of the flesh. Pete, lean with sinewy muscles that stretched over his five-foot eight-inch frame, paced back and forth in front of his audience like a taut wire about to be sprung. He preferred to wear tight fitting black t-shirts tucked into snug black jeans and motorcycle boots; unless he was donning a long white robe and a peaked hat that masked his face. Pete Davison was the unit chief of the local chapter of the Ku Klux Klan.

"What's up Tony? Want a beer?"

"Yeah, sure. We got her, Pete. We got her nailed now," Tony said as he reached for the plastic glass of foamy beer. Excited, he talked loud and fast. "I saw that bitch at the movies today..."

"Lower your voice, Tony!" Pete barked. "There're women and kids here."

Tony, puzzled, took stock of his surroundings as if seeing the family for the first time.

"Sorry," he said. "We got a break today. That Ginny broad was at the movies with a nigger. Then later they were all lovey-dovey in the front seat of a car. My wife took some pictures with her instamatic. I don't know if they'll come out 'cause we were a ways away."

Pete was instantly interested. "Did you recognize the nigger?"

"I never saw him before. But he was all over her, and she was lovin' it." Tony's face contorted into an expression of disgust. "Made me wanna puke. But I think we can use this now, especially if the photos come out. We don't need no nigger-lovin' commie causing trouble in the union, see? She's gonna cost us our jobs."

Pete took a long swig of his highball.

"We can talk it up around the mill, and that might turn some minds around; but I think we're beyond all that. We need to stop her organizing this mess in the union before the company decides AC is too much trouble and shuts it down. And we need to show people what happens when a white woman strays from the fold. Does this monkey work in the mill?"

"Dunno. The way I see it, Pete, right now she's more important than he is. We got to stop her before we all go down." Tony polished off his beer and wiped the foam from his watery lips. "I gotta go, my old lady's in the car."

"I'll get the unit together. We have to act fast." Pete relished the idea. Finally he had an opportunity. If this was done right, he would net some kudos from the Brotherhood and maybe be promoted. At the least he could revisit that tingling feeling that came over him when he watched a whore take her last breath. He'd felt it in 'Nam. It was better than sex.

⌁⌁⌁

"My mother had a serious relationship? With a man I never met?" Cory sat stunned.

"Yep," Blinky said.

Cory sputtered, "I never knew. I don't remember her ever bringing anyone home. I guess she had another life no one knew about."

"That *you* didn't know about," Blinky said, shifting her weight in the straight-back chair. "Parents have lives apart from their kids, right?"

"Yes, of course they do. I'm sorry, I've been having problems remembering my childhood. There is so much I've blocked out. But here is something really big I never knew.

"And the Klan?" Cory asked incredulous. "The Klan was in the mill?"

"Little girl, you gotta lot to learn," Blinky said. "These hate groups are all over the place. They may not have a big following, but you only need one or two to stir up shit."

"They were there, that's for sure," Dorie added. "I don't know how many, but a couple of them tried to recruit me. They figured because I was a white woman from the South that I agreed with that trash. But I never imagined they'd actually DO anything. That is until Ginny went missing."

"They're still in the mill," Sheri added. "I wouldn't put anything past them. They're evil, plain and simple. And if they had anything to do with Ginny, believe me they wouldn't want that news getting out now."

Cory flashed back to the warnings she'd had about some people not wanting to have information dug up twenty years later. Cory decided that if her mother had the courage to carry on the fight, there was no way she could back down now.

19

The rank and file meeting to discuss the latest plans for the protest demonstration had been all business, no time for jokes or chit-chat.

"We've got three weeks to get the word out," Ginny said. "Other locals in the area have contacted me wanting us to send a speaker to their meetings. We have to get the leaflets printed and distributed to our contacts in the mills."

"I've been getting calls, too," Curly said. "The word is spreading fast. I think we should try to meet with the locals in Youngstown and Cleveland. They ain't American Steel, but we're under attack from the whole industry."

Dorie nodded her head in agreement. "My cousin works for James and Laughton in Ohio. The union offered all kinds of concessions, practically had the guys paying to work there, but they're closing it down for good next month. Everybody's pissed off. I think we can get a lot of folks to participate if we can get the word out."

"The easiest way to do that is to have a press conference," Ginny said. "I can send out a notice."

Others in the group agreed to distribute leaflets and talk to workers who were having meetings in their homes, but when it came to public speaking at press conferences or union meetings, they wanted Ginny. She was fiery, smart, and battle-tested, having gone up against the lawyer from the International and that slippery slug from American Steel.

"All right," she said, reluctantly, "I'll drive to Ohio on

my days off, but we need to take up a collection for gas and tolls. I'm busted."

It was nine-thirty when she pulled away from the union hall. She crossed the Rankin Bridge, turned right onto Rte 837 and drove towards Munhall. Suddenly a car with its brights on came up behind her. Within seconds it was at her rear bumper. The interior of her car flooded with light.

Ginny bit down on her lip and pressed the accelerator to the floor. The big Chrysler lunged forward. The car behind her sped up and stayed within an arm's length of her bumper. Ginny's mouth went dry. Suddenly the car swung out into the empty opposing lane and pulled alongside of her. She slammed on her brakes and grabbed the crow bar that she now kept beside her on the seat. She heard laughter as the car flew past her, made a squealing left turn onto Greensprings Avenue and hauled-ass up the hillside.

Ginny pulled off the road and slammed the gear in park. Her hands clenched the steering wheel, her teeth chattered.

Eventually the constriction in her chest subsided and she was able to take deeper breaths. She put the car in drive and patted the dashboard. "I take back all the bad things I've ever said about you, Black Beauty. You're great."

Thirty minutes later she lay sweaty and naked on her bed, the little fan near her window simulating a breeze, and fell into a fitful sleep.

The following week her phone rang incessantly. Mostly the calls were from workers from other mills wanting the latest information about the protest demonstration. At times there would be silence on the other end of the line, at others, just breathing. They gave her the creeps.

One morning she got a call from Tim Fester. She had been invited to a special meeting at the union hall.

"What's it about, Tim?"

"Dunno. It's that guy Chonski from downtown."

"Who else has this invitation?"

"Dunno that either. I'm the last person to know anything. All I know is that it's tomorrow morning and since its union business, you can have the time off from work."

She hung up and rang Blinky. "What do you think he wants?"

"Let me guess. He either wants you to step aside so that the International can take the lead in organizing this demonstration..."

"HAH! Have you lost your mind?"

"Or he wants you to step way out of the way, as in drop the whole thing."

"Yeah, that's what I think, too. How dumb can he be? This demonstration, this whole Fight-Back movement, would take place with or without me."

"You gonna go?"

"You think I should?"

"Go, girl. Find out what's going on. You know, get a read on the situation, do a James Bond, infiltrate the enemy."

"Good grief, Blink, this isn't a Hollywood flick. But I think you're right. Yeah, I'll go."

The next morning she drove to the union hall. Although it was only nine o'clock, the temperature was rising fast. The air-conditioning in Black Beauty had been dead for two years. Ginny's jeans stuck to the back of her legs. The humid air blowing in from the open windows made her hair frizz as if her finger was stuck in a socket.

She pushed open the door to the hall and balked. Three men were crammed into Fester's small office. Fester caught her eye and nodded his head for her to enter. She had no choice but to squeeze in amongst them.

Fester sat sweating behind his desk. "Ginny, you remember Jerry Chonski? He spoke at the Local awhile back."

Chonski looked uncomfortable perched on a wooden

chair. "Ms. Johnson, it's good to see you again," Jerry Chonski said. He stood up to shake her hand.

"And this is Johnny Kelso." Kelso nodded an acknowledgement.

Ginny had a vague sense she had seen him before, but she couldn't remember where. He was a big man with thick neck muscles that made it impossible to fasten his collar button.

"Please, be seated," Chonski said. He sat off to her right, blocking the path to the door. Kelso remained leaning against the wall behind her.

A sudden chill rolled down her spine. Whether it was the air conditioned room or her instincts warning her, she couldn't tell. Ginny was determined that no one in the room detect her nervousness. She clamped her mouth shut and waited.

"How is everything going for you at AC?" Chonski asked.

Ginny shot a glance at him, stupefied. "Is that what this meeting is about? How things are for me at work?"

Ignoring her question, Chonski removed his bifocals and rubbed the oily lenses with his handkerchief. "You've made quite a name for yourself recently. You have been a loyal union member over the past four years. You've accomplished quite a bit for our sisters in the Local."

"It wasn't just me, it was the work of the Women's Committee," Ginny said.

He looked up from his cleaning task. "Yes, I realize that. But committees have their leaders and you are a born leader, Ginny. Is it ok if I call you Ginny?"

She nodded.

"Good." He repositioned his glasses and took a sip from a mug of coffee. "I respect members of the rank and file who aren't afraid to step forward and speak their minds, so long as they keep the good of the union in mind. You are doing that, aren't you? Keeping the good of the union in mind?"

Ginny hesitated before she answered. She wasn't sure if she was being set up for a fall. "No one wants to hurt the union. What we want is for the union to protect us. With the rate that the plants are closing, the union doesn't seem to—"

"Young lady!" he said sharply. "You don't know what you're talking about. That's the problem. What you and the others are doing is dangerous because you don't understand what the union is up against. The steel industry is changing and it's changing for good. With the technology they've got now, they can make steel with fewer workers. That's what their goal is, that and diversifying. That's their right. It may not be morally right, but it's legally their right. We don't own it, it's not our call. We can only try to salvage what will be left."

Ginny felt her cheeks get hot. She leaned forward in her chair and glared at Chonski.

"I agree," she said. "We are caught in the technology trap. Technology's great. It makes life easier, faster, and safer. But it also destroys lives because there's no protection for the likes of us who work for a living. Profits go up. Shareholders are happy. But what are we, yesterday's hash? Are ninety thousands of us supposed to go flip burgers in some greasy fast-food restaurant?"

Chonski began to speak, but she raised her hand to stop him.

"There are no laws that protect us, no political parties on our side to raise the issue of nationalization. I read in the papers the other day about how Canada has a labor party. Did you know that? Maybe that's a good thing."

"Hold up, Ginny, we're going way beyond what this meeting is about," Chonski said, folding his arms across his chest. "We want to discuss with you about the possibility of you helping out the union in a way that can make it stronger."

Ginny's forehead wrinkled in puzzlement. She glanced from Chonski to Fester. "What do you mean?"

"The union," Chonski replied, "the International Steel Workers Union, is going to have to diversify also. We're exploring metals, chemicals, and maybe public employees. It's a whole new ball-game and we need talented organizers like you to come on board and help the union grow. You've got what it takes. We need committed people with guts.

Chonski paused to look at Fesgter, then added, "We'd like you to start immediately. There's a plant of glass workers near Altoona we're interested in. Of course, you would have to spend some time at Linden Hall taking classes. They start next week and last for a month."

Speechless, Ginny sat back in the chair and stared at Chonski, the only sound, the air conditioner throwing cold air into the room.

"Of course," Chonski continued, "the job can have long hours, but the pay is more than what you are making now and."

Ginny blurted out, "Why are you offering me this job? Why *now*?"

"We always need courageous and smart people," Chonski said. "People, like you, who come up through the ranks. You've made a name for yourself."

In that instant the curtains opened and Ginny could clearly see the point of this meeting. She had nothing but disdain for these transparent men.

"The way I see it is you want me to quit my job today, go sixty miles south to the union's private estate for a month of classes, and then go sixty miles east into the country, live in a motel and talk to glass workers? Is that right?"

The room fell silent, except for the sound of Kelso shifting his weight.

Ginny glared at Chonski. *He works for the International, but the guy's a lawyer. What does he know about making steel or fighting for survival?* She turned towards Fester. *He's come up through the ranks, and even though he's got this cushy union job, maybe, just maybe, he can dredge up a memory of what it's like to work for a living.* But Fester was busy staring at his trembling hands.

"That would get me conveniently out of town. Are you hoping that the Fight-Back movement would fall apart? Is this your answer to the catastrophe we are facing?"

Chonski opened hjs mouth to speak, but Ginny cut him off. "You've already written us off, haven't you? In your mind steelworkers have no choice but to go down, so why fight, right? That's what all this diversification is about, isn't it? Good-bye steel, hello glass. You don't get it. It's been so long since this union has mobilized the ranks for a genuine fight against a company that its forgotten how these things are done. This movement is bigger than me. You could send me to the moon and these men and women would keep right on fighting."

She rose from her chair and stabbed her index finger in his direction, her contempt and anger exploding with every word.

"They would do it because they don't have a choice, but you don't get it! Instead of leading, you can only think of beheading!"

Rage contorted Chonski's face. He grasped the arms of his chair, hoisted his bulk up out of his chair, and roared at Ginny, "Now you listen to me, young Lady, this is your last chance!" He caught himself and stopped, his mouth agape.

"Or *what*? Are you threatening me?" she yelled.

Silence encircled the room as the two stood glowering at each other from opposite sides of the desk. A fist full of outrage seized her chest, making it difficult to breathe. She grabbed her purse from the chair, took two strides to the door, and turned to face the men.

"Sorry," she said, "I'm not a good candidate for your job. I don't sell workers out. I wouldn't fit in around here."

She left the room, slamming the door behind her.

Ginny hurried to her car and was about to open the door when Kelso, his jet black hair shellacked straight back like an oil slick, stepped in front of her. He grabbed her shoulder with his beefy hand.

"What's the rush, Red? You got some place important to run off to?"

"Get your paw off me," she said, with more courage than she felt, "and get out of my way."

He snickered but did not remove the grip on her shoulder.

"You made a big mistake back there, girlie. So I'm gonna give you a little time to rethink your position. Your choice is pretty clear. Back off on your own or I'm gonna help you."

She winced from pain as his fingers dug into her shoulder blades. "Do we understand each other?"

Ginny didn't flinch. She stood glued to the spot, her mouth dry as chalk.

"Just remember, time's running out," he said as he shoved her backwards and ambled off in the direction of the union office. She had the car door partially opened when he turned and taunted her.

"Oh, yeah. If you ever see Danny again, tell him I said hello."

Ginny could feel the metal point of an ice pick pricking up and down her spine. She began to shiver despite the

June heat.

"How do you know Danny?" she asked, turning towards him.

He stood there with his legs spread apart, his burly arms folded across his well-defined chest, a smirk on his face. She could see the muscles around his jaw twitching as though he could barely contain his glee. She hated herself for asking because it gave him the upper hand, but he had caught her off guard.

"Everybody knows about Danny. It's too bad he got sent away for killin' that chick he was shacked up with in Michigan. You two losers were made for each other," he laughed as he turned to walk away.

"Hey!" he shouted over his shoulder, "I heard you had his kid! How's the kid doin'? Busy sending letters to Daddy in the nut house?" He howled with laughter as he strode off to the office building.

Ginny tumbled into her car, slammed the door shut and shoved the lock down. Within seconds she was speeding down the highway. The muscles in her body were balled up with tension. As she put some distance between herself and the union office, the tautness gave way to tremors. She leaned forward to rub the wave of cramps gripping her calves. Dry heaves retched up her esophagus.

Twenty minutes later she skidded to a stop in front of Blinky's house. "Please be here, please," she mumbled as she pounded on the door. "Blink!" she hollered. "Open up, it's me!"

Finally the door opened and her friend, sleepy and disheveled, stared back at her.

"Girl, I'm on night turn, can't this wait? I need my beauty sleep." Examining her closer, Blinky said, "Get in here, you look like shit. What happened?"

Inside, Ginny paced around the room. "There're some

things going on that you need to know about and some things about my past that I want you to know. But you have to promise you aren't gonna say anything to anybody. Ok?"

"OK, OK, just sit down, you're makin' me jumpy. I'm gonna put some water on for coffee."

Ginny followed Blinky into the kitchen and collapsed onto a chair. She blew a long rasping sigh through her lips. Blinky sat down across from her and waited.

"Things began happening when that guy Blake from American Steel...." Ginny concentrated hard to put events in chronological order as she described the creepy guy that had asked how Cory was and told her to stop organizing. Then the flat tire with Antoli standing on the other side of the fence sneering about how she might soon be dead. Next were the phone calls at home with no one on the other end. And now this morning's meeting at the district with the job offer just to stop her from organizing Fight-Back, her refusal, Chonski's "or else," and Kelso's threat to stop her physically.

She told Blinky about Danny McCormack and how he had been found not guilty by reason of insanity in the gruesome death of a young woman he had done drugs with. How he had sworn to her on the phone before the final decision of the court that he was innocent and that it was some other guy. And how, since it had happened so far away, his family had found it easy to keep the whole grisly affair quiet.

"I never told anyone what happened to him," Ginny said, "so how did this guy Kelso know about it? And he knew about Cory, too."

"Cory? How..."

"Well, not exactly Cory. He knew that I had had Danny's baby. He didn't say Cory or son or daughter. He just said kid, Danny's kid. There's only one way he could have known. Danny must have told him." She paused to think. "Maybe Danny didn't do it... but when he got put in the mental institution, no one believed anything he said. I mean, I tried talking to him on the phone but he wasn't making any sense. He was seeing stuff, yakking out of his head. After a while I didn't believe him, either. But this Kelso, maybe he followed the case for some reason." Her voice drifted off as her thoughts became entangled in the past.

Trying to relieve her friend's fears, Blinky said, "You don't know any of this for sure. Maybe somebody told him about it years ago. It would have been damn hard to keep that a secret. Maybe he knows somebody in the family. A cousin or somebody. If someone else did kill that woman, maybe he knows who it was or he's just spoutin' off."

Blinky stopped long enough to take a breath and a sip of coffee. Without warning, a jittery foreboding balled up in her stomach. "You better stop working with Fight-Back. Let the others do it. Damn, Ginny, you know we can't win this, we're just pissin' off a lot of big shots. The company... the union..."

Ginny sat quietly, doodling on a piece of scrap paper.

"You hear me, girl?" Blinky continued. "Hell, a lot of guys in the mill, women too, are so scared about their jobs they don't want to make a peep. They think what we're doing is what's gonna lose them their jobs. It ain't worth getting beat-up or killed."

A hush fell over the kitchen as the two friends sipped their coffee. The clock on top of the television set chimed twelve times. Blinky was unsuccessful in stifling a yawn. Ginny stood up; it was time to leave.

She knew she couldn't quit Fight-Back. It would send a message to women not to fight and it would tell men that women can't be on the front lines. Quitting now would be demoralizing for the movement. Plus, to see Fight-Back in a mess would tell the company that steelworkers are push-overs. Worse, it would tell the union that they can use their goons to smash any opposition.

She smiled weakly at Blinky. The quivering in the corners of her mouth belied her attempt to appear confident.

"I can take some precautions, be more aware of what's going on around me."

"You gonna tell Mike about all this?"

"No. He's got enough on his plate right now. Besides, there's nothing he can do and he'd only worry."

Ginny walked to the front window and scanned the patch of dirt and grass that the Housing Authority called a play-ground for the children who lived in the projects. It was noon in the middle of the week. The place was deserted. She opened the door and turned back to hug Blinky.

"If I quit, they win. I can't do it," she said. "I'm in this with everyone else—right to the end."

20

It had been a little over a month since Franklin Blake was run off the stage at Local 1630. He remembered how Tim Fester, that gutless wonder of a union president with his purple veins spreading like cob-webs across his alcoholic face, had frantically rummaged through his desk drawers searching for a bottle of booze. Blake, his stomach roiling, had stood at the corner of the window alternately sneaking peeks at the angry crowd on the sidewalk below and back at the office door. Two union officers had blocked the door while the freakish thug from company security had weaseled his way close to that bitch.

Blake had fought hard to defuse the bomb of humiliation that threatened to explode in his chest. The corporate attorney had been disgraced. Devalued. Made to feel alarm and to retreat from irate idiots. His plan had blown up in his face.

He was relieved that Chairman Richards had taken the month of June to vacation in the south of France. It had given Blake time to calm down and get things in perspective. Now, as he rode the elevator to Chairman Richards' office to give his report, his confidence surged. The entire mess was not his fault.

"Apparently we did not get a good reporting from our sources about the strength of the opposition in the local ," Franklin Blake said. "There is definitely an infestation of radicals there. I don't know how many or how much support they have…"

Richards snapped, "Do they seem as well-organized as that Homestead bunch?"

"At Homestead the entire local leadership is radical. I got the impression that what's happening at AC is more an incipient coalescing of a few disgruntled types. Their main spokesman is a woman." He added grudgingly, "She's smart and articulate. She could be real trouble if this thing is allowed to gain strength."

Blake could tell Richards did not like what he was hearing. The Chairman turned to the wall of glass behind his desk and gazed down upon a city where he wielded tremendous power. "We've got a lot of enemies down there: politicians, economists, professors, unions, workers, housewives. They blame American Steel for unemployment, pollution, you name it." Conrad Richards sighed. "They're going to hate us all the more once they see what downsizing and diversification is going to do."

He shrugged his shoulders. "We don't answer to them. We answer to the shareholders."

In a deadly serious tone, he said, "It is imperative that the plan go forward. We've got the government of the United States in our pocket, for Christ sake. I'm not going to get jerked around by some loud-mouthed female who should be home baking pies.

"I don't need to remind you that we have hundreds of millions of dollars invested in this mill. When we get the caster in there, it will be millions more. We need to act quickly to neutralize any problems.

"I don't care how you do it." He slammed his fist on desk. "Just do it!"

Franklin Blake was conflicted over this new assignment. He disdained violence. It was beneath him, a tactic employed by weak minds, he would say whenever the topic came up. He preferred to win by his intellect. By outmaneuvering his opponent, using humor, charm and craftiness to slowly encircle his victims and then, like the final squeeze of a boa constrictor, bring them to their knees.

Yet, there were moments in his life when fury rendered reason impotent. At those times he was consumed by the need to physically crush anyone who, on rare occasions, claimed a victory over him.

Ginny Johnson had out-maneuvered him and had forced him to cower in the corner of Fester's tacky wood-paneled office. She had humiliated him in front of hundreds, and the shame he felt still burned like an acid-drip in his veins. Blake understood the politics and economics behind Richards's choice of the word "neutralize." Now he would add a personal motive: vengeance.

He put a call through to a friend in the AC's BOP shop, and then to security.

"Come up to my office," he ordered.

Within minutes there was a tap on the private door to his inner sanctum. Blake buzzed his personal assistant to say he did not want to be disturbed.

When the man entered, a sudden cold draft swept through the office. Blake shuddered. He was repulsed by everything the man represented: blind obedience, stupidity, blunt force, cruelty. Yet these were all the qualities that he needed for the job.

"Take a seat, Moe. How's it going?"

The man appeared uncomfortable in his cheap, snug-fitting suit. His face was expressionless. A few thin brown hairs stuck out from under his nose in a failed attempt to disguise a harelip. Moe sat down heavily on a tufted leather arm chair and waited.

"I have an assignment for you," Blake said. A wave of revulsion swept over him. Christ, the man looks like a giant squid.

Moe nodded.

"Remember that red-haired girl at the union meeting?"

Moe nodded again.

"She's causing problems and we want to clear her out of the way. Permanently."

Moe's upper lip shriveled into a grin, exposing small, tobacco-stained teeth.

Blake shuddered at the sight.

"Just keep it quiet." He handed Moe a slip of paper. "Here's her name, address, phone number. She's on midnights this week in the BOP. Saturday midnight is her last night. You need help getting into the mill?"

"Nah. Don't need help. Saturday midnight."

"We don't have a lot of time. She's planning a press conference for Monday morning and we don't want it to take place. So this problem has to be solved before then. Make sure no one can trace anything back here, or anywhere. Got it?"

"Yeah, I got it," Moe said with a nasty little chuckle. He pushed himself out of the chair and lumbered towards the private door.

Blake shuddered. Jesus, he thought, I wouldn't want that big ape breathing down my neck.

❧❧❧

Jerry Chonski was feeling the pressure. Daily reports were coming in from Tim Fester on the organizing plans of the Fight-Back committee. "They're gonna announce the demonstration Monday at a press conference. The damn thing is gonna start at the International headquarters and end at American Steel. Plus, they've been telling steelworkers from around the country to come. This thing could be big, Jerry. Real big."

"Don't worry!" Chonski thundered into the phone, "there isn't gonna be a press conference." He slammed down the phone. It was maddening that the Johnson girl carried on despite his order that she stop, ignoring him like he was some kind of nobody. She's not gonna make a horse's ass out of me, he fumed, though he wasn't sure what to do to shut her up.

Added to that was the reaction of his bosses at the International. Chonski, the legal-beagle, was looking like a chump. Word was going around that he was unable to control some upstarts at a Local. He needed to squash this rebellion before it got out of hand. He needed to show that he could not only prepare legal documents but that he could handle tough situations with upstarts. His promotion—his whole career—depended on it.

He picked up the phone and called Fester back.

They met in the late morning at a noisy diner on Penn Avenue in Pittsburgh. Mashed potatoes, brown gravy, and thin slices of beef were piled high on Chonski's plate. He didn't care what time it was, he was nervous and that made him hungry.

Fester, on the other hand, clutched a coffee cup and tried to stop his hands from trembling. His stomach felt raw from all the booze he'd poured into it the night before. He watched with disgust as Chonski's flabby jowls jiggled while he chewed.

"She ain't gonna stop," Chonski said, wiping a stream of gravy off his chin with his finger. "She's flipping us the bird."

Fester nodded his head in agreement.

"I don't see that we have any choice," Chonski continued. "I mean, we can try to scare her off again, but Kelso seemed pretty certain he'd conveyed the message to her after the last meeting.

"She's the leader of this committee. The others listen to her before they make decisions. Getting her out of the way will definitely—what'd she say, *behead*? It will definitely behead that group."

He paused to shovel a forkful of food into his mouth. It didn't occur to him that Fester was not responding.

"We need to act before the press conference. We can't afford to wave red flags in front of American Steel. That meeting at the Local with their company man, Christ, what were they thinking?"

Chonski cleaned his plate with the last of his bread. "And we can't afford to allow the ranks to get riled up. The last thing we need right now are demonstrations. They could easily spill over into wildcat strikes. Hell, it could become an opposition movement inside the union that vies for leadership. What a mess *that* would be. We're not about battling with the company, we're about doing whatever it takes to keep the peace. This concession package has got to go through smoothly."

Fester finally roused himself. "I just don't understand why she's doin' this. She's like one of them Jap Kamikaze pilots, gonna fly that suicide mission right into AC. Doesn't she see that the company wants to keep AC working but they're not gonna invest in that caster if the local can't be trusted to cooperate? She's shootin' herself in the foot. Doesn't she see that?"

"Some people choose to go down fighting and she's one of them." Chonski sipped the last of his coffee. He rose from the booth. "We've got to do whatever it takes—and fast."

A few hours later Kelso pulled his black SUV alongside a new beige Oldsmobile sedan parked in a Wendy's parking lot. Chonski, having succumbed to the sweltering heat of a July afternoon and the mountain of grease that was percolating in his gut, was catnapping in the front seat. He snapped awake when he heard Kelso's voice.

"Hey, Boss, what's up?"

"The red-head is causing too much trouble. She's gotta go. Try scaring her off one more time. She's got a kid, maybe that's an angle. Can you handle it?"

The hell with another warning, Kelso thought. *She'd had her chance.* His wide mouth broke out into a wicked grin. "Yeah, Boss, my pleasure. I knew she wouldn't stop. She's a big talker but a slow learner." He sniggered. "When and where?"

Chonski's jaw pulsed. He hadn't known Kelso long, but the guy gave him the creeps.

"If it comes down to it, the mill is probably your best bet. Fester says she's on night-turn. Finishes up Sunday morning. Her group is planning a press conference for Monday and it would be bad for the union if it happened. You got a way to get into the mill?"

"The guy owns the security company owes me big time. He can get me in." Kelso broke into a hellish guffaw and slapped the steering wheel. "Ok, Boss. Consider it done."

Chonski growled a warning: "Don't say anything to anyone. Got it?"

"Got it. Don't worry, I'll handle it."

Kelso pulled away and drove out onto the highway. A diabolical calmness came over him as he imagined the horror that would erupt in those big baby blues. He would enjoy toying with her, watching her squirm, listening to her plead. Oh yeah, she'll beg because—for all of her tough acting—she'd never come up against the likes of Johnny Kelso.

21

The cheap Formica table in the church basement was round, giving the appearance of equality, but Pete Davison was definitely the man in charge. Four men, including Tony Blasko, listened respectfully while Pete prepared them for the task at hand.

Davison, his hair shorn military style, spoke in the clipped manner of the Army sergeant he used to be, spittle shooting between his teeth. His platoon had been reduced to these four men and he was missing the terrain maps to spread out across the table, but he had not forgotten how to motivate his troops.

"This is a war on two fronts," he said, his zealousness pulsating in every word. "It's a war to save our white race from being polluted by these niggers and it's a war against communism. We have been preparing for battle and now the time has come. There is a nigger-lovin' commie whore who is threatening to destroy our jobs and that will weaken our country. She's shackin' up with a monkey and that, men, will weaken our race. We will not allow that to happen!" he shouted, slapping his hand down on the table.

His words reverberated off the wall of the big empty room with its cracked linoleum floor. Davison could feel the Calling coming over him, taking over his mind and soul, and he knew that for the next few minutes he would speak words he would not remember saying.

He rose from the metal-folding chair and began to strut back and forth, his index finger stabbing upward toward the heavens. The words shot out of his mouth with a military cadence.

"Race mixing is the work of Satan!" he said loudly. "Communism is the work of Satan. Doing nothing to defend ourselves against this threat is..." He paused, and with the intense expression of someone consumed with the righteousness of his mission, shouted, *"The work of Satan. Are you ready? Are you able? Are you willing to destroy this evil plot of Satan? To destroy that Jezebel and her bastard child? Smite down that whore of Babylon who walks amongst us?"*

The men had moved to the edge of their seats. Their eyes glazed over and their brains took flight as their emotions were captured in the net of fanaticism. To a man they nodded their heads. They felt the effervescent power of Jesus Christ taking root in their hearts and lighting the way to their salvation. To a man they affirmed their readiness to cleanse the world of the foul female.

Pete Davison picked up his tattered bible and waved it in the air.

"The proof of the righteousness of our mission is here in God's word. To doubt it is to abet the devil," he admonished the multitudes that only he saw, the hundreds of parishioners who filled the seats, stood along the wall, and crowded down the aisles. He continued to preach, inflaming his followers, until he collapsed in his chair. His head hung down while milky foam dribbled out of his open mouth.

Having witnessed this before, the men knew to remain silent until their leader returned from wherever Jesus had spoken to him. Slowly he came to reality, void of the piercing heat that had possessed him just a few moments before. He fought to get clear of the fog.

Tony Blasko, who never failed to be moved by these

performances, was anxious to settle the plan.

"We're ready, Pete. Yunz just pick the day and the soldiers of God you want to do the work. We're ready to carry out the plan."

Pete, the sergeant, was all business.

"You said Saturday midnight is her last turn?"

Tony nodded his head yes.

"OK, I'll make the plan. After that the soldiers are drawn by lottery, except for Tony. He's too close. Remember," Pete said with deadly seriousness, "we operate in secrecy. Anyone who talks pays the highest price. Is that clear?"

His platoon nodded in agreement.

22

Ginny watched as her daughter packed a pink duffle bag with pictures of Minnie Mouse on the sides. It was Friday afternoon and Cory was off to spend the week-end with friends from school.

"You want some help?" Ginny asked.

"No, Momma, I've got everything."

"You've got toys and games in there, but hardly enough clothes," Ginny laughed. "How about some underwear and pajamas?"

Cory looked at the stuffed suitcase and frowned. "I guess I forgot. But there's no room left."

"Here, let me help you. We'll put some of these things into a paper bag. Ok?"

At six o'clock Ginny walked her daughter to the curb where a station-wagon filled with little girls waited. She bent down and hugged Cory tightly to her chest.

"I love you, Muffin. You remember that, ok? And you behave yourself. I'll pick you up Sunday around five." She hugged her again. "Don't forget, if you want to come home before then, just call me, ok?"

"Momma, don't worry," Cory said. She climbed into the back seat and was soon lost amongst the giggling girls. Then, as the big car drove off, her head popped up in the back window, her long red pig-tails falling down the bib of her coveralls. "Bye Momma!" she yelled, blowing kisses with both hands.

Ginny grinned and waved back. Without warning she

felt a rush of emptiness pass through her while tears spilled down her cheeks. She couldn't figure out what was wrong. Her daughter going off for two nights was not the end of the world. Yet, she couldn't shake the sense of dread that coursed through her body.

Four hours later she awoke drenched in sweat from the humid heat that wafted through the windows of her pitch black bedroom. She showered, dressed, made her lunch, and turned on the television to kill some time.

Mike rang to say good-night and tell her to be careful at work. They made plans to go biking on Sunday afternoon if she was up to it. "I love you," he said softly as he hung up the phone.

Ginny parked under a lamp near the guard house and walked alone toward the bathhouse. When she passed by the metallurgy lab, she saw Ron Antoli leaning up against the door jamb.

"What's the matter, Miz Johnson?" he sneered. "You afraid to park in the dark?"

Ginny, tired and feeling an unfamiliar kernel of vulnerability in her gut, stared straight ahead.

"I'd be afraid of the dark if I was you, Miz Johnson. Yep, I'd be looking over my shoulder all night long if I was you. Lots of dark places around here, anything could happen."

"Fuck off, Antoli," was all she could muster while a cold shiver of fright licked at her spine.

Antoli erupted in a high-pitched shriek of laughter.

She scurried down the road to the bathhouse like a mouse along a baseboard, keeping her head down as she passed maintenance sheds and dark empty buildings. Shadows, like ink-blots, fell across the lane. Her nerves about to snap, she broke into a sprint and dashed the last seventy-five feet to the bathhouse.

"Hey, Red, what's up?" Dorie was laid-out on the narrow

bench, sucking in her breath and yanking at the zipper on her jeans. "Jesus, I knew I was in trouble when I had to lie down on the bed to zip these things closed. Now, I'm so sticky from this humidity...."

Dorie stopped and stared up at Ginny. "What happened to you? Your face is white as milk. What's wrong?"

"I saw that Antoli bastard, again. The man gives me the creeps. And my tire was slashed the other day." She sat down on the bench and unlocked her locker. "I'm ok."

"Are you sure? You don't look so good."

"No, I'm ok. Just didn't get enough sleep. Have you seen Blinky?"

Her pants finally zipped up, Dorie pulled an oversized t-shirt over her head. "She just finished up daylight. Won't be back out here 'til Sunday afternoon." Dorie grabbed her paper bag stuffed with dirty work clothes, turned towards the door and stopped. "Hey, maybe we could meet Monday before the press conference. Have breakfast. Maybe that'll cheer you up."

"Yeah, that sounds good," Ginny replied as she pulled on her thermal long underwear.

"Work safe," Dorie said, and then she was gone.

It turned out to be a slow night for the pit crew. One of the furnaces was down for repairs, which cut production in half. When Ginny wasn't on the platform with her crew, she spent her time sitting on a bench in a corner of the pit shanty feigning sleep.

"What's wrong, Red?" Curly asked, "You ain't said two words since you walked in."

"I'm ok, Curly," she said feebly. "Just tired. I think I could sleep for a month. Changing turns every seven days is a killer."

"You got that right," Curly said. "Put your head down, get some sleep. I'll wake you when our next heat is up."

When eight in the morning rolled around, Ginny drove out of the parking lot feeling groggy and numb. She relished the thought of her dark bedroom, cool sheets, a breeze from the window fan, and the cooing sounds of a pair of mourning doves that had taken up residence in the eaves of her neighbor's roof.

The house was quiet when Ginny entered. There were no cartoons playing on the television, no toys littering the floor, no little girl clothes draped over a chair, and no Cory running towards her with arms outspread anticipating a big kiss. This is probably why I've been feeling so weird, she mused, passing through the dining room en route to the kitchen for a chocolate brownie. Nothing like a little sugar and a lot of chocolate to settle the demons.

She froze. Something was wrong.

She stared at the back door. It was slightly ajar. The lock chain hung from its hinge, ripped from the wood. She held her breath and listened to the silence surrounding her. Grabbing a large kitchen knife from the rack, she inched down the three steps that lead to the landing where the back door stood open, and strained to hear any sounds in the dank basement. All she heard was the thumping of her heart.

Ginny crept up the stairs, passed through the kitchen and tip-toed down the hallway towards her bedroom. She put her ear against the closed door and listened. She could hear the clock ticking next to her bed. The door knob stuck to her clammy hand as she turned it inch-by-inch. Finally it clicked and she shoved the door open, holding the knife in front of her.

The morning sunshine peaked through the corners of the drawn shades, throwing enough light for Ginny to see. Nothing was amiss. She stood still for several seconds, trying to think, trying to come up with an explanation.

Then she remembered that hissing voice and the vacuous eyes of that creep who grabbed her arm at the union hall. "Your daughter, Cory, how is she?"

She whirled around and stared at the closed door at the opposite end of the hall. She lunged forward and raced along the hallway, knife in hand, her jaws clenched, rage and terror fueling each stride.

She crashed through the door.

"Oh, my God! No!"

All the lights in the room were on, casting a garish hue over the bright colors of what had been Cory's bedroom. The yellow walls were smeared with brownish-red paint that looked like dried blood. Her bright blue Winnie the Pooh bedspread was riddled with slashes from a jagged blade. The pink curtains lay in a shredded mass on the floor. The heads of each doll had been ripped off and tossed on Cory's pillow. Her stuffed animals had been slit up the middle with the stuffing thrown about the room. The clothes in her closet had been drenched in the blood-colored paint.

Ginny gaped at the vanity mirror where the words "Commie bitch" were smeared in the dark red paint.

The room and everything that belonged to her daughter, the one person she was charged with protecting against all harm, had been destroyed. Ginny, trembling, dizzy and nauseous, ran out the back door and vomited on the grass. Her cheeks were awash in tears as her body, bent over, convulsed with sobs.

After a time, the horror subsided, replaced by a simmering anger. She walked to the phone in the kitchen and called the police.

"I want to report a break-in," she said, in a slow, clear voice.

An hour later she sat on the front porch waiting for the

police to finish their investigation. The detective had asked her a lot of questions, honing in on the possibility that someone wanted to send Ginny a message by harming her daughter. She'd already thought of it.

The "what-ifs" had been rumbling around in her head non-stop. What if Cory and Mrs. Gromski had been asleep in the house? What if it had been Cory and me? What if Cory had spent the night with Mrs. Gromski and they had returned to find this? What if Cory had had a friend over for the night? What if...?

"We'll keep a patrol car cruising through the neighborhood for the next few nights just in case. If we get any leads, we'll let you know. It might be a good idea if you can get somebody to stay with you for a while."

The police officer started to go down the porch steps but turned back. "You sure you can't think of anyone who is out to get you? Anyone angry enough to do this?"

Ginny hesitated, not sure how much to tell. She described the veiled threat to her daughter, her tire slashed at work, and the phone calls when the caller remained silent.

She hadn't spoken to Mike, knowing he would be at her doorstep in an instant, and she didn't want the police making assumptions about race being the issue. Maybe it was, but that wasn't what that freaky guy at the union hall had been talking about.

The officer said the remarks could have been innocent, someone wanting to intimidate her, but they would follow up, nonetheless. "You can pick up a copy of the police report for your insurance at headquarters. Be careful," he said and left.

Ginny rang Blinky and told her what had happened.

"I need someone to clean up Cory's bedroom later this afternoon and paint it tomorrow. Can your brother's crew do it? I know it's a lot to ask on such a short notice."

"He'll do it, I'll make sure of it. You going to work tonight? Maybe you should call in sick, take the night off."

"No, I'm going in. It may sound funny, but I feel safer there than here. I'm going to talk to Sara Roberts and see if Cory can stay a few more nights until I get her room back to normal. And I'm gonna tell Mike that I got called out at four this afternoon and have to work a double. That way he'll understand I won't be able to see him Sunday. Tomorrow I'll go shopping for some clothes for Cory."

"Jesus, Ginny, tell Mike. Don't you think he should know?"

"All he's gonna do is pitch a fit and tell me to quit Fight Back and quit the damn job. I don't want him worrying and telling me what to do. Besides I've already made up my mind."

"About?"

"I have to quit Fight Back. I'll finish the press conference on Monday. After that I'll tell Mike I'm through. I'm all Cory's got. For her sake, I can't risk it."

"Girl, you don't have to explain anything to me. It ain't worth it. We're all goin' down anyway. And don't worry what anyone else thinks. Cory is more important than any of this."

"Thanks Blink. I'll talk to you tomorrow."

Ginny hung up, relieved that she would soon be out of the fray and Cory would be out of danger.

23

Ginny might as well have doubled out that night. The furnaces were cooking fast and furious as American Steel sped up production ahead of a scheduled visit from the Occupational Safety and Health Administration. The brutal pace was welcome, she needed to push the dread she felt out of her body.

What horrified Ginny most, besides her alarm for Cory, was her own panic. Never before had she experienced such fright. She had moved through life with confidence; dauntless even when faced with serious problems. She'd taken for granted the inner strength that she relied upon. But threats to her daughter were too terrible to bear.

Now fear had moved in, sending its tentacles to capture and destroy every vestige of her self-assurance. Unnerved and alone, her fear grew at the rate of an avalanche.

When she walked past the guardhouse, she waved her ID card at a guard she had never seen before. A wave of apprehension enveloped her. She felt him watching her as she walked down the road to the bathhouse. It'll be okay, she told herself. Stay calm, keep your eyes open and get through the shift.

Ginny worked at a feverish pace, thankful that she could hide behind it. Her mood was vile. She was curt with the men. In between heats, she sat alone outside the shanty, wanting to be invisible.

After finishing a rim heat at 4 am, she strode towards the elevator that would take her to the women's bathroom on the third floor. As she walked, she peeled off the heavy asbestos coat that hung down to her ankles. Next to come off was the green fire-retardant jacket. Her wet thermal underwear clung to her back and her feet squished inside socks soaked with sweat.

She stopped at the closed elevator door. "Damn them," she grumbled. "We've been asking for a woman's john on the first floor for four years. A pipe, a toilet, and four walls, is that too much to ask?"

She thrust her finger towards the elevator button and stabbed it. Yawning, she leaned against the wall and waited, her bladder on the verge of bursting.

OSHA's visit would miss the levels of toxic pollution being emitted into the atmosphere from tonight's quickened pace. Stinking smoke ripe with chemicals was melding undetected into the sultry night air.

"The daylight crew will have it nice and easy tomorrow," she grumbled. "Maybe they'll have five heats all day. Hah! We've had six in four hours and more to come."

"C'mon!" she yelled, kicking the metal door with her steel-toed boot. At last the doors opened to an empty dark box.

She balked, the taunt from Antoli about dark places fresh in her mind. But there was no time to climb three flights of stairs. She hurried inside and punched the button. The doors slammed shut and the elevator began a sluggish ascent. She stared out at the blackness, tapping her fingers on the wall behind her.

When the doors opened, she walked briskly out onto the furnace floor, turned left and marched passed the labor foreman's empty office. She pushed open a door and entered the deserted office area of the day time staff. The fluorescent ceiling lights cast a harsh glare on the long hallway with its drab green wall.

She pushed open the bathroom door with her shoulder while she fumbled with the buttons on her fire-retardant pants. The door slammed shut. Ginny was instantly enveloped in darkness.

She groped along the wall searching for the light switch. She flipped it up. Nothing happened.

"Damn," she muttered. She tried it again, staring blindly at the pitch-black nothingness, a rising sense of dread gripping her.

A chair leg scraped against the linoleum floor. Ginny whirled around to face it. She heard a deep grunting sound as a body lunged at her.

She opened her mouth to scream. A gnarled fist smashed into her face, shattering her nose and crushing her cheek bones. The back of her head smacked into the cement block wall and split open. Warm blood flowed freely down her neck. Her knees buckled as she slumped towards the floor.

"Is she out?"

"She ain't moving but we gotta make sure she can't make no sounds."

She felt her body being pulled up against the wall. She tried to raise her arms but they hung like sacks of cement against her sides.

Her last sensation, before she succumbed to unconsciousness, was the crunching sound of her jaw bone crumbling from the force of an exploding fist.

The smaller of the two men removed a flashlight from his pocket and scanned the wall. There was a splotch of bright red blood where the back of Ginny's skull had been split open. Two thin streams of blood were slowly weaving their way towards the floor. He grabbed some paper towels, wet them, quickly wiped the wall and stuffed the towels into his pocket.

"We've gotta hurry," the big man said. "They'll be tapping the heat in a couple minutes."

"OK, let's get her outta here."

They wrapped her head in her green jacket to keep the blood from dripping on the floor. Then they flipped off the hallway lights and carried her out onto the furnace floor.

No one was in sight. The furnace crew was busy taking a test on the other side of the massive vessel. The two men dropped her body in a wheel barrel and covered it with her asbestos coat. They pushed it towards the short metal platform that stuck out over the mouth of a ladle that was waiting for the next heat.

"You see anybody up in those cranes?"

"Smitty's up there sleepin'. Let's get this over with fast."

They upended the wheel barrel, plunging her body forty feet to the floor of the ladle.

The two men double-timed it towards the metal stairs. A warning horn blew. Within minutes the furnace would be tilting to pour the next two hundred tons of searing hot liquid into the waiting ladle.

"She's history. There won't be any more trouble from her."

The other laughed. "That's one ingredient that might fuck up the beer can recipe."

"Are you kidding? They won't be able to tell anything. She's vaporized, man. Vaporized."

They raced down the stairs, walked quickly out of the huge building and disappeared into the night.

Barely conscious, Ginny lay in a crumpled heap, her legs twisted and her face broken and bleeding. As the massive iron furnace began its slow downward movement, one word gurgled in her mangled mouth. "Cory."

The molten steel, thick and bubbling, cascaded into the ladle, splashing against the brick lining, licking flames as it filled to the brim.

A lone figure stood paralyzed on the metal bridge above the ladle, his innards convulsing. With bile oozing up from his gullet and gathering in his mouth, he gawked at the hideous scene below.

24

Ginny's pit crew waited at the far end of the steel-pouring platform. Ginny had been so distant from her coworkers that she was not immediately missed. Now, as the crane carrying the ladle creaked down the aisle on its approach, they looked at each other quizzically. Where the hell was Ginny?

The first steel pourer, captain of the ship of that heat, was irritated at her disappearance. He paged Curly on the intercom to come up on the platform and fill in for her until she got back from wherever it was she had gone. As the big ladle moved over the molds emptying its load one-by-one, the men became increasingly concerned.

At the end of the heat the first steel pourer had no choice but to report to the pit foreman that his third steel pourer was missing from the job. Scowling, the pit foreman spit brown snuff juice into a Styrofoam cup, then dialed the night boss on the furnace floor.

"She was here until the last heat. Maybe she's sick or something. Can you check the women's john?"

He buzzed the infirmary, but the nurse, awakened from a deep sleep, reported no injuries or illnesses.

Then he rang the labor foreman and asked for a replacement to be sent to the pit. He scowled as he stuffed more snuff into his lower lip. Crazy broad, what the hell does she think she's doing?

The night furnace foreman rang back. "She isn't in the woman's toilet. No lights and no woman," he said.

The pit foreman sat, banging his pencil on his metal desk, trying to puzzle out what could have happened. He grabbed the phone and called the guard at the gate. The guard picked up the receiver halfway through the first ring.

"Yeah, I seen her," the guard said quickly. "She walked outta here 'bout forty-five minutes ago. Hadn't even changed her clothes. Got into a white pickup and drove off. Why, there a problem?"

"No," the pit foreman growled into the phone, "If she comes back, stop her at the gate and call me." He slammed down the phone. *What the hell?*

Stymied, he strode off towards the pit shanty.

"The guard says she left in a white pick-up just before the last heat. Anybody know anything about this? She say anything?" The men, surprised, shook their heads no in unison.

"Ginny would never just walk off," Easy Money said. "That ain't like her."

"I don't know, she was actin' pretty strange," Champ pointed out. "Didn't hardly say nothin' to nobody,"

Catfish agreed. "Ginny was definitely not Ginny tonight. Somethin' was eatin' at her."

Curly jumped up from the bench where he'd been sitting. "Aw, c'mon you guys, you know Ginny. You know she'd never leave. She'd never stick it to her crew that way. Something's happened."

"What about the pickup truck?" asked another worker.

The certainty of Curly's words slowly faded, leaving him puzzled. Even he couldn't explain away the pickup truck.

At eight in the morning, under a grey sky threatening to burst into a storm at any moment, the men filed out of the mill. Some noticed that Ginny's old car was still in the spot where she had parked it the night before.

~~~

At the same time, Janice Gregorich, a 38 year-old divorcee, mother of a teen-age son and member of the AC janitorial staff, pulled her cleaning cart into the doorway of the women's bathroom. She discovered that the bulb in the ceiling was missing and set about replacing it. When the light came on, a flash of yellow appeared in the corner of her eye.

What the devil? She bent over and retrieved a wrinkled yellow headscarf lying near the waste basket. It had been trampled upon and was streaked with dirt. Janice tried to shake it open but it was caked with dried blood. She held it up to the light to examine it closer. If someone had a nosebleed, they sure lost a lot of blood. She laid it on the top shelf of her cleaning cart and began to remove some supplies from the bottom.

It was then that she saw drops of blood on the tiled floor. Yes, someone had a bad nose bleed, she confirmed; after all, she was experienced with such matters, having nursed her son through several of them.

She finished wiping up the blood drops with a damp mop and gave a quick examination before she turned towards the toilet and sink. But then she thought she saw something on the wall, and moved closer for a more thorough inspection. A dark red crust about two inches long was stuck in the grout between the cement blocks.

She knew immediately that one would not normally find blood from a bleeding nose there. Janice examined the floor and up at the wall again.

"Oh my God!" She took off running down the hallway in search of Chuck Elwood, the BOP boss.

Elwood was locked in his office with two foremen. Janice stood in the deserted hallway and waited her turn.

She caught snatches of a heated conversation taking place between the three men.

"I don't know what happened. She was in the pit just before the heat tapped around four in the morning..."

"...we searched. I even sent a laborer down to the women's bathhouse..."

"For Christ sake, people don't just disappear around here. Even the suicides had witnesses..."

"...guard said on the phone he saw her leave in a..."

"Which guard was it? ...name?"

"Don't know...new..."

"Where is he now?"

"...left after...shift."

"Ok. I'll get ahold of security. Don't say anything, I don't want this getting out, understand?"

Janice, a bony creature with a fragile constitution and timid nature was suddenly overwhelmed with fear. Fleeing back to the women's bathroom, she grabbed a wet rag, and scrubbed the crusted blood from the wall. Janice understood that this was no nosebleed. The drops of blood on the floor had been in one place and one place only: directly under the blood on the wall. And she had already mopped them up. No one would believe her. They would be angry, she might get fired. After all, she had, how did they say it on the TV? She had damaged...no, that's not it...she had tamped...tampered, that's it. She had tampered with the evidence and that was a crime. She scrubbed furiously at the wall, her charwoman knuckles turning as red as the blood she was washing away. Finally, panting from the effort, she stopped and examined her work. Nothing was left to incriminate her. She exhaled a shaky sigh. As the last of her breath escaped her lungs, her glance fell upon the bloodied yellow headscarf crumpled on top of her cart.

She recoiled in renewed alarm. Panic clamped down

upon her chest like the jaws of a crocodile about to snap a body in half, while disjointed images crashed around inside her head. Finally, she grabbed hold of one idea. She shoved the stained scarf into a plastic bag, stuck it into her pants pocket and darted out the door.

The elevator ride to the sixth floor was excruciatingly slow. As the door rattled open, she stepped out onto the deserted floor. Except for an occasional maintenance man, no one ever went up there. It served no purpose except to support the roof above. Mounds of silvery graphite turned the floor into a lunar landscape.

She located a dark corner, jammed the bag onto a steel plate inside a steel beam and piled graphite over it. Although her footprints would soon be covered by the never-ending shower of silver particles, just to make sure, she scooped up fistfuls and dropped them over her tracks.

Janice Gregorich rode the elevator down to the first floor and walked to the nearby canteen. Her hands shook as she dropped fifty cents into the machine and retrieved a cup of black coffee. It was for the better, she rationalized. Whatever happened to whoever it happened to, well, it was too late to fix it now. Besides, she could not afford to lose her job.

Sipping coffee, she felt a seed of doubt burst open and send tiny shoots of guilt into her conscience.

25

Once BOP Supervisor Elwood finished his conversation with the foremen, he dialed the security company. Then, pale-faced and shaken, he called Ralph Owens, the Superintendent of Andrew Carnegie Works.

"Sorry to bother you on a Sunday morning, but I thought I better check with you first." He explained the problem, adding a puzzling piece of information gleaned from the security company.

"They said their man, Ernest something-or-other, didn't check in at work last night. His wife called their office to see if he was working a double because he hadn't turned up at home, either. They talked to the guard that worked three to eleven and he said he never saw Ernest come to work. It was some new man he had never seen before who told him Ernest was sick. The guard that came on duty this morning said the guardhouse was empty when he showed up. And to top it off, the company never heard of the new guy worked the night shift."

"Any signs of foul play on our turf?"

"Nothing. I sent the maintenance foreman down to the bathhouse to open the missing woman's locker. Her street clothes were still hanging in there untouched."

"Give me a few minutes, I'm going to call downtown. It may be Sunday but I've got emergency numbers. And, Chuck, don't say anything to anybody, ok?"

Owens dialed an emergency switchboard number and within seconds Franklin Blake's mellifluous voice could be heard on the other end of the line. "Ralph, how are you? It's been a while. Haven't seen you at the club. You been playing any golf lately?"

"Listen, Franklin, we've got a problem here...." He explained the distasteful business that had found its way into his domain. He was about to suggest the possibility of calling in law enforcement, when Blake cut him off.

"Apparently this security company has a problem keeping track of their employees. That's not our problem, except for the fact that the guardhouse may not have the necessary coverage. It may be time to re-examine their contract; maybe we need to get another company in there.

"As for Ginny Johnson, seems pretty clear she's decided to walk. Makes sense to me, she's been in over her head for some time. Maybe the pressure got to her. Maybe she decided to become a beautician." He chuckled. "Or maybe she found a man. That's the story I'd go with, she walked off the job and into the arms of her new boyfriend. These women don't belong in the mill. What they really want are husbands and babies."

Owens thought about his daughter, who was studying engineering at M.I.T. He resented Blake's sexist comments. At the same time, he was relieved that the answer to the problem had come so easily.

"Just let it be," Blake continued. "If someone comes asking for her, just tell them the truth. She walked out of the mill on her own two feet and left in a white pick-up. And don't worry about the security company, I'll look into it pronto."

Owens was troubled by the phrase "that's the story I'd go with." If it was true, then it wasn't a story. If it was false, it was more than a story, it was a dangerous lie. But since there was no evidence of an accident or a suicide on company property, he felt a certain comfort level. He rang

Elwood and told him how to proceed: say nothing except that she walked away. The security company was lax and would probably be booted out.

Franklin Blake hung up the phone and leaned back in his oversized suede swivel chair. He put his hands behind his head. "Mission accomplished," he snorted.

Tim Fester was at home that Sunday morning when he got the news. "What? Walked off the job? Yeah...ok...no, it's good news. Yeah, thanks for the call."

He shook his head in disbelief. What a break! He dialed Jerry Chonski's office. "Jerry, you're not gonna believe this but Ginny Johnson has gone missing." After he completed his report, there was silence on the other end. Fester was impatient, "You there, Jerry?"

"You're sure? I mean maybe she got sick and went home. You're sure there's no trace of her?"

"Nothing. Got into a pick-up with some guy and drove off. Left her car in the lot, but it was a piece of junk. Her friend Curly went by her house this morning, found nobody there. Guess she decided to take a hike. That's going to be a real kick in the ass to this Fight Back group. I doubt they'll be able to carry on without her. I wonder why she gave it all up."

"Probably found a man," Chonski replied dismissively. He hung up the phone and made himself a Bloody Mary. He took down a bottle of Johnnie Walker Black from the cupboard to give to Kelso on Monday, a small token of his appreciation.

Pete Davison was in a trance as he paraded back and forth across the wooden stage of his plain white church waving his bible in the air. His voice pierced the air as he called upon Jesus to deliver his flock from their evil ways. The small group of parishioners sat obediently, their prayer books at the ready on their laps. They believed him when he called them depraved sinners. The burden of their wickedness bore down on their bent shoulders as if they were bearing sacks of rocks.

Tony Blasko entered the church and slid silently into the last pew. It was nigh impossible for him to sit still. He was bursting with the good news. He'd worked the same night shift as Ginny and knew that trouble-making woman had gone missing.

"Damn," Blasko muttered, slapping his hand on his knee. He knew Davison was a genius but he never imagined he could pull off such a clean job on such short notice. He resolved to never doubt the man again.

He caught Pete's eye as he was bringing his Sunday homily to a close. Pete, his white shirt drenched from his two-hour harangue, gave a slight, almost imperceptible nod in Tony's direction. Blasko read the message clearly: the preacher knew and was pleased.

Preacher Pete raised his arms towards the heavens, waving them side-to-side, as he bellowed from the depths of his deranged soul, "Thank you, Jesus for providing us an opportunity to serve you! Thank you, Jesus!"

∽∾∽∾

A week later the grey bloated body of a Caucasian male in his late forties washed up on the garbage ridden shore of the Monongahela River not far from the Carrie Furnaces in Rankin. He was wearing dark blue pants and a light blue shirt with a patch over the breast pocket that read, "Lorain Security" in bright red letters. Since there were no apparent signs of a struggle, it was ruled a suicide by drowning.

26

It had been a long afternoon for Cory and her mother's three friends. They had talked for hours telling their stories and sharing speculations while rain fell in torrents, pelting the big living room window with drops the size of agates. The small living room was warm and muggy, filled with the gardenia scent from Sheri's perfume. Now all was silent except for an occasional passing car splashing through the pooling water in the street.

It was Blinky who finally broke the stillness. She took a deep breath and exhaled audibly. "Your mother was a brave woman. I think the company, the union, and those backward types, the racists and the women-haters, they knew it. She was a threat to them. A big threat."

"I agree," said Dorie. "I believe in my heart that someone killed her and got rid of her body in a way that no one could ever find it."

"It makes me sick to think about it," Sheri said. She leaned closer to Cory and patted her hand. "I hope this helps, honey. It's not the whole story, but so much time has passed that I don't think the truth will ever be known."

Hearing Sheri's words, Cory began to doubt her original goal. After all these years, was it even possible to unearth the truth? Maybe she should give it up.

Besides, she had become the recipient of riches she could never have imagined. In the past couple of days her mother had come to life, resurrected from the darkness where she had languished under that cement lid, and had taken her rightful place in Cory's heart. Happy memories, long lost in a forest of misguided guilt, were now jumping out of the shadows and startling Cory with their clarity.

The women confirmed what Mrs. Gromski had told her: Cory had been the center of her mother's universe. She wrapped her fingers around the locket and felt her mother's strength pulsating in hand.

Yet, while she experienced healing and newfound calm in one part of her soul, another part was gaining strength by the minute. It was a deep anger, clamoring for the truth as it echoed throughout her being. Cory could not stop now with only half of her mission accomplished. This was no different than cold case files the police kept in basement boxes. She was determined to reopen the case and reexamine the evidence. She was not finished yet. Not by a long shot.

"Thank you, thank you so much, for the time you've spent with me and for telling me about my mother. It has meant more to me than I can put in words." She took Sheri's hand. "But I can't stop now. I hope you understand. I have to take this to the end. Not just for my sake, but for Mom, too."

Nodding their heads in understanding, the women began feverishly talking at once. "I want to help." "I know someone who might know something...." "You need to contact the union, not just the local but the district." "I can help her with...."

Cory heaved a sigh. She had come alone, carrying nothing other than a suitcase of determination. Now she had a committee, contacts, drivers, and a cottage, all organized within a few days. Surely with these resources she could find out who had murdered her mother.

Murdered? The word jumped out at her. Cory was certain, her mother had been murdered.

The women crowded around the doorway saying their good-byes and making plans for another meeting.

"Wait," said Cory. "What happened with the press conference? With Fight Back?"

Blinky shook her head. "We went ahead with it, had the demonstration, too. There were about three thousand steelworkers and their families there. But the Fight Back fizzled out after. We really never had a chance. The union never prepared us, they were too scared to do anything. American Steel ground us up and spit us out like we was sawdust. In the end our contracts were renegotiated, the union gave them everything they wanted, and they kept right on closing mills."

Mr. Mobley pulled up in front of Blinky's house. The big red Impala swayed in the deluge like an unmoored ship. Cory waved good-bye to the women and climbed into the back seat. It was five o'clock and she was exhausted. She began to rub her temples, something she had done for years as a way to ease the pain of her migraines. Her eyes popped open. There was no migraine. There was not even the hint of a minor headache. She had fought for so many years to keep the lid on her feelings and memories that her body had retaliated with migraines. Now that the lid was off and there was no pain.

She broke out into a huge grin.

~~~

In the cottage Cory set to work preparing an enormous salad smothered in feta cheese. She let it sit on the counter while she called Ora.

"Aunt Ora, it's me. Are you ok?"

"Cory, darling, I'm fine—up to my fat fanny in boxes. I decided it was time to clean out the garage."

"Aunt Ora," Cory said in an exasperated tone, "wait until I get back. I can do it. What's the rush?"

"I'm not going to live forever, darlin', and I wanted to find that funeral book I told you about. But tell me, have you learned anything?"

Cory gave her an abbreviated version of what she had learned from her mother's three friends, hoping Ora would not read too much between the lines. Her Aunt, however, was excellent at doing just that.

"My goodness. Do you really think Ginny was killed?" And then with alarm, "You're not thinking of trying to find out who did this, are you? Yes, of course you are. Cory, turn this over to the police. This is their job, not yours."

"Please don't worry, I'm not in any danger. I *am* going to turn this over to the police, but the problem is I have no hard evidence to give them. I can't go in there with hunches, I have to give them something to go on. Right now I just have the impressions of her friends, and maybe one old police report about a break-in."

"Cory, this is more than worrisome."

"Aunt Ora, I promise you I'll be careful. Please, don't worry."

They rang off, promising to talk in two days' time.

After soaking in a steamy bath, Cory curled up on the drab old couch in the living room with her salad just in time for a Law & Order re-run. She crawled into bed at eight-thirty and fell into a dreamless sleep.

27

The swaying motion of the big semi as it rolled over the hills of Western Pennsylvania had lulled Danny McCormack into a semi-conscious slumber. The driver had been disappointed. He liked to talk, but his passenger wouldn't cooperate. Instead, the stranger fell asleep, his head lolling on the back of the seat and his mouth making weird sucking sounds. The driver turned to his CB to pass the time, speaking in cryptic phrases to other big rig drivers as they sped along the turnpike.

It was dark when they drove through Pittsburgh. The sound of the air brakes snorting and hissing and the diesel engine rumbling as they sped through the Squirrel Hill tunnels brought Danny to full consciousness. He was momentarily disoriented as he stared out at the street lights but kept his questions to himself. The rig travelled south into McKeesport, a town that had shrunk to less than half its population after the big iron pipe mill shut down. At one time it employed ten thousand steelworkers. Now it had joined the industry's graveyard.

"This here's McKeesport." The driver rumbled to a stop at a red light on Fifth Avenue.

"Thanks for the lift," Danny said. He stared at the wasteland where the mill used to be, feeling like he, too, was a wasteland. "You happen to know where I can get a room. It's a little late to be surprising my mom."

"You're in luck, Bud. There's a YMCA two blocks up on Sinclair Street. They got rooms."

Danny nodded his thanks and jumped down from the cab. His stomach was growling from hunger, his armpits smelled like a dumpster, and he had two days of dark hair sprouting on his face.

The man working the reception desk at the Y was watching a baseball game on a small black and white TV. "It's ten dollars a night for a room. You pay in advance. There's a hot shower down the hall. How many nights you planning on being here?"

"Maybe a week. I'll pay now for five days." He handed the guy a fifty dollar bill and inwardly said a word of thanks to his sister, Marian. For the past 28 years she deposited fifty dollars a month in his name in a Michigan bank. That was the last time he had contact with her. "Don't call anymore," he had said, "and don't send any money. Give it to Ginny for the kid."

"You'll be out soon. Momma's helping Ginny some. I'm going to help you. No matter what, when you get out, you go to this bank, it'll be waiting for you." She had kept her word.

After showering Danny lay down on the narrow bed. He lay awake for most of the night, turning from side to side. Truth be told, he couldn't remember the last time he'd slept through the night. Violent, psychotic killers were awarded private sleeping rooms the size of broom closets at Ypsilanti State Hospital. They were given meds and shuffled off to bed at nine o'clock. Each night as he stepped into the little cubicle, he listened to the bolt on the lock slide into place behind him. The sound enraged him. It took hours before calm prevailed, just in time to watch the blackness of night turn a miserable grey.

This night was no different. Sleep eluded him as the images of his incarcerated life paraded through his mind. Over the years he had learned patience; learned how to wait for the first glimmer of grey to lighten the dingy window. Only then did he lose consciousness, sleeping for an hour or less.

Danny showered again in the morning. He used an old razor and a rusty can of shaving cream that had been left by someone else. What he saw in the mirror was a tired old man with hate in his eyes glaring back at him. He shrugged. It didn't matter anymore.

Despite the bright sunny day, McKeesport was like an empty hull of a corroded ship. He walked to a drug store and purchased toiletries. At the Goodwill he bought some shirts, two pairs of jeans, and a duffel bag. He needed underwear and socks, but that could wait until he found his sister. That is, if she was still living.

He squeezed his big frame into a booth at a diner, ordered two eggs sunny-side up, fried ham, four pieces of wheat toast with extra strawberry jelly, and a mug of black coffee.

The waitress, a skinny little thing in a faded pink uniform with an unraveling hem, was taken with the emerald color of his eyes.

"Check 'em out," she nudged her co-worker, "ain't they perty? Same iridescent color of a little ol' garden snake."

"He's new around here," observed her friend.

"That green up aginst all that black hair, now that's somethin'."

"Stop it, Belle, you're a married woman. Besides, see how his lips keep puckering. God, that's too weird."

"Might make him a good kisser," she laughed, swatting her friend's butt with a towel.

There was a pay phone around the corner from the restaurant. Danny stood in front of it, uncertain of his next move. Phoning his sister seemed at one and the same time the right and the wrong thing to do.

Danny stood staring at the phone. He needed help and she was the only person he trusted. He picked up the receiver, dropped in some coins, and dialed a number he had never forgotten. It was Friday morning. A woman answered the phone.

"Sis? It's me, Danny." He heard a sharp intake of breath and then silence. "Marian? It's me, Danny."

"Oh my God! Danny, is it really you?" She was crying and laughing and trying to talk. "Where are you? In Michigan?"

"I'm in Mckeesport. Can you meet me here? I have a room at the Y."

"I knew some day you'd call. I knew it," she said breathlessly. "I'll leave right now. It'll take me twenty-five minutes. Don't go anywhere. I'm coming." She slammed down the phone, grabbed her purse and ran out the door.

An hour later they sat across from each other in the diner. Danny felt her studying him as though she was counting the pores on his face. It made him uncomfortable. Wave upon wave of disturbing emotions ebbed and flowed beneath the poker face he had perfected over the years. He knew she wanted more of him. More conversation, more explanations, more descriptions, more about his plans for the future, but he was slow to answer. He found it difficult to meet her eyes, the same color as his, save hers had vitality and warmth while his were lifeless.

Marian seemed determined to reach him; to throw a rope of words across the divide that the years had created.

"I taught second grade at Bessemer for twenty-five years and retired last year. Never married. Just too picky, I guess." She gave a short tinkling sounding laugh that rang hollow with bitterness.

"I guess I got too busy helping Mom and Dad after you... after..." She had unexpectedly wandered into dangerous territory and abruptly changed course. "They're living in

Phoenix in an assisted-living complex there. So far," she tapped her knuckles on the Formica table, "knock on wood, they're in good health. Jeez, Mom's 80 and Dad's 84, but they drive to the mall, play bingo, you know, the stuff that senior citizens do these days."

No, he didn't know. He'd hardly been able to figure out how to work the god-damn pay phone. He hadn't driven a car in three decades, yet his elderly parents were gallivanting all over fuckin' Arizona.

Whoa, calm down, boy, calm down. This is family we're talking about, the same family you told never to call again, remember, asshole?

"You don't need to stay at the Y. I still live in the old house. I spent a fortune fixing it up, and there's plenty of room for you."

"Thanks, Sis. Maybe later."

No way. That's the first place they'll check. Plus, walking into that house would be walking back in time, and if he were to take that journey, he might implode. No, he wasn't going backwards, except for one last piece of unfinished business.

"Oh, here I am chattering away like a Blue Jay. You probably have some questions. I mean, there must be something..." Her voice trailed off. She clasped her hands hoping to hide her jitteriness and waited.

Danny stared at the side of her face. It was the closest he could come to meaningful human contact. Something stirred deep inside his brain; some wispy thread with a silken hook at the end of it. It was a new feeling, something other than anger and, therefore, unidentifiable. It had gentleness to it, and that unnerved him.

Danny noticed the pile of shredded napkin in front of him and frowned. He cleared his throat and tried in vain to control the puckering of his lips. "Do you hear from

Ginny?"

Marian sighed and glanced out the window at the dreary building across the street. She could not avoid the subject, however painful it would be for him.

"Soon after the baby was born, she moved across town. She was a loner, I think, not used to having family about. Anyway, for the first couple of years she would bring Cassandra over once or twice a month. What a beautiful baby! Her hair was the color of carrots and thick as a rug. And her eyes were huge and green..." She looked into her brother's face. "Like yours. Mom just loved her to pieces. But Ginny kept her at a distance.

"Then Ginny took a job at American Steel in Braddock and her work schedule was complicated. Anyway, she just drifted away. She would send a Christmas card every year, sign both their names, but, after a while, that stopped too. We never heard any more."

Danny sat staring at the shredded napkin. Cassandra. Cassandra McCormack. No, she wouldn't have used my name. Cassandra Johnson. Sadness exploded in his chest like Fourth of July fireworks sending a rain of blue sparks over a deep black lake. Somewhere out there he had a daughter he would never know. His shoulders sagged.

"I'm sorry, Danny." Marian reached across the table and wrapped her fingers around his gnarled hand.

His instinct was to pull away, but that silken hook had latched onto the warmth of his sister's hand and wouldn't let go. He nodded, then mumbled, "It's ok. I've been gone a long time. Some things are gonna take getting used to. Listen, Sis, thanks for sending the money. Someday I'll pay you back."

"You don't have to pay me back," she said, patting his hand. "Having you here is enough for me. Come live at home, Danny, at least until you get back on your feet.

There's plenty of room."

The hardness of his resolve returned. His stomach drew taut and his shoulders straightened as he drew back in his seat.

"Maybe later, but not right now. Listen, I need a car. If I'm gonna get work, I need to have a car."

Marian beamed. "Mom and Pop's old car is parked in the garage. You can use that. But...," she faltered, "do you..."

"Yeah, I got a license," he lied. "I got a Michigan license. Got it a few months ago when I was working for a delivery service."

"Good, Danny, that's real good. I know Mom and Pop won't mind you using their car. They are going to be so thrilled when they find out you're back. I bet they take the first plane—"

"Sis, I don't want them to know right now. I got to get my feet on the ground. I don't want them seeing me without a job and having to use their car, so I don't want you to say anything just yet. You understand, right?"

He could see that he had taken the wind out of her sails.

"Yeah, sure, Danny," she said, blinking away tears. "I understand."

"Thanks, Sis. I need some time."

"I can drive the car out here later today. My girlfriend works in Monroeville and she can pick me up when she gets off work. How's that?"

"That's great, Sis. I appreciate it."

She insisted on paying the bill, and pushed her arm through his as they walked back to her car. She smiled up at him.

"Danny, I'm so happy you're home. Things are going to get better. I can feel it."

He watched the car as she drove off. Yeah, things were definitely going to get better—just as soon as he found that son-of-a-bitch that had blown his life to smithereens. Payback time was coming up fast.

28

Early the next morning, Danny sat behind the wheel of the old brown Plymouth and studied a street map, familiarizing himself with main thoroughfares. Three decades of being transported in locked vans had eroded his driving skills.

Hey, relax, it's the same as riding a bicycle, he reminded himself, a few stops and turns and it'll all come back. As the minutes ticked by he became more and more comfortable behind the wheel.

He drove along Carson Street, the main drag of what used to be a rough and tumble working class neighborhood called South Side. The narrow streets of aged row houses had been gentrified, with a new class of young people colonizing the area. The blocks of bars, diners, used clothing, junk and grocery stores had been transformed into pubs, restaurants, boutiques, galleries, and gourmet food stands. Trees had been planted, brick facades sandblasted, bright paint added, ferns placed in windows, and BMWs parked Along the metered curb.

Danny drove cautiously. He was searching for something recognizable. An alien stepping down from a UFO could not have felt more out of place.

Corky's bar couldn't have survived all this, he thought. It had been a funky hang-out that catered to men who liked their beer cheap and shot glasses filled to the brim. Rock and roll dwelt side-by-side with country music in the oversized red jukebox. And the pool tables in the rear saw constant action by amateurs and hustlers alike. The corners of Danny's mouth curled upward in a crimped chuckle as he remembered the hell-raising that went on there.

He drove on, peering through the windshield wipers as raindrops peppered the glass. At last he saw the old neon sign with the "O" missing from "Corky's".

I'll be damned. It's still here.

He parked the car and walked into the dark bar. One thing that hadn't changed was the stench of cigarette smoke and stale beer. At ten in the morning the stools along the long bar were taken up by lonely old men nursing large glasses of piss-colored beer.

Danny stood at the bar not far from the door. A thin-lipped woman with penciled brows and frizzy blond hair wiped the counter in front of him.

"What would you like, Hon?"

"Can I get a coffee?"

"Sure thing," she said.

She brought a mug in one hand and a sugar bowl in the other. The barmaid had sized him up and decided he was a dried out drunk. Those types liked their sugar.

"Here ya go," she said amiably, "You new to the neighborhood?"

He figured she was happy to have someone younger than Methuselah to talk to, though he wasn't all that comfortable with chit-chat.

"Sorta. I used to come here a long time ago. Been living outta state." He was tempted to say he'd been living on another planet, one full of whackos, but figured that would lead to more questions than he could handle.

"Long time ago, eh? Well, Corky's been here for about ninety years. How long ago was it?" She had her hands deep in hot water, washing glasses as she spoke.

"Early seventies. I'm trying to find an old buddy of mine.

We joined the army together in '73 and I lost track of him."

"I sure wasn't around here then. Wasn't around any-where back then, except for the gleam in my daddy's eye." She laughed as she scanned the long bar. "You might be in luck, though. See that old geezer down at the end? He's been coming in here regular his whole life. Kind of a walkin' history book. Maybe he can help you. And if you buy him a shot of rye, he'll tell you lots of tales. Some true, some not."

"He got a name?"

"Beany. Everyone calls him Beany."

"Thanks." Danny picked up his mug and meandered down the bar. She noticed he hadn't used any sugar.

He took the stool on the far side of the old man. "You Beany?"

Beany swung his head in Danny's direction. He looked like a wasted old grizzly bear perched on a circus stool.

"That's me. Who wants to know?" he wheezed.

"Name's Danny. Can I buy you a little rye?"

Beany gave Danny a sly glance, sizing him up. Then he broke out into a toothless grin, his dentures having hit the bottom of a sewer during a drunken fall.

"A little rye, that's the spirit."

Danny watched as the old man lifted the glass with trembling hands and swallowed half the shot. His lips smacked closed, careful not to dribble any whiskey down his chin.

"That's the spirit," he repeated. "To what do I owe this honor?"

"I'm trying to find a buddy of mine. He used to hang around here back in the early seventies. Big guy, lots of muscles. He used to do amateur boxing but quit when some black guy turned his nose into ground meat."

"There's always been a lot of boxers in here. Amateurs all of 'em. Fightin' each other every night, usually over some pool game or pair of tits. You sit near the door, you got a ringside seat." He let loose with a nasty snort and downed the last of his rye.

Danny continued, unwilling to give up the ghost. "He was a big man, over six feet, and he played a mean game of eight-ball. One night he got into a fight with some guy and broke a cue stick over his head, split his scalp open, there was blood All over..."

Beany straightened up. "Knocked the guy out cold. Yeah, I 'member now. Half the cue stick went through the window. Lotta blood all over the place. Ambulance took that poor joker away. Your buddy had a mean streak, could go off on somebody for no reason. He was a big son 'a bitch, wasn't he? With little beetle eyes sunk way back in his head? I 'member that 'cause his forehead hung down low, like an ape, an albino ape. I'd never forget that face."

Beany nudged the shot glass towards Danny. Danny bought him another rye.

"You wouldn't happen to know where he is now, would ya?"

Beany stared at his shot glass as if he half-expected the answer to appear in the amber colored liquid. He raised his chin and scratched the grey stubble on his neck.

"I can't say for sure, but I think he came in here one time some years back with some other men. He was talkin' loud about somethin', somethin' about steelworkers. Yeah, that's right. He was carryin' on about a union. He might have been workin' for a union. Can't say for sure, though. Never forget that face. Ugly son'a bitch."

He gulped down the last of his beer and pushed the glass towards Danny. "Ain't seen him since that I 'member."

Danny set him up with another round of rye and beer. "Thanks, old man. You been a big help." He slid off the bar stool, nodded to the barmaid, and walked out into the rain.

Later that afternoon he stood in a phone booth with

a roll of quarters stacked on the small counter. He had the phone numbers of the International, a District, and a Local. The International was a dead-end; too many different departments. He dialed the District and the line was busy. A man with a gruff voice answered at Local 1630. He told Danny that Kelso hadn't worked at the Local in close to twenty years. "He got promoted. Try District 20 in North Versailles," he said.

"Sorry, sir, he's gone for the day." the chirpy young voice at District 20 said. "He'll be in on Monday."

Danny dropped the phone into its cradle and walked briskly towards his car, anticipation licking at his heels. He was one step closer.

29

At nine that same day, Rashid Mobley ripped around the corner and squealed to a stop at the curb where Cory was standing. He extricated his spidery appendages from the front seat and in four strides was opening the passenger side door.

"Yo, Ms. Co. What be hangin' today?" He readjusted his Pittsburgh Pirates baseball cap, positioned sideways, for the umpteenth time that morning. His baggy shorts exposed bone-thin calves that stuck out like sticks.

"What be hanging?" Cory shook her head. "Wait. Don't say anything. This one is easy. It's what's up? Right?"

"Hey, cool, you got that right," Rashid laughed. "Where to this morning?"

"First, I want to make a quick trip to the main library. And then make a plan for the day." She prepared for take-off by fastening her seat belt and bracing against the seat. Within seconds Pilot Rashid was flying down the runway of Greensprings Avenue intent on a take-off before they hit bottom at Eighth Avenue. Minutes later she climbed out of the car, her face ashen and her red hair a disheveled mass.

"I'll only be a minute." She ran up the steps to the library entrance.

"I want to see microfiche film of the Pittsburgh Press starting from July 5th of nineteen eighty-two," she told the librarian. Soon she was seated in front of the monitor scanning the film until she came upon the article about the death of the security guard who had worked at AC. She wrote down the name, Ernest Chestnut. Then she raced through the obituary sections until she saw the name "Chestnut" on July 13th.

"Mr. Chestnut is survived by his wife, Daisy, and two daughters, Christine and April, of Mt. Lebanon. Funeral services will be held at St. Paul's Episcopal Church, Mt. Lebanon, July 15th, at 10 A.M."

Cory then searched through a Pittsburgh residential phone book. There was a listing for D. Chestnut in Mt. Lebanon . Could it be the wife?

She passed through the front doors punching telephone numbers into her cell phone. A woman answered.

"Mrs. Chestnut?"

There was a hesitation. "Yes. Who is this?"

Cory felt awkward, but pressed ahead. "My name is Cory Johnson. I am trying to locate Missus Ernest–or Daisy–Chestnut. Actually, I am trying to get information about Mister Chestnut. He worked as a security guard. My mother worked in the mill back then. I just read in the obit..." She realized that it was impossible to explain all this on a telephone to a stranger. A widow.

"Would it be possible to speak with you in person? That is, if you are the Mrs. Chestnut that was married..."

There was a sharp intake of breath, followed by a long silence.

"Ma'am?"

The voice sounded far away. "When do you want to come?"

Cory couldn't believe her luck. "Would now be ok?"

∽∾∽

Cory raced down the steps of the library. Rashid was parked directly in front of a "No Parking" sign. She jumped into the car, out of breath.

"Tell me something. When you took the driver's test, did the manual mention no-parking signs?"

"Oh, yeah, the book it shook with lines and signs, but mama dukes says she back in time, so..."

Cory couldn't help but laugh, which, she figured, is probably what he intended in order to get her off his case.

"Mama dukes? You are too funny, Rashid. We are going to twenty-seven, seventy-five Broadmore in Mount Lebanon. You got a bead on that line?"

~~~

The news on the radio played in the background as they sped along. Rashid was mouthing a tune softly and tapping his fingers on the steering wheel. He stopped singing and leaned towards the radio.

"...gang shooting resulted in the death of a five year old boy today. He was shot in the head and died instantly. No suspects have been apprehended."

Rashid snapped the radio off. His fingers drummed faster and louder while his body tensed in an almost uncontrollable jitteriness. Flashbacks to the blood spurting out of his father's head and splashing down upon his upturned face exploded in his mind in vivid color.

He heard Cory speaking, but he was unraveling faster than the speed of sound.

"Rashid, please pull the car into this gas station. Rashid, you are driving with me, Cory, and I want you to stop the car. Can you hear me?"

He could hear her voice and see the pink flesh flapping against his father's skull. He drove over the curb into the parking lot and came to a jolting stop. Cory reached over and turned the ignition off.

He bent over the steering wheel gasping for air, his face contorted in terror.

Off in the distance he heard a calm voice. "Rashid, you are having a flashback. What you see is not happening now. It happened many years ago. Listen to me. Take a deep breath through your nose, that's right, deep, and hold it while I count to five. Good, that's good. Now, exhale through your mouth, slowly, until there is no breath left. Good. Again, inhale...."

Eventually, the tension and jumpiness receded and his breathing became rhythmical. Then he was plagued with a different malady: humiliation. He jumped out of the car, mumbling about using the men's room, and disappeared from sight.

Rashid was subdued when he returned. He wanted to apologize but could not look at her. Instead, he drove in silence.

∽∾∽

"I shouldn't be too long," Cory said as she opened the car door. "OK?"

He stared straight ahead and nodded yes.

As Cory turned towards the house, she saw two women standing on the porch. About twenty-five years apart in age, they had perfectly round faces with pudgy noses. It was extraordinary how they appeared so similar.

"Ms. Johnson?" said the younger woman.

"Yes. Please, call me Cory."

"I am April Beecher and this is my mother, Daisy Chestnut. We are pleased to meet you." They escorted her into a cozy living room, crowded with knick-knacks and memorabilia and sat together on a love seat, like two blue birds fat from feasting after a spring rain.

"Please sit down. My mother said you might have some information about my father."

Cory was instantly apologetic. "I'm sorry. I do not have any specific information."

Their shoulders sank in unison.

"You see..." Cory paused, fumbling around in her mind as to how to begin. "My mother went to work at AC on July fifth, nineteen eighty-two, the midnight shift, and she never returned. I have reason to believe she was murdered. And I have a suspicion that Mister Chestnut, who disappeared on the same night, might have suffered the same fate. That is, unless you are certain he took his own life."

The Chestnut women stared at Cory, their brows knitted in expressions of momentary confusion.

When April spoke, her voice was firm. "My father did not commit suicide. No one in my family believed it then and we do not believe it now."

Cory was not surprised. She had been expecting it. "I'm sorry. I realize this must be difficult for you, and me being a perfect stranger, but do you mind if I ask you some questions?"

"Go right ahead," they said in harmony. April added, "We have been waiting for many years to understand what happened. But, before you begin, let me show you a photograph of my father."

She reached for a framed photograph and handed it to Cory. A large handsome man stood next to his petite wife, his arm resting protectively around her shoulders. His two teen-age daughters stood in front of their parents. The whole group glowed with happiness.

"That is my father. He loved my mother and he loved us. There were no money problems, no scandals, no emotional problems and no marital problems. As a matter of fact, he and my mother were planning to drive across the country for a vacation that July. I told the police exactly that when they said the coroner ruled it a suicide. I remember asking why they thought he would do such a thing."

"How did they respond?"

"They didn't."

"Can you tell me about the night he went to work? What time? When did you expect him home? There may be something helpful even in the smallest detail."

Mrs. Chestnut rubbed her damp palms on her pink polyester slacks, took hold of her daughter's hand, and spoke in a soft, clear voice.

"It was his first night out on the eleven-to-seven turn. He left about ten-thirty. It was only a fifteen minute drive to work from Penn Hills where we lived at the time."

She paused and picked a tiny nub of wool off the sleeve of her sweater. "I was napping in front of the television when he kissed my forehead. He said he'd see me in the morning and asked if I wanted to go to the Eat-N-Park for breakfast." She stopped again and studied her sleeve. When she looked up at Cory, her eyes were wet with tears. "I...I never saw him again. It's like your mom. He went off to work and he never came back."

She cried silently, clutching her daughter's hand. April dabbed at her cheeks with a hanky.

A lump lodged in Cory's throat. She managed a hoarse, "I am so sorry." There followed a silence as the three women treaded water in the sea of loss.

"The day he didn't come home," April said, taking up where her mother left off, "we telephoned Lorain Security several times. They didn't know anything until late in the afternoon, when they phoned to say the man who came on at seven in the morning told them that Dad wasn't in the guardhouse like he was supposed to be. He said no one was there.

"My dad would never walk off his post," she said. "So, when we heard that, we decided to contact the police. They checked at Lorain, and there was no time card for my dad—"

"No *lunch pail*," Mrs. Chestnut interrupted. "And his car was gone. Tell her about the car, April."

"Yes, his car was gone, I guess to make it seem like he drove off. It was never found."

April shifted in her seat and leaned forward towards Cory.

"Seven days later we got a call from a detective. He said my dad's body had been found, that he had drowned in the Monongahela River. I was standing next to Momma when she talked to him. I heard her say *drowned*? Drowned in the Mon? That can't be him. Suicide? And then she collapsed on the floor."

Mrs. Chestnut dabbed at her cheeks. "I couldn't believe it. All that week I kept thinking he was sick in some hospital, maybe he had amnesia, like they show on TV. And when I heard the word suicide, it was just too much."

April put her arm around her mother. "My sister and I went down to the morgue to identify his body." Her checks paled as she fought to keep her composure. "That was the hardest thing I've ever done in my life."

"Did you speak with the coroner or read the medical report?" Cory asked.

"I read the report. It described the drowning symptoms, you know, bloating and all. It said there were no major bruises or cuts or bullet holes. And when I saw his face, he seemed so peaceful."

"What did it mean no major bruises?"

"Well, he had some small bruises on the back of his head and neck. His neck was broken. The report said it was from the way he fell, that it broke when he hit the water.

But he had water in his lungs, so he died from drowning."

"He was a big man," Cory said, pointing at the photograph.

"Oh, yes, he was," Mrs. Chestnut replied. "He was six feet tall, big shoulders...and big feet." Her voice faltered. "Can you tell us why you think your mother was murdered? And what it could possibly have to do with Ernest?"

Cory told them it was possible that Mr. Chestnut was kidnapped before he reached his job site. That told her that the killer or killers needed a failsafe way to enter the mill. So they were coming from the outside. That didn't mean they didn't work there, just that they weren't working that night. Or they didn't work in the mill but knew it, had a map in their head, and just needed to get in, but Mr. Chestnut stood in their way.

"But more important," Cory continued, "they needed someone who would tell the lie that my mother walked out of the gate and climbed into a white pick-up truck driven by a man and took off. They wouldn't have trusted Mister Chestnut to tell that lie, so he had to be replaced by someone who would."

"No," Mrs. Chestnut said fiercely. "He would never have done anything like that. Oh, this is all so dreadful. If you two don't mind, I am going out to the garden."

"Are you all right, Mom?"

"I'm ok. It's been a bit difficult going back over this and hearing Cory's story on top of it. But I feel better for having done it. Now I just want some air." She turned to Cory. "Young lady, you be careful. This may have happened a long time ago, but whoever did all this may not want you asking these questions."

"Thank you Mrs. Chestnut. Thank you for seeing me."

April was mulling something over. Finally, she said, "If he went over the rail of the Rankin Bridge, it had to be a very large man who put him over it, or two men. There's no way he would have gone without a struggle."

Cory had been thinking exactly the same thing. Then something else occurred to her. "They know a lot more about forensic science now than they did back then. I wonder if they could tell whether or not the blow that broke your father's neck came from hitting the water or from someone breaking it."

April shuddered. "You're thinking of an exhumation?"

"I don't know. I'm uncomfortable with the medical report."

"It does seem to raise more questions, doesn't it? But I don't know how my mother would take to this idea."

"I understand. Is it ok with you if we just leave the door open to this idea? I may find something more tangible and it wouldn't be needed."

"Yes. I want to know the truth, and if bringing my father up out of his grave is the only way to do it, then that is what we will do." She hugged Cory. "You are a brave woman, Ms. Johnson. Please be careful."

Rashid and Cory stopped for lunch at a Pizza Hut and then left for Braddock. She was determined to meet with the president of the Local Union 1630, even if it meant camping on the union's doorstep for the remainder of the day.

30

It was one o'clock when Cory walked through the door of Local 1630. Since the installation of the continuous caster in the early 1990's, the labor force at AC Works had been reduced to less than nine-hundred workers. The local had moved out of its spacious headquarters above the Pennsylvania Employment Security Commission offices, often dubbed the "unemployment insecurity office," when it closed. The International had bought a lot and funded the construction of an oblong structure, modest in size yet suitable for its diminished membership.

Cory walked towards the small office at the rear of the hall where two men were talking.

"Can we help you?" The man behind the desk was so pasty Cory thought he might need a transfusion. "I'm Al Luwanski, the president of this local." He extended his arm for a handshake. "This here is the Vice President, Tony Blasko."

Blasko had a bulbous red nose with spidery purple-veins that branched out to his flushed cheeks. He gave a nod and mumbled "how do."

Cory straightened her shoulders and looked down at the two paunchy men.

"My name is Cory Johnson."

"Have a seat. It's not often we get a pretty young lady in the union hall. How can we help you?"

Cory sat on a chair near the door. The hairs on the back of her neck felt prickly.

"My mother was Ginny Johnson. She was a member of this Local in the early eighties. Do you recognize the name?"

"Yes," Luwanski replied, "I remember Ginny. She did a lot for the union, especially the women in the mill."

Blasko grunted and nodded his head, saying nothing. The name "Blasko" sounded familiar to her. But she had heard so many unfamiliar names lately, she couldn't place it. An uneasy feeling circled around her chest as she searched her memory for a connection to the name. "I am trying to find out what happened to my mother back then."

"What do you mean happened?"

"She went to work and never returned." Cory couldn't shake the feeling that she was in a den of slobbering wolves eyeing a little lamb.

"If I remember correctly," Blasko replied, "she went off with a guy in a pick-up truck. Right in the middle of her shift. Ain't that right, Al?"

"Yeah."

"I know that was the *official* story," Cory said, "but I have talked to a number of people who were around at that time and they have a different opinion. I'm just trying to get all the pieces to the puzzle. I was hoping you could share with me whatever information you might have."

Blasko growled from his slouched position, "If yunz was wastin' time talkin' to her old friends, well, they got an ax to grind. They couldn't accept that she would leave 'em for some man."

My, my, Cory thought, he can put together a complete sentence. At the same time she felt something shift internally, a splintering crack in the foundation of a dam. She had lost her patience.

Cory turned to Luwanski in time to see him shoot Blasko a fierce glare. "What he means is that there was a lot of tension in the local back then. American Steel was going through a tough time and the men and women who worked here, well, let's just say there was a lot of infighting. It was a nasty time and some members still have some hard feelings about it."

Cory, who'd grown tired of this 'Mr. Nice Guy' routine, responded calmly to Blasko, "Were there hard enough feelings to commit a murder?"

"Now wait a minute," Blasko said, leaning forward.

"A murder?" said Luwanski. "There wasn't any murder. She left with some guy. In a pickup."

Cory cut him off. "Tell me, Mr. Luwanski, don't you find it a bit odd that her car sat in the parking lot for twenty-four hours before it was towed away? Or that her street clothes were still hanging in her locker? If she wanted to run off with a man, she could have packed her bags and left on her day off."

Luwanski opened his mouth to object, but Cory kept talking, "Or how do you explain that the security guard also disappeared that same night, was he running off too? When he floated up to the shore of some garbage dump, then the story was he killed himself. Quite a coincidence, don't you think? And the story about the white pickup truck came from some stranger who worked Mister Chestnut's shift and was never seen or heard from since. How do you explain that?"

Cory sat alert, expectant. She was surprised at the rush with which the words had poured out. Surprised at the anger that had unexpectedly burst through her containment. But she was not the least apologetic. These two bozos had been trying to play stupid and she had cornered them. Yet Cory had a niggling feeling that she had made a major mistake by playing all her cards at once.

Al Luwanski lost his measured tone. "You're barking up

the wrong tree, missy," he growled. "There was no murder. Your mother skipped out. You may not want to hear it, but that's the long and short of what happened. You don't wanna hear the truth, then we got nothing to say. You better leave." He motioned towards the door.

Cory marched out of the union hall and crossed the street towards the car. It was empty. There was no movement up and down the avenue with its boarded up abandoned buildings. Rashid had disappeared.

31

As soon as Cory left the union hall, Luwansi told the grumbling Blasko to shut up and dialed a familiar number.

"Harley Security. Ed Harley speaking."

"It's Al. You remember our little conversation a few days ago? Well, she just left here and she's on the scent of that security guard."

"*Relax*, there's nothing to worry about."

"Relax? I'm telling you she's dangerous. I bet she knows more than what she's saying." Speaking fast, he told Harley what had transpired in his office. "If she finds out how you got the contract to run security for the mill, we're dead."

Harley lit a cigarette and snapped his lighter closed. His brother-in-law was a big-talking fool with the spine of a fucking noodle.

"Al, anybody in the office with you?"

Luwanski snatched a glimpse at Blasko, who was reading the union newsletter but had probably heard every word. He realized he'd made a mistake. "No," he lied.

"Don't you ever talk about how I got that contract, understand? I don't want any problems."

"We already got a problem. Her name is Cory Johnson."

"Do you know where she lives? If the time comes and it's necessary, I know who can take care of this."

"How the hell would I know where she lives? I run a union and she don't work here."

"Never mind, I'll find out. Just calm down, keep your head on straight and your mouth shut. She's just snooping around. Believe me, if she had anything solid, she wouldn't be talking to you."

Clicking the button to disconnect the call, Harley pushed a speed dial button. Within seconds he was on the line with his daughter, who worked for the electric company.

"Hi Sweetie. Listen I'm kind of in a hurry. Can you get me an address for a Cory Johnson?" He took a last drag off his cigarette and stamped the butt into an ashtray. Within a few minutes, his daughter was back on the line.

"West Mifflin, new account. I got it. Thanks Sweetie. I'll see you Sunday at your birthday party."

Harley quickly scribbled down the number as he hung up. He tried reaching his old buddy, but the friend had gone on a fishing trip for the week-end. There's no rush, he decided. Let's just wait and see.

~~~~~

Rashid was trapped in the union hall. While words had been flying around the President's office, he had walked unnoticed into the men's room. He heard Cory leave the building and was about to follow her when he heard one of the men say, "We got to do somethin' 'bout her. She's trouble."

Rashid stood with the men's room door opened a crack, listening to what the men were saying and becoming more frightened by the moment. He knew he'd heard a whole lot more than he should have and that he had to get out of there fast. He flushed the toilet so it would sound legitimate, heaved open the bathroom door, and made three giant strides to the building entrance.

Blasko shouted, "Hey, what the hell yunz doin' in here." As Blasko lumbered down the length of the hall, his face turning beet red from the effort, Rashid bolted out of the door. Luwanski reared up from his desk and raced to the windows.

Rashid sprinted across the street to the car where Cory was waiting. He unlocked the driver's side door, jumped in and leaned across the seat to open the passenger door. He yelled at Cory to get in, shoved the key into the ignition, and peeled away from the curb.

~~~~

Rashid need not have hurried. Once Blasko saw that the young man was going towards the car where Cory was waiting, he stopped, the blood drained from his face and he strained to keep his bladder from giving way. He gingerly walked back into the building and straight towards the toilet.

Luwanski watched as the car sped off. "*SHIT!*" he exploded. The sound reverberated through the empty hall.

Blasko came out of the john wiping the sweat from his forehead. "Do yunz think he heard us?"

"He wasn't running like that because he was late, you moron. Of course, he heard us." Luwanski fell back into his chair, his blood pressure rising. "That's Charles Mobley's kid, I recognized the car. She must've hired them to drive her around town."

"Mobley? He that big nigger that used to work in the slab mill?"

Luwanski nodded his head.

Blasko sneered. "Well, well, this ain't so bad. Relax. I know how we can handle them." He was feeling better already.

Rashid sped down Braddock Avenue, raced across the Rankin Bridge, made a quick left on Greensprings and flew up the hill. His passenger sat mute, plastered against the back of the seat.

He skid to a stop in front of Cory's cottage, turned the ignition off and jumped out of the car. The young man bent over and puked in the street.

Cory scrambled out of the car and raced to his side. She put her arm around his waist. "Rashid, please, let's go inside. I'll get you a glass of cold water." She tried to lead him away from the car, but he was immobilized with embarrassment.

"No thanks, Ms. Co, I'm ok. I gotta get home." He reached for the door handle but Cory stopped him.

"Then sit here on this cement step for a couple of minutes, catch your breath, and tell me what happened to upset you."

In the retelling it didn't sound so bad, until he got to the part about Luwanski saying he didn't know where Cory lived.

"That dude on the phone must have asked where your crib was." For the first time, Rashid made eye contact. "Now why's he askin' that?"

"I don't know." She tried to sound matter-of-fact. "It's probably just talk. Besides, no one knows where I live except you and your uncle. I'm not going to worry about it. And don't you either. Deal?"

He gave an unconvincing nod. As Cory watched Rashid drive away, she approached the cottage alone. A shiver of fear ripple through her chest.

༄ ༄ ༄

At seven that evening, Charles Mobley found Rashid lying flat out on his bed asleep in his boxer shorts. This was a strange sight. Usually Rashid was on the phone with the TV going, a plate of sandwiches on his lap, and the sound system playing in the background.

"You hungry?" Mobley asked, nudging him on the shoulder.

His groggy nephew sat up and yawned. "Yeah, thanks."

They ate quietly at the big table in the kitchen. Mr. Mobley could tell something was chewing at Rashid's insides, but rather than question him, he waited for the boy to make up his mind to speak. Finally, his nephew pushed his empty plate back and, in a soft voice devoid of street slang, told his story of the day's events.

"What were the names of the two men?"

"Luwan-something and Bas...Blas...something with Blas," Rashid replied.

Charles Mobley, in a prayerful pose, appeared to meditate. He might have known those union guys were up to no good back then and still up to no good today. Maybe he shouldn't have recommended Rashid for this job. But how was he to know? If one or both of these men had been involved in Ginny's disappearance, then it could be dangerous for the girl, especially with that Tony Blasko, and dangerous for Rashid as well. But as much as he wanted to, he knew that he couldn't clear the path of danger for all of Rashid's life. No, he could not. But he could watch his back.

"I'm worried about Ms. Co," Rashid said. "She be sittin' up in that little house, surrounded by trees where anybody could be hiding. But she didn't seem too worried. It was business as usual when she told me to pick her up tomorrow at nine. I told you she's tough, Mister Charles. She don't scare easy."

"That Tony Blasko had a bad reputation long time ago. He used to spout off about the Klan, had a real vulgar mouth." Mobley stirred his coffee. "How you feeling about all this?" he asked, studying Rashid intently. "You don't have to do the driving if you don't feel up to it."

Rashid frowned. "Hey, I'm fine. Ain't no way I'm cuttin' out on Ms. Co."

~~~

Later that night, Cory lay curled up on the sofa unable to sleep. The television cast a metallic glare across the room. It had been a hot, sticky evening, the kind that foretells rain. By eleven o'clock the wind picked up and bolts of lightning were streaking across the sky.

A powerful gust of wind tore through the big oak trees and shook the flimsy building. The wall trembled and the glass panes rattled.

She jumped up to close the window when suddenly a sharp cracking sound pierced the air. She froze and strained to listen as the electricity went dead.

Cory was enveloped in blackness.

32

The next morning men's voices at the back of the cottage brought Cory to full alert. She tip-toed to the back window and peeked through the venetian blinds. They were making a plan.

"There's where the branch came down on the line. So we got to bring a new cable up, and go from pole to pole."

"Yeah, I don't see any other way."

Cory broke into a giggle and then a loud laugh. Surprised, the men whirled around and stared at her. She waved at them. "I'm sorry. I didn't mean to startle you. I'm just glad it's you."

"It's OK, ma'am. We're gonna be here most of the day, so you probably won't have electricity until late this afternoon. It's drizzling now, but if it really starts coming down, we'll have to put this off till tomorrow."

He pointed over to a long, gnarled branch that had been ripped off the tree by the force of the wind. "That's what snapped your line. Couple feet over and it would have come through your roof."

It was eight-thirty. She had thirty minutes before Rashid showed up. *If* he showed up. The poor kid had two serious bouts with trauma yesterday. Cory couldn't blame him if he decided to bail out.

She took a cold shower, washed her hair, and then realized she could not use her hair dryer. Great! She grabbed a towel and was rubbing it vigorously over her hair when her cell phone rang. She noticed the battery was getting low.

"Hey, Shug, how's it goin'?" Dorie drawled.

They chatted for a couple of minutes until Dorie zeroed in on the reason for her call.

"I ran into some women from the church yesterday at the mall. We was gossip'n like women do and they told me 'bout a sister-member who was recently put in a nursing home. Lucy said the poor woman's nerves gave out, but then Annie said the woman's nerves been givin' out all her life. Said her name was Janice. At first I couldn't place her, but then my mind got onto it and I remembered who she was." She paused.

"Go ahead, Dorie," Cory said.

"I'm catchin' my breath, Shug. Well, this Janice used to work as a janitor in the BOP administrative offices. She was a scared little thing, like a wounded bird with a tomcat on its tail feather. Anyway, she started going to my church back then, and one day, about six-seven months after Ginny disappeared, she was sittin' out in the lil' cemetry besides the church bawling to beat the band. She knew I worked in the mill, maybe that's why she opened up to me."

"What did she say?"

"At first she buried her face in her hands, but when she finally looked up, she was all wild-eyed and whisperin' so nobody could hear. I'd heard she had a weak mind so I thought she was just talkin' outta her head. She went on and on about there being so much blood, yellow blood where it shouldn't a been. Said she had to clean it up. And then she got on her knees in the snow and started moving her hand like she had a rag in it and was cleaning the floor, only she was scrubbin' snow. She started blabbin' faster and watchin' over her shoulder like she half expected someone to come up on her.

"She worked herself up into a right good frenzy, wailin'

and chokin', and she kept repeatin' they were gonna get her 'cause she cleaned up the blood. Then she grabbed hold of my leg and motioned that she wanted to whisper in my ear, so I stooped down.

"'Please don't tell nobody, please,' she told me. She was so scared. I mean, all-out scared. She kept saying, it's on the sixth floor...the sixth floor... yellow, it was yellow, now red....

"All of a sudden she stopped talkin' and her eyes rolled back in her head, then everything went back to normal. She looked around where she was sittin' in the snow, real calm, and asked me what she was doing down there. All these years I thought she was, you know, sick in the head. She quit AC right 'bout then 'cause she couldn't hold it together, but she kept comin' to church. Yesterday when I met up with the sisters, I started thinkin' maybe there was somethin' to her rantin'. What do you think? You think there might be somethin' to this?"

"Do you think it would be possible to talk to her? Do you know where the nursing home is? Can you meet me there?"

"Slow down, Shug. I take it you think there might be something to all this."

"It's possible. The thing is, I don't want to frighten her. If you could be there too, it might make it easier for her."

"Yeah, OK. The name of the place is Victory Lane Rest Home. Sounds like a race track now that I say it, though I seriously doubt there's anyone moving faster than a slug in a place like that. I'll meet you there in thirty minutes." She gave Cory the directions.

"Thanks, Dorie, you're a peach."

"Naw, Shug, that's Georgia. I'm a Blueberry," she laughed.

❧❧❧

When Cory arrived, Dorie was talking to a grey-haired woman who was sitting behind the reception desk in the lobby of Victory Lane. If there had ever been a victory here, Cory mused, it hadn't been lately. Multi-colored paint chips had peeled off cracked wall and were scattered about the floor. The white linoleum floor had yellowed with age, while the scent of urine permeated the air.

"Hey, Shug, you made it. This is Miss Beatrice."

"Call me Bee. My, you're soaked, honey. I didn't think it was raining that hard."

"It's not, Ma'am, I couldn't dry my hair this morning, no electricity. Nice to meet you."

"Let's see, it's Miss Janice you're wanting? She's probably in her room, don't hardly come out none," Bee said, shaking her head in disapproval. "It's the last door on the left down the hall."

When they reached the door, they heard a woman's voice humming a gospel tune. Dorie tapped lightly. "Miss Janice? It's Dorie from Precious Light of Love church."

The humming stopped, followed by a long moment of silence.

"Miss Janice?"

The door opened slowly exposing a sparse room: a twin-bed covered with a drab brown bedspread, a dresser, a framed picture of Jesus Christ, a wooden chair, a bedside table and a lamp with a lopsided shade. The pinched face of Janice Gregorich, fifty-eight years old, hollow-cheeked and paranoid, peered around from behind the door.

"Do I know you?" she whispered.

"It's me, Dorie, from the church. This is my friend Cory. We've come to visit you."

Janice stretched her scrawny neck upwards and

searched Dorie's face. A flicker of recognition lit up her otherwise suspicious face.

"I remember you. You go to Precious church." Janice clutched at the top of her grey sweater and covered her trembling chin with it. She made no move to invite them in.

"How're ya doin', Miss Janice? Is there someplace we can go to sit down and talk?"

Janice chewed on the edge of her sweater. These kinds of decisions were always troublesome and frequently paralyzed her mind. The problem was that she could never be sure, absolutely sure, that if she chose one or the other it would be the right choice. She looked each woman up and down with watery eyes, hoping to see their real intentions. They were large women, tall and strong, and that gave them an advantage over her frail frame. But she thought she saw a kindness on the face of the one with the wet hair. Strange, one had dry hair and the other wet—what did that mean? Why did they really come here?

She gave a furtive glance up the hall but saw nothing out of the ordinary. No, she would be flirting with danger if she invited them into her inner sanctum.

But that meant having to risk venturing out to the dining room. Again she checked the empty hallway. It was not lunch time so it would be empty. But the staff would watch her from the window in the kitchen door. They were always staring at her, watching her every move, planning how to rob her room while she ate her meals.

"You better go now," she said. "They'll come and get you if you break the rules."

"Miss Janice..." Dorie began, but Cory touched her arm in a way that said "stop." Janice Gregorich gave one last glance up the hallway and then shuffled back behind the door and closed it firmly.

Cory whispered, "Let's find whoever is in charge."

"What's wrong with her? She's scared to death."

"I don't know for sure, but I'd bet the word paranoid is somewhere in the diagnosis. Here's the administration office."

They introduced themselves to a grey-haired woman wearing a black dress and black oxford shoes that fit snugly under her swollen ankles, the picture of a prison matron.

"What can I do for you?" the woman in the office said.

Dorie opened her mouth to speak but Cory stepped in front of her and spoke up quickly. "My name is Cory Johnson. This is Dorie Samuels. I've come from California to find a long lost family member. You see, my uncle died in Sacramento and he left a sizable estate to my aunt, Janice Gregorich." She leaned forward as if to share a secret. "I'm not at liberty to say how much, you understand. As soon as his will is probated, she stands to inherit quite a bit of money."

The administrator stopped tapping her pencil on a stack of overdue bills. Her expression of haughty disdain transformed into the cunning grin of a Cheshire cat at the thought of a veritable pot of gold falling into her lap.

"Please, sit down," she said, pointing to two straight back wooden chairs. "I'm Barbara Morgan, the owner of Victory Lane Rest Home. Would you like something to drink? Coffee perhaps? No? Well, then, you say Janice, er, Miss Gregorich, is your aunt?"

"Yes, that's right." Cory frowned, "I'm afraid I don't know much about her. I've never actually met her. But my uncle had the name of her church, Precious...ah, Precious..."

"Precious Light of Love," Dorie's raspy voice piped up.

"That is how I got hold of Dorie here," Cory patted Dorie on the arm and beamed at the director. "She has been such a big help."

Barbara Morgan's smile sat uncomfortably on her otherwise stony face. She nodded in Dorie's direction. "I'm sure she has. Now that you are here, how can I be of help?"

"I'm a bit concerned. We just visited with Aunt Janice..."

Morgan sat straight up in her chair. "You *what*? How did you...." Realizing it was probably that unhinged resident Bee, always sitting out at the front desk reliving her days as a secretary who had let them pass, the owner re-established her welcoming expression. "And how was your visit?"

"To be honest with you," Cory said, "she seemed a bit off. You know, in the head. I need to know if she's ok, mentally that is, before funds can be dispensed."

This bit of news presented a perplexing problem for Ms. Morgan. The best option would be for Miss Morgan to be appointed the guardian of a mentally ill resident; in charge of her medical issues and the soon-to-be fattened finances. Yet, if she stressed a mental illness, she ran the risk that the niece decided Janice needed a higher level of care, and, if there was a lot of money, the niece could afford to move her out.

On the other hand, if Morgan said nothing about Gregorich's paranoia, there would be no suspicion as to her mental state and no reason to appoint a guardian. She glanced covertly at Cory. There was no time to dither, she had to make a decision.

Morgan thumbed through a file drawer next to her desk and pulled out the Gregorich chart.

"Janice hasn't been here long. Apparently she has always been rather timid. She has had a number of inpatient psychiatric hospitalizations, but was always able to return home. She has one son, and he visits her often. Oh, dear, but you must understand that her son is mentally retarded and could not possibly take care of his mother's affairs."

"Psychiatric? What is wrong with her?" said Cory.

Barbara Morgan squinted over her reading glasses. "This is confidential information. I'm not sure I should..."

"I understand," Cory said sympathetically. "It's just that the bank—it's a small town bank—they are relying on me to make a recommendation as to how to disburse these funds."

Morgan wasted no time pondering her next decision. "Of course, you need information to help you make a wise decision. Her diagnoses are Major Depression and Paranoid Personality Disorder. That last one means that she believes that people are out to harm her in some way."

"Oh, my, that's awful. She's such a frail, little thing. Is she taking any medications?"

Morgan ran her finger down the page. "Her meds are Haldol for agitation and Zoloft for depression."

"Oh, my."

"It sounds worse than it is. Janice is doing well here. She is no trouble."

Morgan was about to close the chart when Cory asked, "Would it be all right if I took a look?"

Miss Morgan blanched and began to shake her head no.

"Oh, and do you have guardians here? Since I know no one, except for Dorie, who has agreed to be a guardian if necessary, which was kind of her, but it might make more sense to have a guardian that is on site, don't you agree?"

Morgan handed over the chart. After all, what harm could it do, it's just a bunch of psychiatric mumble-jumble. She's not going to make much sense out it.

"It's a lot of technical words. If you need help deciphering it, just ask. And, yes, we offer guardian services here. We have bonded volunteers. We try to help our residents with all of their needs," Morgan said, her expression not unlike a happy shark circling a piece of meat.

33

Dorie busied the nursing home owner with small talk while Cory leafed through Janice's old psychiatric reports. She skimmed the history: suffered physical and sexual abuse from step-father beginning at age six and lasting for ten years; emotional abuse by mother; high school dropout; raped at age twenty-two by uncle resulted in birth of a mentally retarded son; unable to hold permanent employment; periodic homelessness.

Poor Janice! She'd been on the mental health track for years. Cory was particularly interested in the various diagnoses for which Janice had been treated: major depression with suicidal ideations and psychotic features; schizoaffective disorder; bipolar disorder; borderline personality disorder. She was a walking diagnostic manual.

There was no reference to the traumas she experienced. No Post Traumatic Stress Disorder and no ruling out of Dissociative Identity Disorder.

I'd be holed up in my room, too, if this were my life, Cory mused.

She handed the chart back to Miss Morgan. "Thank you very much. You've been most helpful. May I have a business card with your name on it? The bank may want to speak with you direct after I make my recommendation."

"Yes, of course. I hope I've been of some help. It's comforting to know that Janice has a loving family interested in her welfare."

Cory wrapped her long fingers around Dorie's arm and

all but lifted her up off the chair as she stood to leave. They both shook Ms. Morgan's hand and strode out of the office.

"Wow, Shug, you're good."

"Dorie, we passed a fast-food restaurant on Penn Avenue. Do you have time to talk? We could get a cup of coffee."

"Are you jokin'? I want to know what all you're thinking."

Rashid started the car. "Hit me up 'round seven, Boo," he said in a sexy voice to the other party on his cell phone.

"Boo?" Cory teased. "What's that, a ghost?"

He gave her a conspiratorial grin and stepped on the gas. They fishtailed out of the wet parking lot. "Some things are just plain private, Ms. Co."

Ten minutes later they were sitting in a booth with three Styrofoam cups of tasteless coffee cooling on the table. Dorie was about to burst. "What was goin' on back there?"

"This isn't coffee. What'd they do, ladle out some dishwater?" Cory complained.

"Cory!" Dorie was fast losing her patience.

"Ok, this is the deal. We went there to find out if Janice's story about blood that she cleaned up and something red or yellow hidden on the sixth floor was true, right?"

Dorie nodded.

"What we found was a terrified woman. The kind of terror that suggests to me a long history of trauma. I couldn't tell if she was completely out of touch with reality from the few things that she said. That's why I wanted to see her chart, read her history, and get a handle on the diagnoses."

Dorie hooted, "So you hung a fat ol' worm on a hook and dangled it in Morgan's face, and she swallowed the whole thing. Gave you the chart! Unreal!!"

"If what I think is accurate, given all the horrible things that happened to her as a child, what underlies her diagnoses is untreated trauma. It's possible that back when she was talking to you at the cemetery a part of her was reliving a terrifying experience. We know she left her job at AC shortly after my mother and Mister Chestnut were murdered. I think she was trying to tell you, Dorie, but a warning light came on in her mind and made her stop."

Cory swirled a plastic stir in her coffee cup. She was lost in a maze, turning left on this hunch, right on that one. Up to now everything had been easy, listening to stories told by her mother's friends, visits to the library, talking to the police, the union, Mr. Chestnut's family.

But what did she really have? Nothing but hunches. She couldn't point to a suspect until she could prove that her mother had been murdered. And in order to prove that, she needed hard evidence.

"Dorie, does the BOP have six floors?"

"Yeah, it's the only building in the mill that high."

"What's up there?"

"I dunno. Sheila knows. Whoa, what are you thinkin'?"

"I have to get up on the sixth floor."

There was a long silence, followed by an explosion of clamorous objections. Rashid and Dorie were yelling, each trying to be heard.

"*What?*" "Oh, no, you can't do that!" "Have you lost your mind?" "It's dangerous!" "You don't know nothing 'bout that mill." "Never mind its private property, you could go to jail!" "How you gonna get past security?" "That Janice is probably a lunatic, talkin' out of her head. She never left anythin' up there, just made it up."

"Wait! Stop!" Cory cried, trying to be heard over the din. "Think about it. I need hard evidence. At least the Chestnut family has a body. I don't even have that much. Instead of proving who did it, I first have to prove it was done. I need something that says Ginny Johnson did not walk off her job, she was murdered. Here's the proof, now we go find the killer."

"But *you* could end up bein' killed!" said Dorie.

"Never mind that. If Mister Chestnut's body is exhumed and new forensic science can prove that his neck did not break from a fall off a bridge, that someone broke it for him, then that would be evidence for one murder. And it might spark an interest in my mother's case. Or maybe not.

"So I need to find out if Janice Gregorich actually hid something on the sixth floor. Something with blood on it. I'm not going to put any one else at risk for who knows what could happen. This is one thing I have to do alone."

"How you gonna get in there?" Rashid asked with resignation.

Dorie perked up. "Sheila! She's still workin' in the BOP, been there nigh on twenty-five years. If anybody has an inklin' how to do this, she does."

Cory handed over her cell phone. "Would you call her?"

Dorie sighed and punched in Sheila's number.

"Good morning, Sweet Stuff. Are you sittin' down, 'cause this is a shocker?"

While Rashid dug into a second plate of pancakes and Cory sipped at the unpalatable coffee, Dorie gave her friend a blow by blow description of the day's events. "What we want to know is, how can Cory get into the BOP and up to the sixth floor without bringin' the cavalry through them gates?"

The sound of Sheila's voice on the phone boomed across the table. "Is the girl *crazy*?"

"Yeah, well, we kinda been through all that. She's crazy all right, but, trust me, ain't nothin' gonna stop her. So we need some ideas." She handed the phone to Cory. "She wants to talk to you."

"Sheila? How are you?" Cory said with a lightheartedness

she did not feel. "Listen, can you tell me what's up on the sixth floor?"

"Nothing's up there, just the big open tops of the two furnaces. Oh, yeah, and some smoke stacks that suck up the smoke from the furnaces and send it along a big pipe on the roof. Other than that nothing but a lot of graphite and dirt. Cory, why don't you let me do it? When there's some down time, I can go up there and check it out."

"Sheila, thank you for offering, but I can't let you risk your job. I mean, what would happen if someone saw you or you were needed for something? How would you explain it?"

"How are *you* gonna explain it?"

Cory rubbed her forehead. "I don't know right now, but I'll think of something. Maybe just tell the truth."

"Hah! This truth ain't gonna set you free, girl. It's gonna lock you up. Or worse!"

"In a way, Sheila, I have been locked up these past twenty years and so has mom. Now I know I'm close to finding the answer that can set us both free. I don't want my mom buried under a pile of lies. She fought hard for the truth and she took plenty of risks along the way. I guess that's her legacy to me. The truth. That's all I want."

Sheila, suddenly struck with an idea, exclaimed, "I've got it! Oh, yes! It's perfect! Oh, girl, this is gonna work."

"What? What is it?"

"The BOP has a lot of tours from other countries going through since they installed that caster. I heard there's a group of officials from Poland coming on Monday. You could come in with them, pretend to be a part of them, get a tour of the BOP. The tricky part is how you are going to slip away and take the elevator up to the sixth floor. I'll have to think about that. And when you get up there you'll have twenty-thirty minutes at most."

Cory's heart was pounding as she tried to envision the plan. "How would I join the group?"

"They come in on a bus from some hotel downtown. I guess we'd have to check around the big hotels and find out where they're registered. That's easy, you could hang out in the lobby and get on the bus with them."

"But won't they think it's odd, some stranger going along for the ride, and they're sure to have some American Steel guy escorting them."

"Right. You're right." Sheila paused to think. "Hey, I'm on daylight Monday. You can drive into the parking lot with me. When the bus pulls up and the folks climb out, you can join them. I'll get you a white hard-hat. Anybody says anything to you, pretend you don't speak English."

"Sheila, you are brilliant! Absolutely brilliant!!"

"Yes I am, honey. Most of the time I keep it a secret. Make sure you call me on Sunday so we can finalize the plan."

Cory's freckled face hosted a broad grin as she explained the plan to Dorie and Rashid.

Dorie was skeptical. "It's too easy, Shug. There are too many people. Someone is bound to notice you ain't a member of the group. Then what?"

"I just have to walk along behind them. They'll think I'm an employee."

"And the American Steel guy? What's he gonna think?"

"I assume he's going to be walking ahead, leading the way, and I'll duck out of sight just as soon as I can." She hesitated, thinking. "All I have to do is take the elevator up. I don't imagine Janice wandered all over the floor searching for a perfect place to hide something, she'd be too scared. She probably stayed near the elevator."

Dorie was not convinced. "I don't know. It just sounds too damn dangerous." She gave Cory a penetrating look. "I don't suppose there's any turning' back?"

Both Cory and Rashid shook their heads no. "Rashid, what are you shakin' your head for?"

"The deal is done, man. Done. So we can eight-six all this negativity. Ms. Co has made up her mind."

Cory and Rashid dodged puddles as they ran to the car. "Where to now?"

"Braddock. I want to take a stab at the administrative office of Andrew Carnegie Works.

34

Ron Antoli sat in his office scanning production reports for the previous month. Since he had been promoted to Superintendent of the BOP and since the continuous caster had been installed, the pace of production had sky-rocketed. That, plus all the layoffs due to the caster, made AC the most profitable enterprise in American Steel's shrunken stable of steel mills. Antoli smiled. Keep this pace up and in time he would be promoted to superintendent of the mill. Quite a feather in his cap.

The ringing of his phone jarred his reverie. He grabbed the receiver and scowled. It was his boss, ver Plank, the present-day superintendent.

"Do you remember anything about a woman that worked in the BOP and went missing twenty years ago?"

"Woman?" Antoli's jaw began to twitch. "Twenty years ago?"

"Yes. Had red hair."

"Ah, yeah. The red-head. She'd be hard to forget, a real trouble-maker. The way I heard it she left her job site in the middle of the night. Security said they saw a pick-up drive up and she got into it. Never saw her again. Why?"

"Did the police investigate? What did the company do?"

"Well now, I was working in the lab, so I wasn't privy to what the company did. I think Chuck Elwood took the position that she walked out on her own two feet, so this wasn't a company or police matter." Antoli cleared his throat, "What's this all about?"

"I just had a young woman in my office asking questions that I couldn't answer."

"What woman was that?"

"Her daughter."

The air rushed out of Antoli's lungs like a slashed tire. This couldn't be happening. This was some kind of joke.

"Her...her daughter?"

"She said her name. Let's see, I wrote it down here somewhere."

Antoli's fingers drummed restlessly on the arm of his chair while he waited, fear fermenting in his gut.

"Here it is. Cory Johnson. Nice young lady. Smart too. She seemed pretty definite that her mother did not walk off the job. She believes her mother ran into some foul play here at AC. Did you ever hear anything to that effect?"

Antoli tried to sound helpful. "That was a long time ago. There were a lot of rumors going around, but the security guard had the last word. He saw her leave. End of story."

"Apparently not. She said the usual security guard disappeared that night and showed up dead a week later. So the guard who gave out the story about a pickup truck may not have been a guard at all. And she claims no one saw him after that night either. Sounds like she's on to something, don't you think?"

Antoli struggled to find his voice. "That's a new one. She got any witnesses?"

"I don't know. She seemed fairly confident, seemed to be checking things off a well-planned list, if you know what I mean."

No! What the hell did he mean? Did she have any goddamn witnesses? Any evidence? Had she been or was she going to the police? Jesus, what a moron. "Well, that's all I know. She ask about anything else?"

"Yes, as a matter of fact she did. She wanted to know

if any of the men who worked the pit back then were still working now. And she specifically asked if you were still working here."

Antoli shot up out of his chair like he'd been stung in the ass by a hornet and began pacing around his office as far as the telephone cord would allow. He stammered into the receiver, "Me? Uh...why...why would she ask about me?"

His thoughts spun like tires stuck in mud. How the hell did she even know my name? Who has she been talking to? What else does she know?

"I don't have any idea. You?"

"*What the fuck would I know about that?*" he hollered, instantly realizing he'd gone too far. His boss was one of those sanctimonious, born again holier than thou weir-does that didn't allow for cuss words in his world.

"Er...sorry about that. I'm just totally surprised by this. I have no idea why she'd ask about me or how she got my name or what she wants with me. What did you tell her?"

"I told her the truth. It's against company policy to divulge the names of employees. She said she expected that to be the case. That was it. I couldn't help her because I didn't know anything. Now I know a little more. Have a good week-end." He hung up.

For the first time in a long time Ron Antoli experienced terror. He couldn't shake the feeling that he was on a run-away train. She knew something and that something had his name on it, of that he was sure. He spun the rolodex until he found the telephone number, seized the phone and punched in the numbers to a private line in corporate headquarters.

"Yes?" the honey-toned voice of Franklin Blake answered.

"This is Ron Antoli."

"Who?"

"RON ANTOLI!" he all but screamed into the phone. "Antoli. BOP superintendent at AC Works. We need to talk. In person. It's important."

Although Blake had met Antoli a long time ago, he had not spoken with him since.

"Ron, good to hear from you. I hear things are going great guns at AC. You guys deserve all the credit. But, listen, I'm afraid my schedule is extraordinarily busy this month. I don't see how I could possibly meet with you in person. Tell me, what is it that is so important?"

Antoli hesitated. He couldn't believe the bastard was blowing him off. Too high up on Grant Street. A fucking peacock, all puffed up. Cock of the God damned walk. Well, maybe Blake didn't remember the favor he'd done, but Antoli remembered as if it was yesterday. And he wasn't going to be denied the privileges he'd earned. Ok, you cheap suit, you want it over the phone? Here it comes, straight at ya.

"You remember that little problem that needed taking care of a few years back? Well, the daughter was in ver Plank's office twenty minutes ago. Seems she's got some evidence that contradicts the official story. She asked about me, *by name*. She must know something."

"Ah, excuse me, but I don't know what you're talking about."

The fear that had gripped Antoli now gushed over its banks. It constricted his lungs and made his voice squeak as it rose an octave. "Listen you son of a bitch, you're not hanging me out to dry."

"Calm down!" Blake said. "Calm down and listen carefully. There must be some confusion. You and I have never had a problem that we needed to solve together. Now your work out there is and has always been greatly appreciated, and I'm going to send an old friend out on Monday afternoon to deliver a token of our appreciation. Do you understand?"

Antoli read between the lines. He stopped thrashing about as he heard the words that could only mean Blake was throwing a lifeline in his direction.

"Yeah, I got it. Tell your friend to come around four. There's a group from Poland coming through here Monday, I'm gonna be tied up until they leave."

35

The robust color of Blake's tanned face drained away as though his arteries had been sucked dry by a gang of leeches. The last thing he needed was for Antoli to lose it and start blubbering and blabbering.

He rang his secretary. "Marilyn, get hold of the phone company and have them change the number of my private line. I'm getting some crank calls."

Then he buzzed Moe and issued the familiar order, "Get up here."

While he waited, Blake considered his options. Frankly, he was surprised by Antoli's nervous reaction. He'd been told Antoli was fearless. Now he's about to piss in his pants. Well, the man had a lot to lose: big salary, big house, new car, status. Losing all that would scare anybody. Hell, it scared Blake.

He dabbed at tiny beads of perspiration on his forehead. She asked about Antoli by name? How'd she get his name? Icy tentacles circled around his chest. His usual confident demeanor became a ghost in the room.

What other names does she have? What does she know? And the security guard. Christ, Blake, knock it off. The most important thing right now is for everyone to stay calm and for Antoli to get some control. Moe can do that; give him a little reality check.

Moe Perdue hadn't changed much over the years, other than some minor vicissitudes of aging. He was still a lumbering, oafish man with vapid eyes that reflected the void in his brain. The dome of his enormous round head was hairless; his jowls hung loose and rested on the goiter-like sack that used to be his neck. Scraggy brown hairs stuck out above his cleft palate, making the attempt at camouflage ludicrous.

Yet there was nothing flimsy or scant about the hardness of his muscles, the strength of his large fleshy hands, or his capacity to rip into another person's flesh. He continued to be intensely loyal to the company that had employed him all these years and to the man that would, on occasion, break up the monotony of his life, never ask for a report and reward him generously.

Moe walked out of the private elevator onto the plush carpet of Vice President Franklin Blake's office, next in line for the throne. Blake patted him on the back. "Moe, I know you're busy, but I was wondering if you could deliver something to AC Works for me Monday afternoon. Here, have a seat, while I explain."

He kept it simple and to the point. "Do you remember the woman who was causing problems out there a long time ago?"

Moe's brow furrowed as he tried to remember.

"Red hair. Big Mouth. A real agitator."

Moe's mouth shriveled into a grin. "Yeah," he said.

"Well, we thought we'd solved that one but now Ron Antoli from AC calls and says that this woman's daughter is snooping around wanting to blame someone for her mother's disappearance. Antoli is nervous. He's jumping to all kinds of conclusions and I'm afraid, if we don't correct this problem, he might go over the edge."

Blake pulled a red suede watch box out of his top drawer. "Here, put this in the safe downstairs and give it to him when you see him Monday. It's a Rolex. Tell him if he stays calm and keeps his wits about him, nothing will happen. I don't want him going off in some frenzy and doing something that could spoil things for all of us.

"Oh, one other thing, see if you can get a line on where this Cory Johnson is living. Maybe it would be a good idea for you to pay her a little visit, convince her that no news is good news, eh?

"But, the first order of business is to stop Ron Antoli from saying or doing anything rash."

༄༅༄

Bob Lofton, District Twenty Director, had been gloomily watching the rain splash against his office window. It had rained so much this week that the acre of grass around his split-level house resembled a jungle theme park. There would be no mowing it this weekend either. But Lofton wasn't just brooding over bad weather. He buzzed Johnny Kelso.

"Hey, Johnny, you leaving early?"

"Yeah. I'm going fishing with some buddies from church. You need me for something?"

Lofton didn't believe his fishing story. Not in this weather. He had met Kelso for the first time when he took over as Director of District Twenty. "He comes with the furniture," someone had told him. Kelso had aged with the furniture, too. Years of being a barroom brawler and doing dirty jobs for that renegade Local in Braddock had turned him into a punch-drunk goon with a meaty nose, swollen ears and scars on his face and hands. But times had changed, and Kelso's special services were obsolete. He was a liability to the Union. A liability quietly waiting retirement in the back office at the District HQ.

Now, however, a spotlight was threatening to cast an ugly glare on Johnny Kelso with his killer-instinct and slicked back black hair and quite possibly the ISU.

"Come in and sit down," Lofton said. Kelso, light on his feet for a big man in his mid-fifties, walked into Lofton's office and sat down across from his desk. His black eyes were like the dark tunnels of a double-barreled shotgun.

"I got a call the other day from an edgy Al Luwanski at Local 1610. Apparently a young woman name of Cory Johnson came into the union hall asking questions about her mother, Ginny Johnson. She said her mother disappeared one night from work about twenty years ago. Luwanski sounded worried, said she might be coming out here. You know anything about this?"

Kelso's bushy brows arched. "Comin' here?" he asked, letting slip the one piece of information that was of any interest to him.

"Probably. Do you know anything about this Johnson woman?"

"Naw, not much. I saw her one time at the local when some guy from the International spoke there. She and some others were raisin' hell. Had to cut the meetin' short. Then Jerry Chonski offered her a job as an organizer. She turned him down flat and left. That's about it," he said, staring at Lofton with a disconnected gaze.

"You never heard anything about her leaving work one night and never coming back?"

"Oh, yeah. Everyone in the Local knew about it. Word was she'd walked off the job." His fat lips curled into a sneer. "No one saw her again. Took off with some guy."

"The problem is that her daughter seems to have some evidence that her mother was murdered."

Kelso flinched. "What kind of evidence?"

"I'm not sure. She seemed pretty convinced."

"If she's got evidence, why ain't she gone to the police? What's she doin' yakkin' to the Local? Naw, she ain't got no evidence, she's on some fishin' trip. Maybe I should invite her to go fishin' with me." Kelso laughed a demonic, deep-throated laugh that sent chills up Lofton's spine.

"You know anything about a security guard that showed up dead a week after the woman disappeared?"

A small crease appeared in Kelso's heavy brow. "Don't know nothing 'bout him," he said.

Lofton wondered how he knew it was a man. There have been female security guards for a long time now. Hell, maybe it was just a figure of speech.

"You think she'll come here?" Kelso asked as he stood up.

"Maybe. Maybe not. Luwanski said she was pretty deter-mined, a dog with a bone were his exact words. If that's the case, I imagine she'll be showing up here — could be today."

Lofton thought it curious that Kelso asked twice about the girl showing up at the District, he rarely showed an interest in anything, even his job. An ugly idea began to germinate in his mind. As Kelso moved towards the door, Lofton felt compelled to issue a warning. "If she comes here, I'll handle it. These are good times for the union. We don't want any trouble, understand?"

Kelso left the office without bothering to answer. He had a different opinion. It was three in the afternoon. If she came today, he'd only have to wait a couple hours, max. He didn't have anything else planned anyway. Why not have some fun?

36

At three-thirty the big Chevy sloshed into the District Twenty parking lot. Cory slipped the hood of her yellow rain jacket over her head. Her new sandals would be coming apart at the seams in all that water. Clearly an error in judgment, she reflected.

Rashid, who had shut the engine off, reached for his cell phone.

"If the last stop was any indication, I'll be back in the car before Boo has time to answer." She took a deep breath, pushed herself out into the storm, and ran through the flooded lot to the front door.

Dripping water on the shiny tiled floor, she interrupted the effort of a young receptionist to repair a chipped fingernail. "Can I help you?"

"I hope so. I want to speak with someone who might know something about an incident that occurred at Andrew Carnegie Works some twenty years ago."

"I'm sorry?" the girl said. "Who do you want to speak with?"

Cory tried again. "Something happened to a worker at AC a long time ago. I want to know if anyone here remembers the incident and would be able to give me some information. The worker was my mother." Cory said apologetically. "Sorry, but that's the best I can do."

"Please have a seat, I'll check and see who is here. It's Friday afternoon and the men usually leave early for the week-end." She trotted off in her stiletto heels.

"Mr. Lofton? There's a woman out front who says her name is Cory Johnson and she wants..."

"Did you tell her I was here?"

"No, I said—"

"Good, tell her we've gone for the week-end. Tell her to make an appointment for next week." He had to stall while he thought this through. "I can't deal with her right now."

Cory waded through the parking lot wishing she was wearing rubber boots.

"No one's there. Place is deserted. How about we call it a day?"

"I'm straight with that," Rashid said as he slowly drove the Chevy out onto the main road. They merged into the busy rush-hour traffic. It began to pour, making windshield wipers less and less effective. The glare of oncoming headlights was blinding. Cory put her head back and took deep rhythmic breaths. Rashid, tapping his fingers on the steering wheel, softly sang a tune. They were resigned to a long, slow drive back to West Mifflin.

They did not notice the black SUV pull in behind them. Nor did they notice that it followed them right to Cory's cottage, headlights off as it stopped beside the curb a few houses back. The driver watched as the tall, skinny woman, her long hair spilling out of her hooded jacket, bent down and said a few words through the car window. Then the red Chevy drove off.

She scampered up the long walk, trying not to slip and fall in her unglued sandals.

"Damn it!" she shouted when the light switch failed to work. "No electricity. Shit!"

After lighting two fat candles she had purchased for just such a happenstance, Cory poured a glass of wine and sipped it slowly while she chopped vegetables for her salad. The only sounds she could hear were the plump drops of rain beating down on the roof of the cottage. The candles cast shadows on the bare wall, weird shapes that moved to the rhythm of flickering light. It unnerved her.

She felt a sudden urge to speak with someone who knew her. Cared about her. Then she remembered that the cell phone battery had died and, without electricity, there was no way to recharge it. Her apprehension grew as she realized she would spend the next twelve hours alone and in the dark.

Cory peeled off her soggy clothes and left them strewn on the bedroom floor. The hot water tank, victim of the lack of electricity, offered up a modicum of warm water, which spurted and gurgled out of the corroded faucet. Her lanky, freckled-frame sinking down into the tub, she put her head back on a folded towel and waited.

Slowly her neck and shoulder muscles responded to the warmth and began to loosen the taut grip that had been there the entire day. The fatigue that she had ignored throughout the week enveloped her.

She did not hear the footsteps crossing her wooden deck or see the shape of a man's head as it peered through a small slit in the Venetian blinds. Nor did she hear the raspy intake of breath as he, immersed in the sight of her naked flesh and his twisted cravings, imagined what he would do to her.

Cory bolted awake, confused and dazed. The water had become cold and she was shivering. She yanked out the plug and felt the last of her energy swirling down the drain. It was eight-thirty when she put on her sleeveless t-shirt and tumbled into bed. Rain clouds darkened the sky. A cool breeze blew through the opened window. Cory drifted off to sleep, thankful that she had made no plans with the Mobley men for the next day.

❧❧❧

The man stood still at the front door. Turbulent feelings surged through him like an electrical current. He reached for the doorknob and stopped. A car turned the corner, casting a beam of light on him. He lowered his head and stepped back. It was too early in the evening. Too risky. He could come back another night. Besides, if he waited, he could extend the delicious feelings that came with imagining all the details, playing and replaying his fantasies, visualizing what he would do, how she would respond, how he would react, on and on in repeated performances.

He would wait a day, maybe even two, no need to hurry. He could feel the excitement, the tingling anticipation, all his senses opening up. It was the only time that he felt alive.

37

Jeff Staniewski yawned as he flicked his cigarette out the cavernous back door of the BOP. He was not looking forward to the week-end on this Friday afternoon. Forty-eight hours of waiting. Thinking and waiting.

Thinking about the past made him feel raw, filleted open on a butcher's table, with a sign that read: "Shame for Sale, Cheap."

Christ, he'd spent all those years trying to obliterate the past and all he'd done was add more foul memories to the garbage heap that was his life. The future wasn't any better, it was blank, insanely blank. The furthest he could see ahead was Monday, the day he would put an end to Mr. Bigshot.

A spark flickered in his eyes and just as suddenly went out. Even that didn't hold the promise it had a week ago. Redemption seemed to require more of the human spirit than he had to offer.

～～～

Mr. Mobley set his alarm for six in the morning. Tomorrow was going to be a busy day: a visit to his wife's grave followed by shopping with Tildie in the Strip district. He grunted as his bulky body leaned back on the queen-size bed.

He pulled the sheet up over him and sighed. Yes, he imagined the day would slip by mighty fast tomorrow, especially since the Pirates were playing a double-header.

But the first thing he had to do early tomorrow morning was check on Ms. Johnson. She had told Rashid she needed to do some thinking, spend some time alone, and wouldn't need their taxi service. Mobley didn't intend to intrude on her privacy, but, he was concerned about her. She was digging around in an old mine field where an explosion might happen at any moment.

So after an early breakfast, he would take a ride over to West Mifflin and drop off the tube of lipstick she had left in the taxi. It gave him the excuse he needed.

He yawned and folded his hands on top of his expansive chest. "Our Father who art in Heaven," he intoned, "hallowed be Thy name. Thy Kingdom...." Mr. Mobley's hands fell gently to his sides as his chest rose and fell in the rhythm of a peaceful sleep.

~~~~

Sheila and Dorie met at the KFC in Wilkinsburg for dinner. The rain had kept the usual Friday night customers away, so they had the buffet all to themselves. Dorie piled mounds of deep-fried chicken wings on her plate.

"Some fool tried to tell me that the wing is the unhealthiest part of the chicken because it's the fattest. Like I care!" Dorie laughed, adding two more to her stack. She found enough room on her plate for baked beans and potato salad.

Sheila pulled the skin off the chicken breast, sprinkled vinegar on her salad, and nibbled on an ear of corn.

"It's no wonder yer as skinny as a dang yardstick," Dorie said with mock disgust. "What do you have against eatin'?"

"I'm saving myself for chocolate," said Dorie.

"Heck, I'm not savin' myself for nothin'." Sheila pinched

her lumpy thighs and shook her head. "I'm past savin'." She snatched another wing off her plate. "Did you get the hardhat for Cory?"

"Yep, but the problem is that group isn't coming until around two in the afternoon. So she can't go with me in the morning. She'll have to go with one of the Mobley's and hope that the bus unloads outside of the gate. I tried calling but her phone must be dead."

"You think this plan will work?" Dorie asked, wiping the grease from the corners of her mouth. "I mean, she could get seriously hurt if they ID her."

"It's the only idea I could come up with. So long as she comes and goes with the group, she should be ok. It's her plan to go up to the sixth floor alone that's got me scared half to death."

"Lord," said Dorie, "I'd never do it, would you?"

"I guess it would depend on how badly I needed to know," Sheila responded.

～～～

Danny McCormack sat in a corner of the recreation lounge at the McKeesport YMCA. A slap-stick comedy was on the television that others in the room found hilarious. While they giggled and guffawed, Danny sat with a somber mien. Though he stared at the screen, he was watching a different program, a script that he had written over the years that was not the least bit funny.

At times he would think of Ginny and how she could make him feel like he was the master of his universe. She told him that he owned his world and could do most anything if he set his mind to it. The problem was she saw more in him than he saw in himself. He failed her, repeatedly.

He thought about his daughter. Cassandra. Carrot-top

Cassandra with green eyes. What is she doing in her life? Is she married? Does she have children? Does she live around here? Every unanswered question exposed his severed life, cut off and rotting like a compost heap.

The week-end stretched out in front of him. Forty-eight hours before he could get back to his singular goal: the execution of the man who had obliterated his life.

∾∾∾

Blinky leapt up from the rocking chair where she had been catnapping through a World War II documentary on the History channel. Good God Almighty, she moaned, they need to rename it the War channel. Then she laughed out loud. They already have War channels, it's called the news.

It was the word "history" that had set her mind in motion; something about history. History and Ginny Johnson. Memories of the years she had spent with her unlikely sidekick whirled in her head. Wait a minute! That's it! I know what it is!!

She raced upstairs to her bedroom.

"Tashika," she yelled, "come give me a hand, girl!"

Blinky marched straight into her closet, dropped down onto her knees and began pulling at stacked boxes, desperate to get to the carton on the bottom.

Tashika strolled down the hall.

"You go any slower, girl, you're gonna fall over."

Tashika had an inkling her grandmother wanted some physical effort on her part, which caused her "basic nature of mulishness," as Blinky often pointed out, to kick-in. She leaned against the doorjamb and glanced around the room with a sullen expression.

"I ain't goin' in there," she sulked. "Might never make it

back out."

"You don't step up here and help me move these boxes, you be right about one thing...not making it out." She twisted around and glanced up at her granddaughter. "Want to play gin rummy with me all week-end?"

Tashika put her backside into moving boxes. "You lose a stash of money you done forgot about?"

At last Blinky reached the bottom cardboard box. She tore the lid open and rifled through its contents. At the bottom was a leather-bound black book. She hadn't meant to keep the book, just borrow it long enough to write some names down. But the aunt had whisked Cory away and there hadn't been time to hand it over.

She ran her finger down the list of signatures on the first two pages. There it is! The one name she hadn't recognized back then, and didn't know now.

Who the hell was he? Why was he there? Where is he now?

～～～～

Mrs. Gromski moved slowly about her kitchen as she took stock of her groceries. She hoped the rain would stop by tomorrow. She jotted down the items she needed to get from the supermarket on a piece of scrap paper so she wouldn't forget them.

Planning what to serve Cory for lunch on Sunday gave her a sense of purpose. It reminded her of happier times when a little girl's laughter would ring through the house. She couldn't get over how Cory had gone from a gangly newborn foal to a graceful thoroughbred with a long mane of red hair.

Mrs. Gromski was anticipating an afternoon with her. That is, if she made it to Sunday. These days, at her age, it was a dim bulb who thought too far ahead. After all, she chuckled, she no longer bought green bananas!

She switched off the kitchen light and shuffled slowly off to bed. She would do her shopping early so as not to miss the first inning of the Pirate game. A double-header against Chicago!

～～～

After coming straight home from the movies, Rashid Mobley sprawled out on the living room sofa. The television could barely be heard over the patter of rain on the roof, but he didn't care, he wasn't paying any attention to it. The day had gone from bad to worse as far as he was concerned, and it wasn't the weather he was thinking about.

This plan of Sheila's was serious, man, real serious. AC is a worl' of its own. Its private. Got its own rules. Own cops. Ain't nothin' good gonna come of this. What if she gets caught in there?

And to top it all off, now he had to come up with some lie to tell Uncle Charles why he was gonna do the drivin' on Monday. Ain't no way Master Charles can be droppin' her off or pickin' her up, however the hell this plays out. He ain't gonna go for this plan, no way.

And she keeps poppin' in on these guys. Sooner or later she's bound to spook somebody out of their cage. Somebody who knows something or knows someone who knows something. The world just ain't that big. Look what happened at the union hall, that Luwanski was just about crappin' in his pants after she left.

If someone offed her mother, they sure as hell ain't gonna think twice 'bout offing her. And yours truly sittin' in the driver's seat. They weren't gonna think twice 'bout shootin' my black ass either.

262

He laid there staring at the ceiling. He wanted to tell his uncle but he couldn't because Charles Mobley would put a stop to him driving Ms. Co right quick. That would only make things worse for her.

As if that weren't enough bad shit weighing him down, Rashid didn't like the way he'd been acting lately, scared out of his mind over little stuff. Even the movie had him tied up in knots, too much killin' with their Glocks and explosions. He couldn't take it anymore, made him sick to his stomach. He was beginning to think he was losing his mind, and that just set his nerves on edge all the more.

Rashid turned on his side and buried his face in a pillow.

38

At one o'clock Monday afternoon, the sun's rays streamed through the kitchen windows of Cory's cottage. With the electricity returned to normal that morning, she had charged her cell phone. She shoved it into the pocket of her snug-fitting black jeans and paced around the kitchen waiting for Rashid.

Sheila had stopped by the day before to tell her that the Polish group would arrive at two in the afternoon, too late to ride with her. She gave Cory a white hardhat along with a hand drawn map of the first floor showing where Sheila worked and where the elevator was located. "I don't suppose I can talk you out of this plan of yours," said Sheila.

"No, I have to go forward."

"Just watch your back," she warned.

Cory made arrangements with Rashid to pick her up at one-fifteen. As she strode back and forth in the small kitchen, her chest pulsed with the rapid beat of her heart. She was scared.

Her wild red hair, lassoed into a long braid, was wound into a tight bun at the nape of her neck. Despite the heat of the day, she chose a long-sleeved blouse to cover her freckled arms. But she was stymied by the multitude of light brown freckles that blanketed her face.

Cory removed the hardhat and examined herself in the mirror on her dresser. She opened the locket and studied her mother's face. Today, Momma, we will find that missing piece of evidence.

"Ms. Co?" Rashid called through the screen door. "You ready?"

"I'm coming." Cory took one last appraisal in the mirror, tapped the locket with her fingers and whispered, "Keep me safe, Momma."

When she joined Rashid, she was struck by his unusually somber mood. "Good grief, Rashid, are you sick?"

"No, I'm fine," he lied, "just didn't get all my beauty sleep."

They walked down the hill towards the car.

"Oh, here, you're gonna need this." He handed her a generic yellow name tag that said "American Steel Visitor" in large black ink. "Sheila dropped it off this morning."

Cory slipped it over her neck and climbed into the car. Rashid drove slowly down Greensprings Avenue, even slower towards the Rankin Bridge, and all but stalled out from lack of acceleration as he crossed it.

"Are you sure you're ok?" she asked, eyeing the speed-o-meter.

"Yeah, it's just we got some time to kill." He winced at the word 'kill.' "No need racin' there just to sit and wait."

"Right." She knew he was scared. Scared for her, and for himself. The last thing she wanted to do was add more fright to a simmering pot.

"Rashid, do you remember what I told you about breathing in through your nose and out through your mouth?"

He nodded.

"Good. Do you think that, after you drop me off, you can practice that while I'm gone? There's nothing else to do except wait in the car, so it's a good time to try it, ok?"

"I'll try," he said, apprehensively. "I'm gonna park down near the old high school so's I'll see you when you come out."

She wrapped her arm around his shoulder and squeezed.

"Thank you," she said.

He pulled up to the curb on Eleventh Street out of sight of the guardhouse and turned the ignition off. They waited without speaking. She was pleased to see that he was breathing just the way she had told him. That was all she could do for him now. When this was over, she was going to have a serious talk with him about getting some counseling.

Twenty minutes later a big silver bus turned off of Braddock Avenue and drove towards them. As Cory watched the oncoming bus, her heart began to pound and her legs trembled.

Breathe! Breathe!

She squeezed Rashid's arm. "I'll be back in a couple of hours, max. Don't worry."

"You call me, any trouble shows up! Hear?" said Rashid.

Cory gave him a thumbs up as she jumped out of the car and willed her legs to sprint down the block. The bus stopped across the street from the guardhouse, the doors opened, and a dozen or so people chattering in Polish and wearing white hardhats descended the steep steps. With the bus blocking the guard's view of the visiting delegation, Cory stood on the outskirts, occasionally smiling or staring down at the sidewalk, hoping her act of belonging was working

"Please follow me," a young man said to his Polish interpreter. The little group crossed the street and passed by the guard.

"This, Ladies and Gentlemen, is one of American Steel's premier steel mills." The young man swept his arm in a wide arc indicating the width and breadth of the mill. "Andrew Carnegie built this mill in 1873, making it the oldest steel-making facility in the country. At one time it employed over nine-thousand men, but today, thanks to technological advancements in steelmaking, there are less than nine-hundred employed here.

"This mill has the company's newest double-strand continuous caster and has the capacity to produce almost three million tons a year. The big building ahead and to my left is where the steel is made. It's called the BOP, or basic oxygen processing.

"Now please watch your step and stay close together in the group."

They passed a large gaping doorway where two cranes facing each other picked up big pieces of scrap metal with thick magnetized pads. The scrap was dropped into enormous iron dumpsters. Cory glimpsed inside hoping to see Sheila, but the area was too dark and dusty.

"First, we are going to take a walk around the ground floor, and then we will head up to the basic-oxygen furnaces where we will be joined by Ron Antoli, the BOP superintendent. Stay in the group, please, and follow me."

Cory's plan meant for her to slip away from the group as they passed the small entrance door that lead to the elevator. However, the mere mention of Ron Antoli's name caught her off-guard. She hadn't realized he worked in the BOP. Before she knew it, she had passed the door and had no choice but to continue along in the back of the group.

Some of the Poles took out notebooks and jotted down facts and figures. One furnace was cooking while the other lay silent. The group moved down the wide dirt aisle. The massive iron hooks of a crane hung in the air, a fork-lift unloaded a palette of bagged chemicals, the slab caster was idle and waiting for the upcoming heat, and one ladle lay on its side at the far end of the aisle.

∿∿∿

A lone man had just finished shooting fireproofing materials with a powerful hose into the ladle's interior wall. While he wound up the hose, he watched the group of strangers approach. Suddenly he froze, arms extended, back bent slightly forward, searching for the freckled face that had suddenly appeared like an apparition.

She was easy to spot, standing on the periphery of the group, tall and thin while the others were short and squat. He stared with horror at the ghost that had haunted his nights for twenty years. He could see her struggling to confine long strands of red hair that had blown free from under her hardhat.

Jeff Staniewski tried to swallow but his throat was clamped shut. He stepped back quickly into the darkness of a corner and lit a cigarette with trembling hands. He scrutinized her every move until the group turned back up the aisle.

"Who are those people?" he asked the passing forklift driver.

"Some foreign government officials checking things out. We get these groups now and then. But the guide must be new 'cause they don't usually have them wandering 'round down here. They usually go straight up to the furnace floor, see the fancy computers and stuff."

The driver strained forward in his seat, "Hah, what'd I tell ya. Here comes Antoli all red in the face."

Jeff watched Ron Antoli high-stepping it towards the group, flailing his arms about like a traffic cop. The visitors were herded out of sight towards the elevator. He noticed that the girl hung back and walked with her head down. She's trying to hide herself. That's it. She's afraid someone will see her. He slipped his hard hat further back on his head and scratched his scalp.

❧❧❧

Since the elevator was too small for all of the visitors. Cory waited to ride with second group. Antoli also waited. He was explaining steel-making to the translator, but he was having trouble staying focused on his subject.

A growing unease began to spread in his chest. His instincts were trying to warn him of imminent peril. Is this a heart attack? He stretched his left arm searching for a sign of pain. Nothing. What the hell?

Then, as he gestured upwards towards the furnace floor, he recognized the source of his discomfort. It was hard to tell if his sentence was cut off by the shrill sound of a siren warning that the heat was about to tap or if he had been struck dumb in mid-sentence.

He saw her make her way around the group to the elevator. The doors opened and she walked to the rear and stood with her head down. Then the jabbering Poles crowded in. Antoli, still trying to fathom the unfathomable, was the last to enter. He stood with his nose an inch from the door.

It took less than a minute to arrive at the third floor. In that time Antoli became more agitated. What was *she* doing here? Who told her about this visiting group? What connection or connections did she have at AC? Did she know who he was? Maybe she heard his name downstairs. No, he hadn't said it, there hadn't been time for introductions, so she wouldn't know. As he exited the elevator, the tightly knit group followed close behind him.

All except for one.

39

Cory did not exit with the others in the tour. Instead, she pressed her back against the side wall and pushed the sixth floor button. The door creaked closed and the elevator began its rumbling ascent. Cory exhaled a long shaky breath. Alone in the enclosed space, where the sounds on the outside were eerily unfamiliar, she fought to keep her nervousness contained.

The elevator bumped to a halt at the sixth floor. As the door opened, Cory peered out at a silvery landscape. She punched the button to send the elevator back to the third floor. The doors closed behind her and the elevator began its creaking descent.

She stood motionless as silver flakes floated down upon her. The air was thick with heat, dust, and graphite.

The floor ran down the center of the building. About thirty feet to her left was a metal railing. Beyond that, a sheer seventy foot drop to the ground floor. Down below was the charging aisle where the iron and scrap were loaded into a furnace. On the right side was another metal railing and a perilous drop into molten steel as it poured into the continuous caster.

Cory felt light-headed. Graphite clung to her clammy face and her dank clothes.

"Get a move on Cory or you'll be buried under this stuff," she said aloud. A quivering smile of relief emerged when she saw a broom and a shovel leaning against a steel column. Sheila had said she would put them there.

Now that she saw the vastness of the floor, separated in the middle by the red hot open tops of the two furnaces, she had a sinking feeling that this was worse than any needle in a haystack. Having no idea where to start, she grabbed the broom and began to sweep the floor around the base of the pillars nearest to the elevator.

She swept furiously around the columns, racing against the time it took for the furnace to empty its load onto the caster. About fifteen minutes remained before it was necessary to rejoin the group.

All at once a siren screamed, echoing off the ceiling and wall. Cory bolted forward and bumped hard into a vertical iron column, causing more graphite to fall on her. She regained her balance, spit out graphite, and looked sheepishly about to see if anyone had seen her. It was then she realized the vertical columns had narrow iron plates forged between their outer edges to firm them up.

Of course! Janice wouldn't have just put whatever it is directly on the floor. And she wouldn't have been able to reach the horizontal girders. She must have stashed it on one of the plates.

There wasn't enough room on a plate for twenty years of graphite to pile up, it would have slid off. But there was just enough room for three to four inches of the stuff to accumulate and hide something beneath it.

Moving quickly, she raised the broom to about six feet and began downward sweeping motions to clear away the graphite that had built up on the narrow plates inside the columns, first one side, then the other. Coughing and sputtering, she frantically moved from column to column. Dirt, dust and flecks of silver flew through the air.

"Where are you?" she muttered between her clenched teeth. "What are you?"

Then something other than graphite flopped to the floor.

Cory dropped the broom and stared at the transparent plastic bag. She sank to her knees and picked it up. A frayed yellow handkerchief matted with faded blood and strands of hair was balled up inside.

Oh my God, this is it! Tears of relief mixed with the dirty sweat on her face. She wiped her cheeks with the palm of her hand. Another siren began to screech. She had to get out of there, her time was running out.

"Don't move," a voice snarled from behind her.

The cement floor pressed hard against her knees, but she stayed put.

"Well, well, well. What do we have here? Could it be Mizz Cory Johnson? And what have you found? Just put it on the floor behind you."

Cory trembled as a sudden down draft of terror whipped across her body. She slid the plastic bag along the floor behind her.

The man standing behind Cory bent down and picked the plastic bag Sheila had left for her. "What's so important about...." A bolt of lightning charged through Ron Antoli's wiry frame. How did this get up here?

Confusion reigned as his thoughts twisted and turned in an agonizing maze. Someone must have found it and hid it up here. Who? Who knew? And why didn't that person ever say anything? Why now? Whoever it was must have told her where to go. And now *she* knew.

He reined in his panic, transforming it into aggression. It was an old tactic that had served him well in times of crisis.

"Oh, this is too bad, Johnson, too bad." The screech of a wharf rat escaped his wet lips as a snicker quickly turned to a high-pitched howl of laughter. "Yeah, too bad you had to go sticking your nose where it doesn't belong. Just like your mother, asking for trouble. And now you got it."

Pain from Cory's knees pressing on the cement floor shot up her thighs. She shifted her weight ever so slightly. Antoli's keen sight, adept at watching for signs of resistance, misinterpreted her movement. He grabbed the shovel Sheila had put there and brought it crashing down upon her head.

She heaved forward, smashing her face against the floor and cracking her nose like a dry wishbone. The hardhat rolled off just as the shovel came down a second time. She stared unseeing at the blood that pooled in the graphite-littered floor.

The half-mad assailant raised the shovel above his head for a final, fatal blow, when he heard a voice of the shop supervisor blare from the loudspeaker: "RON ANTOLI! REPORT TO THE OFFICE IMMEDIATELY!"

Antoli dropped the shovel and whipped around, his chest seized with fright. Quickly he tore a sleeve off Cory's shirt, bound her hands and feet, gagged her mouth and propped her against a steel column.

His shirt dripping with sweat, he rode the elevator down to the furnace floor and dashed to his office. He slammed the door shut and flung himself into a chair, panting in quick raspy beats. Jesus! God!! What the fuck...he had to get control...slow down...think.... He bent over and covered his face with his hands. The darkness helped to slow his brain and calm his agitated bowels.

Ok, Ok. He had to change his shirt. What time is it? Shit! Any foreman could come through his door. He had to get control of himself, change his shirt, act normal. That asshole Moe will be here later. He couldn't deal with Cory Johnson until night-turn anyway, there were too many people around now. Then he remembered. Oh, God, what happened to that group?

He jumped up and called the BOP foreman. "Those

people still here?" he barked into the phone. "Ok, ten more minutes, Ok, listen, tell them I'm sorry I couldn't stay with them, tell them...tell them I had a problem I had to take care of."

When he slammed down the phone, he saw drops of blood that had sprayed onto the sleeves of his shirt. In a fit of frenzy, he ripped the shirt off, sending the buttons flying, and stuffed it into the bottom drawer of his desk. He shoved his hand into his pants pocket, pulled out the plastic bag containing the bloody handkerchief and thrust it under the shirt.

Rummaging through his gym bag, he found a wrinkled polo shirt and pulled it over his head. Antoli, his world unraveling, slumped into a chair behind his desk to wait for Moe Perdue.

40

The big SUV drove through the gate and parked next to Ron Antoli's yellow Corvette near the entrance to the BOP. Moe Perdue tossed his security ID card onto the dash and hoisted himself off the leather seat. He lumbered toward the elevator, beads of perspiration popping out on his bald head while a stream of sweat ran down his hairy back.

Perdue found Antoli sitting hunched over some paper work.

"How yunz doin' Ron?"

Antoli glared at the hulk that loomed over his desk. The corners of his lips curled into an expression of contempt. In a mocking voice, he answered, "Things couldn't be better."

"Good. Glad to hear it." Moe took the red suede box out of his pocket and put it on the desk. "Blake sent this along. Said it was a token of his 'preciation for all yunz done."

Antoli picked up the jewelry box and rolled it around between his fingers. "Appreciates my work, eh? That's good to hear." With a snarl he said, "If he appreciates me so much, why didn't he bring it in person?"

Moe studied the man for a few seconds. Even he could see that Antoli wasn't right, what with his eyes jumpin' from wall-to-wall and his skin breaking out in blotches. He had that desperate look of a trapped animal that Moe recognized from his years of hunting.

"Blake said to tell yunz he's real sorry he couldn't come. He's outta town today. But he wanted yunz to have that." He pointed to the box.

Antoli flipped open the box and stared at the Rolex watch sparkling on a black velvet cloth. He snickered, snapped the box closed and flicked it across his desk. "It's a little late for gifts," he said.

Perdue plodded along. "Blake said not to get yunz drawers in a knot about this girl. Said the important thing was that yunz stay calm and not do nothing that could end up bad..."

"Blake said...Blake said..." Antoli jumped up and began pacing the room. "Tell me something, Schmoe, do you ever think for yourself? Here, sit down. Let me tell you why you should do a little independent thinking."

He jabbed at Moe's chest with his finger, pushing him backwards towards a chair. "What if I told you that the girl knows her momma didn't drive off in no pick-up truck? What would you think then?"

Moe's brow furrowed as he wrestled with this new information.

"Would you think that she would have the balls to come into the mill—right under my nose—searching for evidence?"

Moe shook his heavy head.

"No? *No?*" Antoli sneered. "What would you do if you saw her with the evidence in her hand?" He grabbed Moe by the shirt collar and screamed, "Huh? Tell me, what?"

"Ron, Blake says yunz got to calm down. She ain't gonna do none of those things yunz said—"

"She already did it, you dumb asshole!" he shouted, the veins in his neck popping with rage.

"Wha...what happened?"

"C'mon, I'll show you, because you're gonna help me take care of her."

Whether or not to bring Moe into the inner circle of his evil deed was a decision that needed to be made in a more tranquil state of mind. But the coil of Ron Antoli's composure was about to spring loose, threatening to unload his hysteria. He moved rapidly down the hall towards the elevator with Moe rumbling along behind him.

The elevator groaned as it strained to reach the sixth floor. Antoli raced to the right and disappeared around the corner. Puffing behind him, Moe Purdue stopped abruptly and gawked at the crumpled body of a woman.

"Is she dead?" he asked.

Cory's mouth was lost to the brackish colored blood that oozed from her twisted purplish nose. Her eyes, red and seeping, were swollen shut. When she heard Antoli move closer, her body convulsed, pushing her further against the column.

"Not yet, but she will be. Gimme a hand." He bent down and grabbed her legs and began to drag her towards a metal shed where the electrical grid for the BOP was kept under lock and key.

Moe took hold under her armpits and grunted as he picked her up. They carried her to the shed. Cory groaned as they shoved her into it. He slammed the doors and snapped the padlock shut.

"Not much air in there. She won't last long," he said matter-of-factly.

Moe stood staring at the metal doors. "Blake ain't gonna like this. He said for yunz not to—"

Antoli gave him a deadly glare. "He ain't gonna know anything because you ain't gonna say anything. You and I are gonna go about our business and meet back here at three in the morning when half the mill is asleep. She'll be dead by then and all we gotta do is get rid of the body."

Antoli's demeanor was menacing. "You got that? Say nothing and be back here at three. Just tell the guard you're on a special assignment for downtown."

Antoli didn't trust Moe, but his back was up against the wall. With his heart pounding and chest constricted, he couldn't see any other options. Just get the big thug back here at three and then he would take care of business.

∽∾∽∾

Jeff Staniewski had stood in the canteen and watched as the group of foreign visitors filed out of the BOP and clambered aboard the bus. The freckle faced girl was not among them. He figured she wouldn't be there.

He frowned. Now what? He had seen how Antoli's expression had changed when he first saw the girl. It was subtle, a slight hiccup in his otherwise smooth performance. Antoli recognized her, and that meant it must be Ginny's daughter, that gangly little red-haired girl he had met a long time ago.

But what is she doing here? And where is she now? He paced around the small canteen, at a loss for ideas.

He was startled to see a black SUV the size of a hearse drive through the guarded gate without stopping to show any ID, just a wave of his hand. It pulled up to the BOP door and parked next to a yellow Corvette. A bullish looking ape climbed out from behind the wheel and swung his heft towards the BOP door.

Jeff frowned. It didn't take a genius to figure out that the big ape was someone's goon. His frown deepened. What's going on?

Suddenly Jeff bolted out of the canteen and raced towards the huge opening of the service aisle. He cut back to a fast walk and went straight for the elevator. The doors were closing when he arrived and he watched as the overhead red light rose to the third floor.

He's going to see Antoli. He'd bet his life on that.

Something big is going on, but what?

Jeff couldn't linger in one spot for long. He had no business being anywhere but at his work site. The third floor, the administrative offices of the BOP, was definitely off-limits to the likes of Jeff Staniewski, an employee of a sub-contractor.

Think, damn it. *Think!*

He checked his watch. It was almost four-thirty, a half hour past quitting time for office personnel. He walked briskly back outside and around to the front door and charged up the metal stairs to the third floor. The door had a glass window giving him a view straight down the hallway, in time to see the goon disappear into an office.

Jeff opened the door a crack and listened. The only sound was the forced air blowing through the air conditioning. He pulled the door open and took a tentative step into the hallway. Now he was thoroughly exposed with no place to hide. He bit down hard on his lower lip and inched slowly towards the office.

He heard Antoli saying something about it being too late for gifts. Jeff leaned forward straining to hear.

Antoli sounded angry, but there was something else, something Jeff didn't normally associate with Antoli. He sounded scared. His voice kept getting higher and more demeaning. He said something about the girl knowing her mother didn't climb into a pick-up, and then he was yelling about her finding evidence on the 6th floor and calling the goon a dumb asshole. Jeff heard a chair scraping.

Someone was on the move.

Jeff spun around, took giant strides back to the door, slipped through it and ran down to the next landing. He stopped and waited. Hearing a door slam shut, he ran up the stairs and peeked through the glass. The goon was loping clumsily behind the trim Antoli, who was sprinting down the hallway towards the furnace floor.

The elevator. Jeff bounded down the steps and ran to the service aisle entrance, almost colliding with a forklift unloading materials from a cargo truck. "Sorry, bud!" he yelled to the driver. "I left my lunch pail."

He sprinted into the building and stopped in front of the elevator. The floor light stopped at the sixth floor.

What the hell is up there?

High up along the sides of the building were the tracks for the big cranes to move lengthwise up and down the aisles. But in the middle were floors and, from his vantage point, it was impossible to see what was on them.

He hesitated, thinking hard, trying to pull up old memories. These furnaces were not sealed vessels. They had gaping holes at the top so that when they were tilted, iron and scrap could be loaded into them. When they were upright, the oxygen lances were lowered into them.

That's it! That's it!! From the sixth floor you could see into the fiery furnace.

His mouth gaped open in a silent scream. The vise of terror clamped around his brain. Again, he stood paralyzed, unable to move, as he watched her tumble down, down, down....

"Hey, Jeff, you doubling out tonight?" It was one of the pit guys.

There was no telling how long Jeff had been standing there. His throat was dry. Sweat cascaded down his forehead and crept into the corners of his mouth. The floor indicator above the elevator doors had returned to the third floor. He couldn't get up to the sixth floor until Antoli and the goon left.

"Yeah, I got lucky," he said, his voice catching on a hook deep in his throat. "Pulled some overtime." He cleared his throat. "How you doin'?"

"I'm heading for the canteen. Got some time?"

"Not much. Let's go."

They walked out of the service aisle towards the canteen. Jeff stood in a corner near the door, a cold can of Dr. Pepper pressed against his temple. His attention was riveted on the door of the BOP while he listened to the pit guy ramble on about baseball.

"I gotta get back," the guy said, chucking his soda can in the trash. "See ya later. Hey, maybe some time we can go watch a game."

"Yeah, that's sounds great," Jeff said, absent-mindedly.

It was close to six when Ron Antoli and Moe Perdue walked out of the BOP. Jeff grabbed the receiver from a pay phone on the wall and put it to his ear. He cracked the door open. He mouthed words pretending to talk on the phone and leaned as far as possible in their direction hoping to hear something.

Antoli was in the middle of admonishing Moe in a high-pitched screechy voice, "...remember, three o'clock, don't be late," when a horn blasted through the BOP warning that a ladle of hot iron was being picked up by a crane.

Trying to read their lips, Jeff looked straight into the contorted face of Antoli, who stopped his tirade and glared at him. Jeff turned away from the two men and went on mouthing words into the receiver. He shrugged his shoulders and nodded his head. After waiting a few minutes, the receiver gripped in his sweaty hand, he peeked out the door and caught sight of the Corvette's tail-lights as both cars drove past the guardhouse.

Within seconds Jeff was riding the lumbering elevator to the sixth floor.

Three o'clock. Antoli said three o'clock. Three o'clock what? Tonight? Tomorrow? Or was he reminding that big bruiser of a time last week?

"C'mon, hurry up," he yelled, slamming his fist against the elevator wall in frustration. When the doors opened, he bolted out and stopped dead. His eyes swept from left to right while his ears strained to hear anything remotely human. In the distance was the bright red glow of molten steel hovering above the open mouth of the second furnace. The oxygen lances had yet to be lowered.

Panicked, he raced to the first furnace, which was standing idle, having just relinquished its hot liquid into the continuous caster. He raised his arm to cover his face and tried to edge closer, but the searing heat forced him to back away. He dashed off to the second furnace even though he knew he wouldn't be able to get close.

"No! God, NO!" Jeff screamed, as the lances were being lowered. He backed up to the metal rail and gaped at the furnace as it began to cook.

This could not be happening. Not again. Please, God, not again!

Numb with shock, he stood and stared at the furnace. Then, his shoulders slumped in despair, he turned and trudged back towards the elevator. Graphite floated through the air and fell upon him like a mantle, condemning him to a lifetime of shame. This was the end. He needed a drink. A lot of drinks.

Wait. What's that? He stooped down to see. A footprint was pressed into the graphite on the floor. Then he saw another larger one. He could barely make them out in the dim light. The prints were leading in the opposite direction of the furnaces. He came upon a wide area where footprints moved in a confused pattern. A shovel lay on the floor not far from where skid marks began. They stopped in front of a large metal shed with padlocked doors and a glaring red sign that read "Danger! Authorized Personnel Only."

He put his ear against the metal and shouted. "Miss

Johnson? Are you in there?"

He heard a muffled sound. "Don't move. I'm gonna help." He ran back, grabbed the shovel and thrust the blade into the seam under the upper hinge of the shed door. He worked the shovel back and forth furiously until the hinge broke, then he ripped into the lower hinge until it too snapped off. He pulled the metal doors open and dropped to his knees.

"Oh my God!"

Cory was slumped against the side wall of the shed. Her head hung limp against her chest, the gag a bloody wad in her mouth. The hair on the back of her head was caked with blood where the shovel had cracked her skull. She tried to raise her arms to ward off a blow, but lacked the strength to go higher than her thighs.

"Miss Johnson? Can you hear me?" She gave a slight nod and groaned. "It's OK. You're gonna be OK. I need to move you away from this grid so you can get some air. It'll just take a minute."

He put one arm under her knees, the other behind her shoulders and lifted her out of the shed. Her clothes were soaked with sweat. As he put her on the floor with her back to a column, her head rolled back and it was then that he saw her swollen, misshapen face.

"I think you've got a broken nose," he said, bending down and removing the soggy rag from her mouth. "You are Ginny Johnson's daughter, aren't you?"

Cory gulped the air, nodding. Her lips were parched, her tongue swollen. "Water..." she pleaded.

"OK. Water. I have to go back down to the canteen to get it."

Her swollen eye lids opened a crack. She grabbed at his shirt.

"No," she whispered in a raspy voice. She tried to move

closer to him, like a frightened cub burrowing under the belly of its protector. "Don't leave. Please...don't leave."

Jeff sat down next to her and put his arm around her shoulders. He tried to squash his own panic and focus on her. Maybe she was bleeding inside. She was definitely dehydrated; cracked lips, soaked clothes, and, from what he could see through the dust and graphite, her skin was the color of a bleached sheet. He needed to move fast.

He knew that Antoli would be back, probably with the goon, and they were planning on incinerating her.

But when, three? Or were they already on their way up? How much time did he have? He needed help but trusted no one. Who else was in on this? The guard at the gate? The furnace foreman?

No, he couldn't trust anyone, especially any boss man. But he couldn't wait for a solution to fall from the sky either.

"Water...please...," she murmured as she squeezed his shirt tighter, not daring to let go.

He had to risk it. He had to make it to the canteen where he could get water and use the pay phone to reach the police. Jeff gently pried her fingers loose and lowered her hand to her side. He bent over her.

"Miss Johnson, listen to me. You need water and an ambulance. I have to go down to the canteen to call the police. I won't be gone more than five minutes, I swear to you."

She squirmed against him. "No...no...my pock...pock...."

"What? What did you say?"

"Pocket," she said, and then she keeled over.

Jeff freaked. "Jesus. Don't you die! Don't you die on me!" He pushed her back up. Frantically he patted the pockets of her jeans. On the far side he felt a small oblong object and pulled it out. A silver cell phone glimmered in his hand. He punched in 911.

After making the call he fell back against the column and moved her upper body against his chest. A long shuddering sigh escaped from his lungs. There was nothing left to do but wait.

41

Moe drove to his office in the towering American Steel building. He had to make a big decision and found the task daunting. He had spent most of his working life following the orders of one man: a man who expected that special assignments be carried out successfully, with no need to report back.

As a matter of fact, his boss had always specifically instructed Moe to never report back. "Just get the job done," the boss always said. But this was different, wasn't it? Or was it? If he reported Antoli's deeds to his boss, Blake was sure to explode. But if he didn't tell him and things turned out worse, he could go off like a cache of dynamite. It was a side of Blake that most people had never encountered. Certainly not the corporate elite or his country-club cronies.

Moe Perdue, a man with little intellect but with powerful animal instincts, sensed that Franklin Blake possessed a heinous core capable of grotesque violence. Moe was a jittery fat man attempting a high-wire act. But he lacked the one necessary quality for a man in his profession: duplicity. Not that he was morally opposed to lying. Lying simply required a higher level of mental gymnastics than he could lay claim to.

In the end he picked up his office phone and dialed Franklin Blake's new private line.

The smooth voice answered, "Good afternoon. Franklin Blake speaking."

"Uh...Mr. Blake, its Moe. There's a problem...."

Switching abruptly to a different persona, Blake demanded, "Where are you?"

"In my office."

"Meet me downstairs in the executive parking area."

Blake hung up and boarded his private elevator. Something went wrong. He knew it. Moe wouldn't call unless there was a problem—a big problem. How could he be surrounded by such fools? Such imbeciles? Anger rose up in his throat like so much grease, until it created a burning sensation that pricked at the roots of his silver hair.

Moe was standing by the big Mercedes when an angry Blake strode out of the elevator. "What the hell happened?"

Moe's mouth twitched nervously as he reported, in halting phrases, how the girl had gotten into the mill and found the bloody headscarf, that Antoli had whacked a shovel into the back of her head, that she was barely alive, and that Antoli expected him to come back at three in the morning to finish the job.

Blake struggled to make sense of what Moe was telling him and, at the same time, control his warring emotions. Waves of fear and rage competed for dominance. Stupid! He had been so stupid, relying on these small-time goons.

Different scenarios rampaged through his mind. They all ended up with his hands strangling the life out of that worthless piece of shit, Ron Antoli. But he had to get control of himself and the situation.

He focused on his reflection in the shiny fender, reminding himself of who he was and the power he possessed. Slowly, with a tremendous force of will, he regained his inner composure, making room for a solution to the problem to emerge.

In the end, it was so simple. So clear. Blake climbed into his car. Perdue, who had been standing in the same spot, long arms hanging limp at his side, a doltish expression reflecting nauseating loyalty, opened his mouth to say something.

Blake didn't give him the chance.

"Antoli put us way out on a limb, but his idea is the best we've got. Meet him at three and take care of the problem. And make sure whatever it is she found goes with her, understand?"

Moe nodded.

"Report back to me tomorrow. I want to know how this turns out."

42

At three in the morning Ron Antoli drove his Corvette through the plant gate. Moe Perdue sat in his SUV dozing, his flaccid cheeks hanging like popped balloons. Antoli pulled up alongside. The ugly son-of-a-bitch gave him the willies. Antoli hopped down from the cab. "C'mon," he said, banging on the window, jarring Perdue awake. "Let's get this over with, I need some sleep."

They rode the elevator up in silence. Dim-witted Moe lacked the heat of passion, the intensity that comes with the taking of a life. This was merely a job to be done, a task to be dispensed.

Antoli, on the other hand, may have seemed calm, but inside he felt tethered to the end of a bungee rope. Things seem to be unwinding before he had a chance to think. There were variables he couldn't control, and that always pushed him closer to fits of uncontrollable rage.

When the elevator doors opened on the sixth floor, Antoli pushed the stop button and locked it in position. He marched off towards the electrical grid, Perdue huffing to keep up. Antoli took the key to the padlock out of his pocket and grabbed hold of the lock. The metal doors tumbled forward, almost knocking him to the ground.

"What the..."

Both men gawked at the empty space where once their victim had laid half-dead. Dazed, Antoli turned slowly, searching out over the floor, hoping to find her crumpled in some corner. Then he caught sight of footprints in the graphite, lots of footprints, moving here and there, until they marched as one towards the elevator.

The taut cable that had been holding him together snapped. He spun around and glared at Moe, who hadn't moved since his initial flinch at the black empty space.

"Who the fuck have you been talking to, huh? *Who*?"

He reached inside his poplin jacket and pulled out a .357 magnum. He pointed it directly at Moe's heart and advanced towards him.

"Who'd you tell about this?" he snarled, his lips contorted in a grotesque grimace.

"Nobody. I didn't tell nobody." Moe was backing up, his hands rising to his chest, open, placating. "Honest. She's around here somewhere. She didn't get far."

"CAN YOU SEE THIS?" Antoli screamed, waving the gun at the floor. "You dumb fuck...see all those prints? There's been an army up here. Who you been blabbing to? *Blake*? You two got some plan to blame this on *me*?" He poked the gun into Moe's stomach.

Moe took a few steps further back. The top of his bald head was pimpled with sweat. "Listen, Ron," his harelip twitched up and down, up and down, "I didn't...yunz can't...yunz gotta believe..."

Froth bubbling up in the corners of his mouth, Antoli kept advancing. "There's only been one mistake from the beginning and that mistake was you. You're so goddamn dumb!"

Moe kept walking backwards until the searing heat from the furnace began to singe the fine hairs on his neck. "Don't do this. Yunz got it wrong."

The strident peel of a siren trumpeted through the BOP just as the bullet ripped down the barrel of the gun and blew a four-inch hole in Moe's distended gut. Antoli fired again and again, as though he were taking down a bull elephant, until Moe Perdue fell backwards into the gaping furnace, arms flailing, and mouth agape, waiting for the scream that never came. He sizzled for less than a second before he was reduced to carbon ash.

Antoli, his reservoir of heinous acts spent, stood staring at the red glow along the lip of the furnace. Then he threw the .357 magnum into the furnace. The tension that had wound him up and set him in motion, gushed out of him like water from a whale's blow hole, leaving him exhausted and confused.

He needed to think. Make a plan. But first he had to go back to his office and get his bloodied shirt and that plastic bag. Those were the only things that connected him to anything. She wouldn't be able to identify him; after all, she'd never really seen him. Yes, that was it, get back downstairs. He whirled around, took a step forward and stumbled to a stop.

Franklin Blake stood in his path, a Glock pistol in his hand.

"Nice piece of work," he snickered at Antoli. "You've lightened my load by fifty percent." Over Antoli's shoulder he could see the open mouth of the furnace. "Too bad about Moe. He was a special kinda guy. Never asked any questions. And never, never made a plan on his own. Problem was he knew too much. Same as you. You know too much."

Blake's smirk evaporated as he brought his laser eyes to bear on Antoli's face. "That was your undoing, Antoli. You imagined for a minute you had a brain. What were you gonna do next, join the country club? Drink martinis in the lounge?" A spurt of derisive laughter escaped. "Forget it. You're dumber than old Moe. At least he had enough sense to follow orders."

"Blake, we've been in on this since the beginning. You

and I took care of that Johnson bitch, didn't we? You got millions in stock options and I got a nice advancement. There's no reason why we can't.... I mean, everything was going great until her daughter showed up here, snooping around. I, I just thought we could scare her. Then Moe got too rough. He just about killed her! We didn't have a choice. We came back here and she was gone."

Blake's throat tightened. "*Gone?* What do you mean 'gone'?"

Confused, he turned his head slightly towards the darkened corner. It was just the hesitation that Antoli needed. He sprang at Blake, a rattler shooting straight out from a tight coil, fangs extended. They hit the cement floor, arms and legs entangled. Blake was bigger, but he was no match for the fiendish Antoli, who was ripping a chunk of flesh from Blake's ear.

"Police! Don't move!"

A powerful hand grabbed Antoli by the neck and dragged him, kicking and spitting, off of Blake, who was writhing on the floor holding a hand over his bloody ear.

Chief Brayton was bent over wheezing.

"You're a lil' outta shape, boss," a younger officer teased. "Six flights of stairs and I'm just warmin' up, but the boss here is 'bout ready to croak."

"Don't you worry 'bout me," gasped Chief Brayton, "I plan on living a long time so's they keep deducting my pension payments from your check."

He wiped the sweat from his brow with a plain white handkerchief. "Let's cuff these two bozoes and get 'em outta here."

43

At noon the following day Cory was propped up in a hospital bed. A large padded bandage covered her broken nose. Her face was puffy with blotches of black and blue bruising spreading out beyond the gauze.

Blinky, Sheila and Dorie crowded together in the doorway. "Good Lord, you look terrible," Blinky said.

"Sssh, that ain't no way to talk to the sick," said Dorie.

"It's no lie. She could be in a horror flick."

Dorie glared at her friend. "Stop it," she hissed.

"It's OK, I look a lot worse than I feel. I even have a hole in my head."

Cory turned slightly so they could see the shaved spot in the back of her head where twelve stitches had been needed to close the gash from the shovel. Her mass of red hair was a matted mess of graphite and blood. "The good news is they are going to release me today."

The curtain that separated Cory from the bed next door was drawn closed but loud snoring could be heard erupting in fits and starts.

"What's that, a construction site?" Blinky asked. She peaked around the curtain's edge. "Get up, boy, what're you doin' in that bed?"

Rashid jumped up as fast as a jack-in-the-box. "Sorry. Miss Cory, you OK?" He pulled the curtain back far enough so that he was reassured by the sight of her, and then sat back down.

"I'm fine, Rashid, really, I'm fine." Then, in a whisper,

"He's been up all night watching over me. Had quite a scare at home."

"And you had quite a scare right here, didn't you little girl?" The booming voice of the diminutive Chief Brayton resonated off the wall as he strode into the room.

Rashid leapt from the bed.

"Ah, there you are!" Chief Brayton bellowed. "Your uncle is needin' your help down the hall, boy."

"I'll be right back, Miss Cory," Rashid said. "Don't you go nowhere without me." He dashed out of the room.

She spoke quietly to her friends. "He won't leave my side, except to check on Mister Mobley, who's on the other side of this ward."

Blinky said, "It's a good thing someone stays right up under you because you are one big magnet for trouble."

Cory smiled at her friends. "Wait till you see what happens next," she teased. Then she turned to Chief Brayton. "Did you get him?"

"Yes, ma'am, he's here." Chief Brayton nodded his head towards the hallway. "Mister Jeff Staniewski, there's a request for your presence."

Jeff, timid and self-conscious, inched his way into the room, his hands fidgeting with his baseball cap. He appeared so much older than his forty-two years: a thick body ravaged by alcohol, drugs, and grinding hard labor.

Chief Brayton made the introductions. "Cory, this here is Jeff Staniewski. Jeff, this banged up little lady is Cory Johnson."

Blinky's mouth opened wide. "You're Jeff? Staniewski?"

"Yeah, I'm Staniewski," he said in a self-deprecating voice, as though he were announcing a new strain of deadly virus.

"Good Lord. It's your name that's in the book, ain't it?"

"Book?"

"You were there. You signed the book."

"Sorry?" He was bewildered.

"The meetin' about Ginny twenty years ago. The meetin' where all her friends came. You remember, don't you? You signed the black book. Yours was the only name I didn't recognize."

Blinky explained how she had always wondered who he was, how she had searched for the book and found it in a box in her closet. She turned to Cory, "I think your aunt put it out for people to sign but she forgot to take it with her." Then she turned to Jeff. "It was you, right?"

Jeff's head dropped. "Yes, ma'am, it was me."

Cory saw another piece of the puzzle, the missing book, fall into place. "Jeff...may I call you Jeff?"

"Yes, ma'am."

"Please, call me Cory."

"Yes, ma'am." He hesitated, and then directed his gaze at her face. "Are you OK?"

"I know my face is freakish, but I feel much better." The tenor of her voice dropped. "Thank you for saving my life."

Jeff was in turmoil. He hadn't wanted to come, but some unfamiliar and long unrecognized spirit deep inside of him had played his hand. Part of him, the part that had been driving his bus for two decades, responded to her gratitude with a smirk. If she knew the truth she wouldn't be thanking him, she'd be havin' him locked up.

Yet there seemed to be a current of possibility upon which the other part of him had tossed his last life-line. And so, suspending his fatalism, he grabbed hold of the line for dear life.

"Yes, ma'am." He breathed a sigh. "I wasn't sure you were gonna make it."

"I never would have if you hadn't shown up."

Chief Brayton cleared his throat, which succeeded in

magnifying the sound of his voice even more. "Exactly how did you show up, Jeff?"

The door of redemption flung open and Jeff Staniewski stood at the crossroads. He felt buck naked, the ugly scar of cowardice beaming across his chest. He had tried for too many years to obliterate the truth from his awareness. But as he watched the police and the EMT's race towards them on the 6th floor, something had shifted in his soul. Perhaps there was more than one truth.

"I knew your mother when I worked at AC. I saw her die."

He told his story to a hushed room. Blinky, Sheila and Dorie sat side-by-side on the hospital bed, Chief Brayton leaned against the wall while Rashid hovered in the hallway listening. But the only person in his sight was Cory, her intense gaze bearing witness to his pain. At times he grimaced with agony. His hands opened in gestures of entreaty. The words gushed out of him like a busted sewer line spewing out toxic waste.

When he finished, he felt bone-weary, used up, with hardly enough energy to pump his heart. The room was silent as he whispered the last of his tale.

"I went to that meeting where her friends were—that's when I first saw you. I went because I wanted to tell somebody what I'd seen. They were all talkin', wonderin' what had happened to her and did she really just take off with some guy. And there I was, knowin' the truth, standing in a corner too scared and guilty to say anything. So I signed that book to pay my respects and left." Shaking his head disconsolately, he added, "I should have done something to help her."

Cory motioned for him to sit next to her on the bed. Her eyes were brimming with tears, as much for him as for the tragic death of her mother.

"You are a brave man, Jeff Staniewski. Thank you for sharing my mother's last moments with me." She squeezed his hand. "I don't know what you could have done differently. You're not responsible for her death. These men killed her. And they wouldn't have thought twice about killing you, too. Just think who they are. Twenty years later and they're still at it. They were playing for keeps."

She kissed her fingers and put them to his cheek.

"Thank you for everything you have done." Cory looked around the room. "But, where is Mister Mobley? He's OK, isn't he?"

44

Rashid had slipped into the room and was leaning up against the wall, cell phone on his belt, hat on sideways. His expression, however, was anything but youthful.

"How is Mr. Mobley?" she asked.

"What's wrong with Charles?" Blinky asked. "Is he sick?"

"Charles Mobley is another hero we have in our midst," Chief Brayton said as he patted Jeff on the shoulder. "Rashid, you were the first on the scene. You wanna tell this or you want me to tell it."

"No, sir, I don't even want to think about it. I'm goin' down to the snack bar. Anybody want anything? Ms. Cory? No? OK. I'll be right back."

Chief Brayton had a reputation for telling good stories. He puffed up his chest and began.

"First I want to say that this plan y'all cooked up damn near ended with Cory here in the morgue. Now I already gave my lecture to her, and she tried to take the responsibility, but I know she couldn't have pulled this off without you abettin' her in doin' it." He waved a finger at Sheila and Dorie. "Don't you ever do anything like this again, hear?" They nodded their heads in agreement.

Chief Brayton hitched up his meticulously pressed pants and began to pace the room.

"After Rashid dropped Miss Johnson off, he figured she'd be about an hour, so he went visitin' his girlfriend. Problem was he lost track of time like young folks do, and got back to the mill just in time to see the bus pullin' out onto Braddock Avenue. He went to where he told her to meet him, but she wasn't there. So he took out after the bus.

"He figured the bus was goin' downtown, but it got on the Parkway and drove towards a motel near the airport. It was in the middle of rush-hour with traffic backed up and moving mighty slow. Took him well over an hour to get there. He pulled up behind the bus and waited for her to get off. No Miss Johnson. He lost it."

Cory could picture Rashid behind the wheel, all ten fingers tapping, knees jumping, body twitching. He must have felt like an unraveling ball of twine in the claws of a malevolent cat.

"He got back on the Parkway and had no choice but to creep into town and then merge with the traffic heading out to the suburbs, which made him an hour and a half gettin' back down to Braddock."

Chief Brayton raised his voice and pointed at Cory. "Of course, you, little lady, were nowhere to be found. He waited some, but when you didn't show, he raced off to your house in West Mifflin. But, as we know," and here he shot a stern glance at Sheila and Dorie, "you weren't there neither.

"So he sped back home just in time to see a cross startin' to burn in the front yard. He set the hose on it and right about then he heard some yellin' in the back yard. He ran back and there was Charles Mobley, a bloody cut on his forehead, sittin' on top of the man who had set the cross to burning."

Chief Brayton chuckled. "Imagine, a whale sittin' on a porker and the porker was squallin' at the top of his lungs, them that was still workin' anyway, 'cause I think he was 'bout squashed flat."

At this, Chief Brayton's infectious laughter rolled about

the room, gathering everyone in its wake.

"Who was it?" Blinky asked, gently dabbing at a gleeful tear with the back of her hand.

"Turns out he's the Vice President of Local 1630, name of Tony Blasko."

Dorie asked her friends, "Who's that?"

"Don't you remember?" Blinky said, "he transferred into the BOP from the blast furnace. He's the one gave Ginny lots of trouble 'bout workin' in the pit."

Dorie cut her off, "Yeah, now I remember. He had a bad reputation. Some said he was a member of the KKK. Guess they was right."

"He ain't so tough anymore," the Chief noted. "He's in a jail cell singing like a canary. Can't shut him up. Funny thing is he says he knows who killed Ginny Johnson."

"WHAT?" Everyone yelled at once.

"Yeah, says it was the Klan killed her but he doesn't know exactly who because they always done things in secret. He's hell bent to give me a list of names of possible suspects. Plus, he said to check into Harley Security. He thinks they got the security contract after they put a guard in the booth the night Mister Chestnut disappeared and Miss Johnson died. Might be another murder charge coming down the pike what with the death of Mr. Chestnut."

"Why do you suppose he's confessin' to stuff that ain't true? I mean the Klan and all," Dorie asked.

Chief Brayton scratched his head. "Could be he's tryin' to save himself from a hate crime prosecution for burnin' the cross, give up some evidence to get a deal. It's a Federal crime, stiffer sentences. Problem is his story don't make no sense. We got the killers, even though that Blake guy keeps spoutin' off 'bout some guy named Moe who did the killin' with Antoli. Antoli ain't saying nothin' much 'cept Blake was in on everything."

They sat quietly for a few minutes, absorbing this latest information. Finally Blinky broke the silence, "Is Charles going to be OK?"

"I'm as good as can be expected, but my tackling days are over," sang the deep bass voice of Mr. Mobley as he walked into the room. A long cut on the left side of his forehead was being held together with butterfly bandages.

He shook hands with Jeff and Chief Brayton, waved a thick index finger at Dorie and Sheila in a teasing admonishment, and patted Blinky on the shoulder. He turned to Cory and frowned. "Miss Johnson, I have to say, you look terrible."

Blinky stuck an elbow into Dorie's ribs and giggled.

Charles Mobley continued. "Rashid said you were being released today, too. Thought we would drive together since I don't think Rashid could stand it if he didn't see to both of us."

"Mister Mobley, that would suit me just fine," Cory answered, grateful for the feeling of safety that he always brought with him.

45

When they dropped Mr. Mobley off at home, his lady-friend Tildie was waiting for him on the porch. The only sign of the wooden cross was some charred blades of grass.

"Now don't you worry none, Miss Johnson. Rashid is going to make a list of whatever you need from the store and, after you're settled in, he'll run down the hill and pick some things up for you. Chief Brayton has notified the police in West Mifflin to drive by your house on a regular basis this week. Probably no need for it, since they got everybody in the jailhouse, but he wasn't gonna settle for less."

They waved good-bye and Rashid, radio off, drove the speed limit over to West Mifflin.

"Are you feeling all right?" Cory asked.

"Me? Yes Miss Cory, I'm straight. You OK?"

"Yes, I'm straight, too," she replied.

He helped her into the stuffy little cottage, opening all the windows and turning on the overhead fan. Feeling entitled to a great deal of pampering, she made a list of her favorite ice creams, chocolate sauces, and fresh nuts. Her salad supply would last another two days.

"Here's thirty dollars. That ought to cover it. Don't go speeding around now, I'll be fine. I'm going to take a shower and wash some of this blood out of my hair."

Her body ached from the muscles in her neck down to her calves. Her black jeans and blouse were caked with dirt and dried sweat. When she got a whiff of herself, she thought the Mobleys had been kind not to have made her ride in the trunk.

As she removed her blouse she shuddered at the graphite flakes that floated innocently through the air. They were in her hair, under her fingernails, in the pockets of her jeans, inside her socks. The more graphite she saw, the more her skin itched until she was scratching and hopping her way into the hot shower.

Two hours later she sat on the floor leaning against the couch with a pillow behind her and a three-scoop fudge sundae in her lap. Chief Brayton was holding a press conference on the TV, announcing the arrest of Franklin Blake, Chairman of American Steel, and Ronald Antoli, Superintendent of the Basic Oxygen Processing department at Andrew Carnegie Works, suspects in the 1982 slaying of steelworker Ginny Johnson and the recent attempted murder of her daughter, Cory. Also arrested was the Vice President of USWA Local 1630, Anthony Blasko, who was apprehended by Charles Mobley after setting fire to a cross on Mr. Mobley's front yard.

"Oh, no!" she shouted. "This will go national. I have to reach Aunt Ora before she watches the news."

She rummaged around the dresser for her cell phone and called her beloved aunt.

"Cory? Is that you? Darlin', are you all right? I just saw the announcement on the TV news. Whatever in the world happened?"

"I am absolutely fine. I'm sorry you had to hear it on the news first."

"It gave me quite a scare. I was running around here trying to find your telephone number. I put it someplace for safe keeping but can't remember where."

Cory gave her a brief explanation, omitting the frightening hours she had spent locked in the metal container.

Ora's voice cracked. "I was so worried about you. And poor Ginny. But when will you be coming home?"

"I'm not sure," Cory replied. She could hear the worry in her aunt's voice and she hated having to prolong it, but she needed a little more time. "There's someone I want to find. His name is Mike Samuels. He's a school teacher. At least he used to be. He and Mom were in love back then. I'd like to tell him what happened in person. I'll call you tomorrow when my plans fall into place."

Cory curled up on the couch and watched a Law and Order rerun. Finally, she drifted off to sleep, the sound of a cricket serenade filling the night air.

And then her heart began to pound. A thud followed by a grunt sent Cory flying off the sofa. Something violent was happening outside on the deck.

She stood motionless in the middle of the room. The drawn blinds engulfed the room in blackness. The swelling around her eyes had knocked out her peripheral vision. She stared straight ahead at darkened shapes and shadows.

A sour taste flooded her mouth as a deck board creaked. Whatever it was, it was closing in on the front door.

Arms extended, Cory groped across the room to the kitchen. She patted her hands down the wall until she found the clawed garden tool. She tip-toed to the wall opposite the front door, sucked in her breath and waited.

In an instant the door latch succumbed to a kick and flew through the air. As the door crashed open, a hulking black silhouette filled the frame. Cory gasped. Slowly he turned in her direction.

"Are you scared of something, Miss Johnson?" he cackled. "I was kinda hoping you'd be in the tub."

Cory, her pulse echoing in her ears, backed into the corner near the couch. She was overcome with a ferocious rage. No way was this sick bastard going to lay a finger on her. Not without a fight.

She needed to get outside, but in order to make a break for the door he would have to move further into the room. With the clawed tool above her head, she began to move sideways across the front of the couch.

"They are always afraid. All of 'em. Afraid of me. Crying and begging me to stop. Are you afraid of pain, Miss Johnson?"

He took another step into the room and stopped. His grizzly head moved slowly from left to right while his nose sniffed the air.

Cory took another step to her left. Her bare foot caught the edge of the ice cream bowl and sent it clattering under the couch.

The bulky frame lunged at her. A blast of his hot breath hit her in the face. She plunged the claw into his chest, dragged it downward, and then ripped it out. A hideous roar filled the room. He reeled backward in shock, then forward in anger, grabbing her T-shirt with his left hand and throwing her sideways against the back wall.

She crumbled to the floor, gasping for air. A voice in her head warned: *Get up, Cory! Get off your hands and knees. Get up!*

She couldn't do it. She couldn't breathe. Her chest was heaving but her lungs couldn't get air. A mass of unruly hair hung down over her face while drops of blood seeped into the bandage over her nose.

Groaning sounds were coming from the middle of the room where his dark shape was standing. Cory clutched the metal claw and stood up on wobbly legs. She lurched to the opposite wall, the open door ten feet to her right.

"I met your mother once. Did you know that? She was full of herself, just like you. I never got the chance to get up close and personal. You know what I mean—real personal."

He paused, his breath wheezing. "She upped and disappeared. But now I can make up for it. With you."

Facing him, Cory took a wide side step to her right. The television was a couple feet away. She would have to step closer to him in order to get around it. She was about to take the initial step when he laughed again, a terrible guttural sound that stopped her short.

"I knew your ol' man, too. Knew the whole fuckin' family." He stood upright, legs apart, taking up most of the middle of the room like a pissed-off gorilla. His meaty nose was once again trying to sniff her out.

"I helped him out of a jam one time. But then he got right back in a bigger one. Ended up in a nut house. All because he wouldn't listen."

Cory saw the silhouette of his head swivel in her direction. He paused long enough to send an icy sensation down her spine, and then swung in the other direction.

"He was a party boy, a druggie. Hopped up on mesc and LSD. Went and got mixed up with a NARC. I kept tellin' him, that whole weekend I kept tellin' him, but he wouldn't listen. Naw. He was the original smart ass."

He stopped talking and pulled his torn shirt away from his bloody chest. "That NARC was my first." Again he stopped, gulped a breath. "The problem was all them drugs she took made her half dead...she couldn't feel much." He inched closer to Cory. "It was a disappointment, I guess you could say, 'cause that's where the fun is—watching their eyes light up when my teeth bite into 'em."

He whipped his left arm out to his side and grabbed her throat. He swung around to face her and squeezed the fingers of his beefy hand, cutting off her oxygen. His face, rank with the smell of sweat, closed in on hers.

Cory raised the hammer up to strike him again, but the monster grabbed her wrist with his other hand and smashed her hand against the wall, forcing Cory to drop the hammer.

Suddenly she heard heavy footsteps running along the deck. Cory stared with horror as another large frame ripped open the screen door and bounded inside.

She heard a click and the ceiling light flooded the room. Cory, still in the monster's grip, tried to see who could be coming into the cottage.

"Don't worry, I'm not going to hurt you, it's him I want."

Cory felt the thug's grip loosen. Struggling to fill her lungs with air, she saw the new intruder step closer to the man who came to kill her.

When the thug turned to see who was threatening him, the intruder raised a short piece of pipe above his head and landed a powerful blow across his face. A second strike drove the man to his knees.

"I've been looking for you. Seems I showed up a little late. But not *too* late." He raised the pipe high above his head to land the fatal blow, but Cory called out, "No! Don't do it. Let the police have him!"

Her savior looked into Cory's eyes. She stared at the stranger, an eerie feeling that she knew him taking hold. She shook her head. Impossible.

The man bent down close to the thug's face. "Remember me, Kelso? It's been a long time."

Kelso groaned.

"You're in bad shape, bud. Too bad I can't put you in your grave, but I guess I gotta take good advice for a change."

"Kelso?" Cory asked.

"Yep, this is Johnny Kelso. I been followin' him." The man looked at her. In the glare of the light Cory saw her reflection in his emerald green eyes.

Trying to find her voice, she stuttered, "Are...are you... Danny?"

"Yeah, I'm Danny," he said.

"Dad?"

46

Cory, phone to her ear, watched Rashid through the kitchen window as he bounced an imaginary basketball around the deck. She figured he was listening to her conversation, gauging when his turn would come. The longer he waited, the faster he dribbled. She quickened her speech.

"Yes, Aunt Ora, I'm going to help Danny—dad—with his evaluation in the hospital. The hospital has done a thorough mental status exam and, if all goes well, he'll be released tomorrow. Except for the Tardive Dyskinesia and some arthritis in his hands, he's doing as well as can be expected. At least he hasn't mentioned suing the State of Michigan. Yet."

She scribbled her diagnosis, "Hallucinogen Persisting Perception Disorder," on a piece of paper. It explained the lingering after-effects of his drug abuse, symptoms that may have easily been misdiagnosed as psychosis.

Cory poured a glass of lemonade, listening as Aunt Ora asked when she was coming home. "I don't know when I'll be back. I have to give the DA's office a taped witness statement about Antoli, Blake, and Kelso. Then Dad and I have to go to Michigan so we can give statements to the police against Kelso in the murder thirty years ago. They all have murder and attempted murder charges against them. Dad and I are going to have plenty of quality time together marching from court room to court room."

She took a sip and waved at Rashid through the kitchen window. "Right now I'm off to a trauma specialist with Rashid. He's agreed to have therapy for his PTSD. Then tonight I'm having dinner with Mike Samuels, my mother's fiancé. And tomorrow I am having coffee and cookies with Mrs. Gromski."

"Yes," she said, her voice softening, "I have a full schedule. But I'll be home as soon as I can."

Two hours later she was sitting in the small private lobby of a clinical social worker waiting for Rashid to finish with his first appointment. There was a large aquarium against a wall that emitted gurgling sounds as the pump hummed and water bubbled at the top.

Cory watched the brightly colored tropical fish glide from end to end and back again. The tension that had accumulated over the past several days began to ebb.

In its absence a quiet energy flowed throughout her body. Clasping the locket that hung around her neck. she heaved a deep sigh. Cory's journey had ended. With the weight from the past lifted, for the first time in twenty years she felt whole, and supremely happy to be alive.

About the Author

Linda Nordquist is a writer, photographer and a clinical social worker who specializes in the treatment of psychological trauma. In the 1980's she worked in the BOP shop (Basic Oxygen Processing department) labor gang at US Steel's Edgar Thomson Works, Braddock, PA. Her short stories have been published in literary journals and her memoir, *The Andes for Beginners*, is available on Amazon and in Peru. She resides in Rapid City, South Dakota. She is a member of the American Federation of Government Employees.

TITLES FROM HARD BALL PRESS

Caring – 1199 Nursing Home Workers Tell Their Story

Fight For Your Long Day – Classroom Edition, by Alex Kudera

Joelito's Big Decision, Ann Berlak (author), Daniel Camacho (Illustrator), José Antonio Galloso (Translator)

Love Dies, a thriller, by Timothy Sheard

Manny & The Mango Tree, Ali R. Bustamante (author), Monica Lunot-Kuker (illustrator), Mauricio Niebla (translator)

Murder of a Post Office Manager, A Legal Thriller, by Paul Felton

New York Hustle – Pool Rooms, School Rooms and Street Corners, a memoir, Stan Maron

Passion's Pride – Return to the Dawning, Cathie Wright-Lewis

The Secrets of the Snow, a book of poetry, Hiva Panahi (author), Zoe Valaoritis and Hiva Panahi (translators)

Sixteen Tons, a Novel, by Kevin Corley

We Are One – Stories of Work, Life & Love, Elizabeth Gottieb, editor

What Did You Learn at Work Today? The Forbidden Lessons of Labor Education, nonfiction, by Helena Worthen

With Our Loving Hands – 1199 Nursing Home Workers Tell Their Story

THE LENNY MOSS MYSTERIES by Timothy Sheard

This Won't Hurt A Bit

Some Cuts Never Heal

A Race Against Death

No Place To Be Sick

Slim To None

A Bitter Pill

Someone Has To Die

UPCOMING CHILDREN'S BOOKS

The Cabbage That Came Back, Stephen Pearl (author), Rafael Pearl (Illustrator), Mauricio Niebla (translator)

Hats Off For Gabbie, Marivir Montebon (author), Yana Murashko (illustrator), Mauricio Niebla (translator)

Singing The Car Wash Blues, Victor Narro (author & translator)

The Garbageman's Gift, Cynthia Hernandez (author & translator)

UPCOMING GROWNUP BOOKS

Woman Missing, A Mill Town Mystery, by Linda Nordquist

Legacy Costs, an industrial memoir, by Richard Hudelson

Throw Out the Water, a novel, by Kevin Corley